Love is a Four-Legged Word

Also by Melinda Metz

Love is a Four-Legged Word

Melinda Metz

KENSINGTON
PUBLISHING CORP.

kensingtonbooks.com

People say it takes a village to raise a child. Turns out it can also take a village to get an author (this author) to finish a book (this book).

Here's to my village: Vivian Anderson, Jo Carothers, Cindy Cole, Donna M. Davis, Gary Goldstein, Shirley Kwan, the members of BCI, Dave Radin, Robin Rue, Debbie Schmitzer, Amanda Smit, and the president of the village—Laura J. Burns.

I couldn't have done it without each and every one of you.

PROLOGUE

Welcome to the world, pups. There are a few things you should know. First, you are Good Dogs. Not one of you is a Bad Dog, no matter what you do. Pee on the carpet? Puppy's gotta pee. Chew on a chair leg? Puppy's gotta chew. Someone calls you a Bad Dog? They're wrong. Ignore them. And the next time you have to pee, choose one of their shoes. And the next time you need a good chew, go for the shoe you didn't pee on.

Second, there are Bad Humans. My first humans—I shouldn't call them that. You choose your humans. I didn't choose those first humans. Salvador, stop chewing on Mackinac's ear and listen. Back then, I didn't even know I could choose. That's how much of a pup I was. The first humans I knew, they were bad. They didn't care if I lived or died. No, it was worse than that. They wanted me to die. They tossed me into the desert when I wasn't much older than all of you, with no food or water. They had to know I wouldn't make it. Don't start whimpering, Savannah. You can see I'm fine. I'm right here in front of you.

You want to know how I made it? Because third—and this is an important one—there are Good Humans. Good Humans saved me, then I decided I wanted those Good Humans to be my humans. I chose them. They became my pack. There was also a rabbit in the pack for a while. Fourth thing you should know? Rabbit poop is delicious. Fifth, cat poop is delicious, too. It tastes almost like cat food. Sixth, never pass by a bowl of cat food. People call it that, but I promise you it's an enjoyable snack for us dogs.

Seventh, after you choose a person, you have to get them to choose you back. There are several ways to do this. The easiest and maybe the best is the puppy eyes. Even adults like me can make puppy eyes. You just make your eyes as big and round as you can and you stare up at the human you want. If nothing happens, don't stop staring. Don't look away and try not to blink. Just like that, Georgia—good job. If the human you're staring at doesn't give you a hug in less than a minute, they are probably the wrong human. It happens. We all make mistakes. Consider choosing someone else.

The pathetic whine is also a great way to get the human you've chosen to choose you. It should be soft and high, and if you combine it with the puppy eyes, you're golden. Although sometimes you might need to take it up a notch and break out the howl. If the human you've chosen walks away from you, howl as loud as you can for as long as you can. If you've chosen the right human, they will come back.

Sometimes humans are confusing. Sometimes you'll know in your gut that the humans have chosen you. But they still might leave you someplace. Not the desert. We're talking about Good Humans. The place they'll leave you will have food, water, a soft place to sleep. But don't settle for that. That's not good enough for my puppies. If that happens, just use your noses and your feet. Sniff them out and run until you get to them. When you do, the humans will understand that it's already happened. They are yours, and you are theirs. You are a pack.

And you're all asleep. That's puppies for you. They can learn so much from my life story, and they've only heard the beginning. I'll have to tell them more tomorrow. Then I'll probably have to tell them the whole thing again. Sometimes you have to tell a puppy something five, ten, a hundred times. But that's okay. We all learn what's best for us eventually.

CHAPTER 1

Riley Bernard wished she could take a video of this moment and send it back in time to her nine-year-old self. Here she was, cruising down Highway 179, those gorgeous red rock cliffs rising up to meet the bluest of blue skies. It was like she was living on page seventeen of *Beautiful America*. Nine-year-old Riley wouldn't believe it. To that little kid, page seventeen might as well have been Wonderland, not a place anyone could actually visit.

And her sixteen-year-old self? Forget about it. That girl might have had a hard time even believing she was still functioning at thirty-three. According to Chloe Campbell, she of the legendary parties and equally legendary grade point average—who knew everything, or thought she did—twenty-five percent of foster kids don't graduate from high school. She also had lots of interesting facts about what the rest of Riley's life would be like: before former foster kids turn twenty-one, ten percent end up dead; fifty percent develop a substance abuse dependence; twenty-five percent become homeless; twenty-five percent are incarcerated; seventy percent of the female ones get pregnant; and less than five percent ever get a college degree.

Maybe Riley should write Chloe a thank-you note. Having those stats shoved in her face had motivated her to come up with The Ultimate Plan, which was to live in every one of the most beautiful places in that book. And here she was. Driving through page seventeen, "Paint It Red" blaring from the top-of-the-line stereo, an order of carne asada bacon fries from Señor Tommy's on the seat next to her. If Riley hadn't been determined to prove Chloe wrong, who knew where she'd be?

Riley powered the windows down a little farther, even though it had to be a hundred degrees out there. The High Sky van couldn't smell like all that yummy carne. The resort was strictly vegetarian. If a guest complained to Ms. Aguilar about a meaty odor, Riley would probably, no, definitely, be out on her butt. It's not like she planned to make a career at the place. In fact, she had a new gig as activities coordinator at the Spruce Summit resort starting in just about a month, next stop in T.U.P. She was handing in her two weeks' notice in a couple days. But her car had been spewing farts of dark exhaust that smelled like rotten eggs every time she drove and wasn't going to make it from Arizona to Vermont without a new catalytic converter, which she couldn't afford at the moment. She almost had enough, but it would take those last couple of High Sky paychecks to get the Kia fixed up and ready to go, which meant she had to keep Ms. Aguilar happy until she had the cash—not exactly easy, since the manager had a long list of zero-tolerance don'ts for employees. That's why Riley not only had the windows halfway down, she also had two Febreze Linen & Sky car air fresheners in the vents. No way was she messing up T.U.P. She kept her eyes on the prize.

She'd reworked the itinerary dozens of times, practically wearing the ink off the pages of *Beautiful America*, until she'd perfected the plan. So what if zigzagging from Arizona to Vermont, and after that, Montana, wasn't exactly efficient. Riley loved a road trip, and even though she'd come up with the plan seventeen years ago, back when she was only sixteen, it still worked, and she still wanted to make that sixteen-year-old's dream come true.

It had taken her more than a decade after graduating from high school to get T.U.P. started. Working minimum wage for a bunch of those years had made adding to a travel fund almost impossible. But she'd clawed her way from fast-food fry-flinger to activities director at a four-star resort, and now she'd lived in San Francisco, Magnolia Springs—sixteen-year-old Riley had thought living in a place where mail was delivered by boat would be so cool, and that Riley was right—Medora, Ocracoke, and Cape Elizabeth. And how'd she accomplished that? Eyes on the prize, baby.

As she pulled onto Schnebly Hill Road, she reached back into the take-out tray of compostable sugarcane—Sedona being extremely eco-conscious—for a couple more of the loaded fries. They'd be too hard to eat once she hit the unpaved section. She had the bite halfway to her mouth when a flash of movement on the highway grabbed her attention. She slammed so hard on the brakes that the van skidded sideways, dumping her fries on the floor, upside down.

A dog. She'd almost hit a damn dog.

Riley pulled in a sharp breath, heart skittering in her chest, then started back down the highway. She was going to have to do a high-speed hazmat-style cleaning on the van. She had a vortex tour scheduled in less than an hour, and—

Wait. What was a dog doing out here? Had somebody dumped it? There was nothing between here and the summit, where the resort sat overlooking Verde Valley. She stopped and put on emergency flashers, even though there wasn't another vehicle in sight.

The tour was supposed to start at 3:30. Sharp. Ms. Aguilar

had zero tolerance for lateness. And lateness involving guests? Riley didn't know what was less than zero tolerance, but whatever it was, that's what her boss would have for making guests wait. But Riley had zero tolerance for letting an abandoned dog die out in the desert.

Riley climbed out of the van headed back along the road. "Doggie, doggie, doggie!" She walked a few more feet. "Come on, doggie!" Doggie didn't appear. And the clock was ticking. Animal control. That was the solution. She'd tell them where she'd spotted the dog, and they would come out and search, and she could get herself back to High Sky on time. She pulled her phone out of her pocket, but before she could do a search for the number, she heard heart-piercing yelps, unmistakably an animal in pain. She ran toward the sound, stumbling over the rocky ground, rounded a clump of yucca plants, then jerked to a stop as she spotted the little brown-and-white dog. No, not a dog. A puppy. A puppy with at least three cactus quills stuck in his body.

Anger surged through her. There were such things as animal shelters. Dropping off the pup would have taken, what, half an hour? He would probably have gotten adopted in a couple days, maybe a couple hours. Cute little things always went fast.

Eyes on the prize. Thinking about how things should have gone was pointless. What she had to think about now was damage control. What did she need? A way to carry the animal without causing it more pain. "Right back," she promised the pup, who was still wildly yelping. She raced to the van. She'd been on her way back from Edible Alchemy with every type of small-batch salsa they made for a tasting the next day. She took jars out of the wooden crate, grabbed a piece of bacon from the mess on the floor, and headed back to the pup, moving as fast as she could over the uneven ground. The puppy cowered as she approached, the yelps turning into a pitiful whimpering. Riley slowed down. She had no experience dealing with dogs. But she had lots of experience dealing with people, some of whom acted like they'd been stabbed by a cactus if, say, the pool was not a perfect seventy-eight degrees.

"You're going to be okay," she said, making her voice as calm and soothing as she would for an upset guest. "I know you're not right now, but I promise you, you're going to be okay." She inched closer and set down the crate, then held out the bacon as a good-faith offering. Human or dog, bacon made everything better, right? The puppy snatched it away, sharp little teeth grazing her finger. How long had he been out here without food? And what about water? She noticed the puppy was panting, and the tip of his tongue was out. It looked dry, at least drier than she thought it should be.

"I'm going to touch you now." The puppy lowered his head, but kept his dark eyes on her, the whites showing. "Please don't bite me. Remember I gave you bacon." She laced her fingers together underneath his belly, feeling the tremors running through his tiny body. She managed to lift him without touching his sides. He didn't try to get away as she maneuvered him into the crate, probably hurting too much. "You're okay, you're really okay," she repeated over and over as she slowly returned to the van, trying not to jostle the pup. She put the crate on the floor of the passenger seat, grinding the carne fries into the floor mat.

Now what? Would Ms. Aguilar understand that Riley had no choice but to bring the puppy back with her? Big no. Okay, more damage control. From the resort, it took five or six minutes to drive up to Riley's little cabin in the employee quarters, then she'd have to drive back, so that was a no-go if she was going to meet the tour group on time. She definitely couldn't take the pup with her on the tour.

Riley took out her phone and pulled up the reservation app. One of the casitas was open. She could stash the puppy there. The van had a first aid kit, and she was pretty sure it had tweezers. She'd get the spines out and leave the puppy in the casita's bathroom, where it couldn't hurt anything. It would only be a couple hours until she could retrieve him. Risky, but the best option.

"I really don't need a casita. If there's a regular room, I'm up for it." Daniel Acker tried to look at everything at once, without being obvious about it. The colors made him want to pull out his pencils and do some sketching, something he hadn't done in, wow, at least a year, maybe two. He couldn't remember why he'd stopped.

Whoever had designed the place had echoed the landscape, using muted green like the cactuses, blood red like the cliffs. There was even a pop of the brilliant blue of the sky in the stenciling around the rounded arch leading to the dining room. There was a dining room. His apartment at home didn't even have a dining room. He hadn't been expecting all this when his parents told him Ben Osborne owned a resort near the rehab and was going to put him up.

"I want you to have it. Even though I haven't seen your parents much since I moved up here after the divorce, there was a time the four of us—" Ben shrugged. "Long time ago."

Daniel's parents had told him Ben moved out of the neighborhood when Daniel was only a couple years old. He had a vague memory of a visit, a dinner out at Original Joe's, when he was maybe ten. What he remembered most was the chocolate cherry ice cream, him and Sam scraping and scraping away at the little silver bowls so they could get every bit of it, and their mom telling them to knock it off. He thought Ben was about his dad's age, sixtysomething, but he looked a lot younger, only a smattering of gray hair and some laugh lines at the corners of his eyes. Who knew what Daniel's dad would look like if he hadn't had to deal with so much.

"My mother's probably in the midst of baking you her special zucchini bread." Her go-to thank-you gift. No one had ever told her it sucked.

"I remember that bread."

"Diplomatic response."

Ben laughed. "I know it's a cliché, but it really is the thought that counts." He handed Daniel a key card. "If you need anything, call the front. Meals are all part of the resort package, so don't worry about that. The dining room's open until nine. I got you set up with a few things in the fridge, too. High Sky is vegetarian, but if you have a meat jones, there are tons of great restaurants in town. You can ask the concierge for suggestions, or any of the staff. They won't judge if you want a burger or a steak. Wish I could take you out tonight. Definitely, while you're here though. You think Sam would want a visit?"

"Yeah, I'm sure he'd be glad to see you." Actually, Daniel wasn't sure, but it felt rude to say that. Sam was a people guy, always happiest when he was the center of a group, but a rehab visit from a friend of their parents—that might be the exception. The last time Sam was in rehab, Daniel had been in high school, and he hadn't gone to see his brother. Sam still threw that in his face sometimes, but their dad hadn't wanted Daniel to go, hadn't wanted him to see Sam that way. Not that Daniel hadn't seen Sam probably looking worse than he had in rehab, though his father hadn't known that. "He can't see anybody the first week, though."

"Yeah. Been there. Literally. That's why I thought of the place when your dad told me what was going on with Sam. I did a stretch at Ironwood. The beginning of turning myself around and ultimately buying this place. Sam's going to be okay." He clapped Daniel on the shoulder.

"I'm sure you're right." The words sounded hollow, but what else was he supposed to say? Anyway, it was good practice for when he called his parents. *Mom, Dad, I'm sure Sam's going to be okay,* he'd tell them, trying for Ben's tone and inflection. He'd throw in what Ben had just said about himself. That should make them feel a little better.

"You have my number. Use it whenever. I have another place near Phoenix, and I go back and forth. I'm heading there tonight, but I'll be back in a week or so, and we'll get that dinner set up."

"Thanks again."

"I hope that second thanks doesn't mean I get a double batch of the zucchini bread," Ben answered, then headed out the sliding glass door that led to the patio.

Daniel set down his bright purple bag, a promo from when he'd joined—briefly—a gym. It looked like a Milk Dud in a box of Godiva chocolates. Which is kind of how Daniel felt. He was more of a Days Inn kind of guy, which was fine by him. Even if he made a ton more money than he did doing bookkeeping for Data Speedway, he'd probably never have stayed at a place like High Sky. The level of luxury made him itchy.

Or maybe the itchiness came from the reason he was here. But at least he'd been able to do this. He'd gotten Sam to rehab. No, that was giving himself too much credit. To Sam, Daniel would always be Little Brother, even though Little Brother was now thirty-one years old, and Little Brother didn't have much influence over Big Brother. A court order had gotten Sam to rehab. What Daniel had done was drive him there. And now he'd be living in this uncomfortably posh place for the next month, seeing Sam as often as the rules allowed, showing up for family group therapy. He wasn't even going to think about what that would be like. His parents had asked him to stay close, and here he was. That was pretty much the best he could do. Sometimes his best sucked.

Daniel sat down on the couch. The upholstery was thick and nubby, almost like a rug—was it a rug?—with a geometric print.

It was comfortable, but that itchy feeling made it hard to sit still. He stood, paced. A weathered—artfully weathered—desk stained a cactus green stood along one wall. He didn't bother with a desk at home, just used the kitchen table. He grabbed his computer bag and set up a workstation, which took about five minutes.

It was hours until dinnertime, not that he was hungry. He and Sam had stopped at a 7-Eleven first thing and loaded up on junk food. They'd been eating M&M's, Red Hots, Pringles, and Slim Jims the whole way from Fort Garland, washing them down with mega Cokes, pretending they were just on a regular bro road trip, not mentioning their destination. Not mentioning stuff was their family go-to.

He rubbed his hands together, feeling restless. The snackage meant that in addition to the itchy, Daniel was wired, semi-nauseous, and riding a sugar high. Maybe he should stretch his legs, take a look around, but he felt a little grubby to be seen by the spa-goers. He'd grab a shower first.

Daniel felt his eyes widen as he stepped into the bathroom. The shower was insane. It had to be twenty square feet, with what looked like hand-painted Mexican tiles. He pulled off his clothes, got in, and started experimenting with the control panel. It had a control panel. After a couple tries, he got a warm waterfall pouring down on him. He added some massage jets and laughed when he realized the shower came with mood lighting—music, too. He stumbled on "Stacy's Mom," which he'd listened to about a million times when he was in—what, fifth grade? Sixth grade?—and cranked it up. Listening to it always upped his mood, at least a little, and he could use that.

When his fingers and toes started to prune, he turned off the numerous knobs and buttons controlling the whole shower experience, then grabbed a towel, the softest, fluffiest towel he'd ever touched. It shouldn't even be called a towel. That's how far it was from the ones he had at home. After he dried off, he wrapped another of the towels around his waist. He'd forgotten to bring fresh clothes into the bathroom.

He reached for the door handle, but before he could touch it, the door swung open, putting him almost nose-to-nose with a tall, rangy, blue-eyed woman cradling a crate in her arms, a first aid kit in one hand. "What are you doing in here?" she demanded, backing away fast, until she hit the edge of the bed.

He took a few steps forward, planning to help steady the crate she held, but then decided a half-naked man advancing on a strange woman wasn't a good idea. "Ben Osborne—he's the owner, but he's only around part-time, I guess—anyway, he's letting me use the room, I mean casita, obviously more than a room." He was using way too many words. He tried to get a grip. "But I can move to a smaller one. I definitely don't need all this." He threw out one hand to indicate the bigger-than-king-size bed—he knew there was a name for that, but couldn't remember it—with the dozen-plus embroidered throw pillows. The motion made his loosely knotted towel slip a little. "Uh, right back."

Daniel retreated, shutting the bathroom door. There were two thick bathrobes hanging, conveniently, just outside the shower. Hadn't noticed those before. After putting one on and making sure the belt was tightly tied, he returned to the bedroom. The woman was exactly where he'd left her. Now that he had the chance to really look at her, he could see the tension in her body, shoulders high, hands gripping the crate so tightly her fingertips were white. "Are you—" Before he could finish asking if she was okay, she interrupted.

"I need to apologize. I thought this room was empty, and you surprised me." She spoke quickly, her eyes locked on his. Those eyes made him want to get his pencils again. He'd use blue slate, layer in cloud blue, and for that thin, thin ring around her iris, indanthrone blue. Daniel realized that one, he was staring, and two, he'd zoned out for a second and hadn't been paying attention to her words.

She was still apologizing. ". . . acted like you were the one in the wrong. I'll let you get back to enjoying your stay." She started to turn away, and a yelp came from the crate.

"What you got in there?"

"A puppy. Someone abandoned him in the desert."

"Is he hurt?" Good. He was managing to restrict himself to essential words.

"A couple cactus spines, but he's okay."

"You want a hand with them?"

"Oh, no thanks. I got it."

Obviously, she was one of those people who didn't ask for help, but he was pretty sure getting the spines out would be a two-person job. He stepped up to her and plucked the first aid kit out of her fingers. Not the right move. Surprise flashed in her eyes, then her mouth tightened. He could see her work to get hold of herself, and almost immediately, she'd tamped the annoyance down far enough that it wasn't visible on her face. "If you're up for it." Her voice was calm and even.

"How can I not be up for helping a wounded puppy? I'm not a monster." He gave the word *monster* a mad-scientist spin. Didn't get a smile, but she lowered the crate to the floor.

Daniel crouched down and looked inside. A brown-and-white puppy cowered in the corner, three cactus spines jabbing into his body. "That's gotta hurt," he said to the little animal, trying to make his voice soothing. "But no worries. We're going to fix you up."

The woman sat down on the other side of the crate and took out her phone. A few seconds later, she pulled up a YouTube vid on how to remove the spines, and tilted the phone toward him so they could both watch.

Was it wrong that he noticed the way she smelled? Not that he wasn't paying attention to the rundown of different kinds of spines. He didn't know what to call the scent. It smelled green. That's the only way he could describe it. Not flowery, just green, sort of like if you rubbed new leaves between your fingers.

"He got lucky," she said. "Those aren't cholla spines. The groundskeeper showed me those my first day. Those spines come off really easy, so that's what people usually get stuck with. They're barbed, so they're tricky to remove. It looks like these are saguaro, so they should pull straight out."

Daniel opened the first aid kit. "Do you want to hold him?" He found a packet of alcohol wipes and used one to disinfect the tweezers.

"You hold. I'll pull." She took the tweezers out of his hand.

Daniel gently stroked the puppy's chest to get the animal used to his touch, then cradled the pup's head with one hand, and positioned two fingers on either side of one of the spines with the other. The little animal quivered, and began letting out soft, high whimpers, but didn't try to pull away. With one quick, sure motion, the woman pulled the first spine free. The puppy gave another yelp. "You're such a good boy, such a good brave boy." Daniel rubbed a dot of antibiotic cream into the tiny puncture wound. He repositioned his fingers, and in moments, the second spine was out. "You're like a pro," he told the woman as he put cream on the new spot.

"I just pulled in the same direction as the spine, like they said to." She removed the last spine, cleaned the tweezers, and returned everything to the kit, then took a deep breath and met his gaze. "Here's the thing. There are no animals allowed at the resort, and my boss doesn't do exceptions. I brought the puppy in here because this room was supposed to be empty. I guess Mr. Osborne didn't bother with registering you before he let you in. Probably just did it on his way out. I'm supposed to take a group on a vortex tour in"—she glanced at her phone— "six minutes. I know it's a huge ask, but—"

Daniel didn't make her finish. "The dog can stay with me." He kept one hand on the puppy, stroking gently. He'd stopped trembling but was still making soft whimpers. Poor guy.

"Just until I'm off. I'll be back here by—" She cursed under her breath. "I can't be back until about ten. I'm in charge of tonight's S'mores and Stargazing. Is that too—"

He interrupted again. "I've got this."

"I'm sorry to shove him on you. I couldn't leave him out there in the desert, and I didn't have time to make a plan other than stashing him here. I know it's not your problem."

No, it wasn't his problem. Unlike his problem, this was something he could easily solve. "No worries. Go on. I got this."

"I'll be back as soon as I possibly can," she promised, before she strode out of the room.

Daniel looked down at the puppy. "How would you like the fluffiest towel in the universe to lie on?" He figured the poor thing might be soothed by the sound of his voice. Also, he tended to talk a lot, even when talking to himself. Unlike the woman—why hadn't he gotten her name?—who wasn't quite abrupt, but not chatty, although maybe just because she was stressed out. "I think you deserve it. You've been through a lot." He quickly pulled on fresh clothes, grabbed one of the towels, and returned to the pup. "I'm going to pick you up, okay? Why am I asking when you can't answer? Just because I want to keep talking to you."

As he reached into the crate, the puppy gave his hand three fast licks. "I guess that's an okay, which means you can answer, which means I was right to ask." As gently as he could, Daniel cradled the puppy to his chest with one hand and got the towel in place with the other, then set the puppy back down in the crate. "There. I bet that's better." The dog was panting. Daniel thought all dogs panted, but these pants were hard and fast. He must be so scared after being dumped in the desert. In the desert. He also had to be crazy thirsty. "I'll be right back."

As quickly as he could, Daniel filled a bowl partway with water. He didn't think it would be good to give the puppy too much at once. "I'll give you more in a little while," he promised when the pup quickly emptied the bowl. "What do you say we watch a little TV?" He got settled on the bed with the crate next to him, remote in one hand, and started petting the puppy again. He wasn't whimpering anymore. That was something.

Daniel found an episode of *Ted Lasso*, although back at home he'd recently discovered *Prison Break* and had been binge-watching it. He didn't need anything heavy-duty right now. His life was feeling heavy-duty enough. He kept up a running commentary for the puppy. When the episode ended, a thought struck him. "You hungry? If I were you, I'd be hungry. And I think it's time for a refill on your water. Right back." As soon as Daniel pulled his hand away, the puppy started to whimper. "Really, right back." Daniel stood, and the whimpers turned into long, high howls. "Okay. You can come." He picked the puppy up and brought him to the kitchen. He filled the bowl partway with water, then sat down on the floor and put the bowl and puppy down.

He twisted around and opened the fridge without getting up. "A few things, that's what he said," Daniel told the puppy. "We got hummus, we got yogurt, we got fresh strawberries, blueberries, and blackberries, we got salad, we got pasta salad, oat milk and almond milk, homemade granola. . . . My stomach would probably explode if I put so much healthy on top of the M&M's and Pringles and all the rest, and I don't see anything for you." He stood up and shut the fridge. "Want to go for a ride?"

The puppy looked up at him and cocked his head, the quintessential *huh?* dog look. "Someday, you're going to go nuts every time you hear the r-i-d-e word." He'd never had a dog, but he'd been around enough of his friends' pets to know that much. "Trust me, your answer is yes. You need some food and some treats, another word that will soon make you lose your mind."

Got a hungry puppy? Go to a pet store!

If only all problems were so easy to fix.

Riley sprinted toward the employee parking lot. She wasn't going to have time to clean the van and make it to reception on time. Her brain spun, trying to come up with damage control. She could yank out the floor mat, but she'd risk being seen if she tried to stash it someplace. Maybe she could dump a jar of salsa on top of the carne carnage. It might disguise the meat smell enough. Maybe she could take the floor mat from the driver's side and stick it on top of the mess. No other possible solutions came to her mind. She raced around the corner and stopped just in time to avoid smacking into Ms. Aguilar. Sometimes it felt like the resort manager had the ability to be in three or four places at once.

Ms. Aguilar gave a pointed look at her watch, ran her hand over her perfectly smooth slick-back bun, then shook two wintergreen Tic Tacs into her mouth.

"Just dropping off the hike schedule to the Fullwiders." Riley tossed out the name of the couple staying in the nearest casita.

"Cutting it a bit close." Ms. Aguilar picked a white hair off Riley's black shirt, frowned, then picked off two more.

"Can you believe it? I'm only thirty-three and I'm going gray. Runs in the family." Obviously she had no idea if anyone in her family went prematurely gray, but she thought the detail made her lie more convincing.

"Invest in a lint brush." Ms. A added two more Tic Tacs to her mouth. She must go through a box every couple days.

"Definitely. Good advice. Don't want to be late for the tour."

Riley took off at a fast walk, not wanting to give Ms. Aguilar the chance to formulate a question—like why she hadn't told the Fullwiders they could find the schedule in their casita's welcome package.

She did another time check as soon as she reached the van. Less than two minutes. She pulled open the passenger door and was hit with the scent of eucalyptus and lemon. The spot where the carne asada bacon fries went *splat* looked a bit damp, but spotless.

She was almost positive she knew whom she had to thank— Garret Ruiz, the head groundskeeper. She hadn't seen him when she'd been getting the puppy out of the van, but he'd been close enough that she'd heard him giving an emotional rendition of "It Must Have Been Love." Garret insisted different plants appreciated different kinds of music, just like people, and claimed the beargrass near the parking lot preferred power ballads. Now that she was thinking about it, the scent in the van reminded her of the natural insect repellent he mixed up. Yeah, Garret had to have cleaned up after her.

Thank you, Garret. Thank you, Whatshisname.

That guest of Ben Osborne had saved her butt, and she didn't even know his name. Whatever Whathisname was, he was a good guy. A good guy who looked good in a towel.

Not what she should be thinking about now. Eyes on the prize.

CHAPTER 2

Uh-oh, Riley thought when she saw Starla Piehl's tear-streaked face. Clearly this was a damage-control day. Riley wasn't the only one who'd be able to tell Starla had been crying. It would be obvious to the guests, too, which would make it hard to create the peaceful vibe Riley wanted for S'mores and Stargazing.

She wasn't too worried about the source of the tears. Starla had a, hmm, tumultuous relationship with her boyfriend, Bumper: lots of crying, lots of hot sex. Riley lit the candle inside the tin lantern on the last of the little patio tables, making the cutout stars and moons glow, then hurried over to the s'more station, where Starla was putting skewers into a vase with one hand while using the other to wipe her nose with a soggy Kleenex.

She looked as pathetic as the little pup. Only a couple more hours and Riley would be able to pick him up. He'd started to whine when she'd left him, like he was losing his best friend. Poor guy. And poor Starla.

"Bumper?" Riley asked.

"Bumper." Starla's answer came with fresh tears.

Riley decided to go with a little distraction. Maybe she could get Starla's mind off the boyfriend and onto work. Starla, while sometimes a bit flaky, was a conscientious worker. "The vases are from Sedona Swirls. I thought putting a few out would give us a chance to talk up the pottery class the gallery is going to be doing for us. You could mention that the red and white colors are inspired by Sedona's rocks, and the way the colors twist together is inspired by the vortexes." It wasn't only a distraction tactic. Riley always liked to give out a few talking points to entertainment staff before events, although Starla never had a problem chatting with guests. At least when she wasn't in the middle of a crisis.

Starla sniffled, then wiped her nose on the disintegrating tissue again. A piece of it plopped down onto the flagstone patio. Guess the distraction was a no-go. Guests would be arriving in about fifteen minutes, but Starla needed her right now. Riley picked up the tissue and jammed it into her pocket to dispose of later, then grabbed one of the brightly colored *servilletas* and handed it to Starla. She unfolded it and pressed the whole thing to her face. "I broke up with Bumper."

Personally, Riley thought anyone over three years old who allowed himself to be called Bumper *should* be broken up with. And it was actually something Starla did repeatedly. In the five months Riley had been working at High Sky, Starla had cut him loose at least nine times. A few days later, she'd take him back, and it was lather, rinse, and repeat. Which meant all this drama and soggy Kleenex was unnecessary. But she knew it didn't feel that way to Starla.

Riley didn't really get it. Personally, she liked to keep her relationships easy-breezy. It's the only thing that worked, since she only stayed in each town for six months. That was the timeline that would allow her to complete T.U.P. a few years before she turned sixty. The downside was that her lack of experience with emotional drama made her feel helpless when attempting to deal with someone else's. She hated feeling helpless. At least with the puppy, she'd been able to google "how to remove cactus spines from dog," and get step-by-step instructions. She'd tried the Google method the first time she'd had to deal with Starla heartbreak, but the results that had come up for "how to help someone going through a breakup" hadn't been all that helpful. She'd taken Starla shopping for new bedding as advised, but Starla and Bumper had ended up rolling around on the new sheets that same day.

"Do you want to talk about it?" Sometimes venting seemed to help.

"We were watching *The Texas Chainsaw Massacre*, which was only because Bumper wanted to. I keep telling him horror movies can dull your emotional and spiritual receptors, but he says he doesn't have them, even though everybody does." Starla's words came out a little muffled because she still held the *servilleta* over her face.

Riley tugged it down. "That's why you broke up with him?"

"No, so we were watching, and I asked if he thought Nell Hudson was hot, and he said, 'nah, not really.' Can you believe that?"

Starla sounded outraged. Riley felt confused. Before she could formulate a question, Starla rushed on. "He lied to my —" Starla pointed to her face. "Of course he thinks Nell Hudson is hot. He's a guy with a pulse. How does he not understand that honesty is much more important? Truth is one of the five virtues, and I've told him that. He knows truth is essential to me." Tears started welling up in her light brown, red-rimmed eyes.

The venting strategy might have been a mistake. "Do you need the night off? I could probably get Peggy." Riley should have started with that.

Starla shook her head, setting the ends of her shoulder-length bob—blue on one side, black on the other—swaying. "I need to be around people."

"Especially people carrying Spicy Mayan Apocalypse Marshmallows, am I right?" Lori Finn, the resort chef, walked over to them and held out a tray to Starla. "Infused with cocoa and dusted with cinnamon and cayenne pepper. I also made some prickly pear chocolate." Starla took a marshmallow. Lori looked over at Riley. "Plus I have store-bought Jet-Puffed and Hershey bars for the traditionalists."

"Perfect, as always." Riley never had to worry about Lori. She was the above-and-beyond type with the ability to anticipate the needs of everyone around her, including right now, helping Riley with the Starla sitch.

Starla wiped her face. "Can I have a Hershey and the prickly pear, and did you make the red chile kind?"

"Always."

"Good, because tonight I need all the chocolate."

Riley made a mental note. *Next Starla breakup, offer chocolate first.*

"Let's all go get some, then you two can help me bring the rest of the stuff from the kitchen." Lori added the tray to the station and rearranged the marshmallows so there wasn't a gap where Starla's had been. "I'm putting out grilled avocado tonight, too. I would love to add bacon."

"Don't let Ms. Aguilar hear you say the *B* word," Riley warned, thinking of all that *B* that Garret had cleaned off the van floor.

"Never." Lori led the way into the kitchen and waved at the trays of chocolate lined up on the sleek marble countertop. "Have at it."

Riley's stomach was too tight to fit in even a piece of Lori's melt-in-your-mouth chocolate. She always felt a little nervous before an event, and knowing there was a forbidden animal at the resort was making it worse, not that she'd had a choice. The casitas were pretty far apart. No one should be able to hear the pup, but what if he got out? What if someone saw him through a window, although no one should be getting close enough to look through a window? Having him on the grounds was low-risk, but with Ms. Aguilar as her boss, Riley needed no-risk. She wasn't going to start feeling okay until S'mores wrapped and she had the puppy out of Whatshisname's casita and safely back at her place.

"Cacao is heart-opening." Starla popped a piece of chocolate in her mouth. "This will help me let go of things that have been blocking me from living my ideal life. Like Bumper. I am truly better off without him."

"Glad it could help." Lori tucked a stray lock of her curly gray hair back into her ponytail and picked up a tray. "Starla, why don't you go wash your face and then meet us out there."

Starla situation handled. Riley was getting assistance from everywhere tonight. She gave Lori a grateful smile. High Sky had a great team, unlike the Cape Elizabeth crew, who had mostly been slackers except when the boss was watching. Riley was going to miss them when she moved on.

"Garret must be in serious need of your chocolate, too," Riley said when they returned to the patio. The head grounds-keeper was standing in front of the s'more station. "He should have been off work hours ago."

"I thought you might want to try out these s'more skewers." Garret held one up as they approached and pushed a button on a box soldered to the handle. The skewer began to spin with a loud *pock-pock-pock* sound. "This makes for a perfect golden brown 'mallow on all sides. What do you think of it, Lori?" He offered her one of the gadgets. She didn't take it.

"I need to go get the avocados."

Garret switched off the skewer as he watched her walk away, clearly disappointed. "They're very cool," Riley told him. "But I think the guests at the resort are mostly trying to get away from tech for a while. Let's let them do it the old-fashioned way. Bet they would do great at the Sharper Image, though. Make sure to get that patent. Put in enough, and one of them is going to take off." Garret's life ambition was to get a mention in *Invention Today.* He put in patent applications about as often as Starla broke up with Bumper. But that's how you did it. Keep your eyes on the prize, and never look away.

"I'll do that. Take one to try out at home." He handed her one of the skewers.

"Thanks. And I think I might have something else to thank you for. . . ."

"Just call me your Gardener Angel." He laughed at his own joke.

Yep, she'd been right. He'd been the one who saved her butt. She should figure out something nice to do for him. Him and Whatshisname. She hoped Whatshisname hadn't noticed her body-check him. But, come on, he'd only been wearing a towel. It was a reflex response. He wasn't chiseled like Ethan, her gym-bro semi-boyfriend back in Cape Elizabeth, who had spent more time thinking about his body than hers. But Whatshisname was solid, strong-looking, and her eyes might have lingered a little, but not for long. She'd had a puppy to rescue. He probably hadn't noticed.

You're at work. Keep your mind on work, she told herself, then did a slow turn, taking in the space. Looked good. Riley patted her pocket. The constellation trivia questions were ready, but it still felt like something was missing. Music! She pulled up the Soundtrack app on her phone and selected the stargazing playlist she'd created. A few seconds later, Alice Phoebe Lou's "Galaxies" began to play from the speakers disguised as rocks. Bellamy and Luis were each positioned by one of the fire pits. Noah had the bar stocked and was in place. The only one missing was Starla. She shouldn't still be in the bathroom.

Hoping Starla hadn't already lost the chocolate-induced revelation that she was better without Bumper, Riley went to fetch her. Just as she was about to knock on the bathroom door, she heard sounds coming from inside and froze. They weren't crying sounds. They were sexing sounds. This might be a new record for Starla and Bumper getting back together. Well, she wasn't giving Starla the night off for the reunion. "Starla! I need you out on the patio in five," she called.

"Yes!" Starla called back, perhaps answering Riley, perhaps in response to something Bumper had just done. Riley decided to assume it was the former and returned to the patio. She had a couple minutes before go time, so, breaking the no-phone-at-work rule out of desperation, she did a quick stealth search for the Sedona Humane Society. Damn. It wasn't accepting any animals for two weeks. There was a respiratory infection going around at the location. She couldn't wait two weeks to get the puppy situated. In two weeks, she'd be getting her car repaired and deciding what to pack and what to give away. She liked to travel light.

"I'm back!" Starla announced as Riley slid her phone back in her pocket.

"And you sent Bumper home?" Ms. Aguilar had a no-exception rule about visitors on site.

Starla nodded. "But wasn't it romantic of him to come here? He could have called or texted, but he said he had to see me. And he said he understands what I meant about trust. And he said he *does* think Nell Hudson is smokin' hot! Isn't that awesome? It's like as soon as the cacao opened my heart and I realized what I needed for my ideal life, the universe sent it to me."

That made no sense. Bumper would have had to be on his way over before Starla ate the cacao, and besides, she'd said the cacao told her she needed to remove Bumper from her life. Riley didn't bother pointing that out. Logic wasn't one of Starla's five virtues. Still, she couldn't stop herself from asking, "You do remember you were completely miserable fifteen minutes ago?"

"Sure, but that's what love is. You can't get the ups without the downs. It's the people you love who make you feel so good, so it makes sense they are the ones who make you feel so bad. I can't remember one day I didn't see my parents fighting about something, and they just celebrated their thirtieth wedding anniversary." Starla smiled. "Speaking of love, look who's over there. Have you noticed how often Garret just happens to show up around Lori?"

Starla saw love everywhere. "He's here because he came up with a mechanical s'more skewer and was hoping we'd let the guests try it out."

"But see how he's looking at her, how he's leaning toward her. They'd make a super cute couple. They're about the same age. She always laughs at his dad jokes. They're both creative. She's always coming up with new flavor combinations in her recipes. He's always coming up with inventions."

"By your theory, though, they should be fighting all the time if they are supposed to be together." Oops. Riley had slipped into trying to use logic with Starla. It's like they spoke different languages. Riley's was fact-based; Starla's, emotion.

"Because they aren't in love yet. The potential is there. He can sense it. The way she's holding on to the edge of the table, though? That shows she's hesitant. Her heart isn't open to it, at least right now."

"Shouldn't her heart be wide open with all that cacao she eats?" Riley teased.

"I'm serious. I wonder what the blockage is. Lori's been at High Sky since before I started, and I don't know anything about her. I know tons about Garret. Divorced about nine years ago. Son about my age. College for a few semesters, but didn't like sitting in a classroom. Broke his arm twice going down the slide rock, but still keeps going back. But about Lori, I've got nothing." Starla narrowed her eyes at Riley. "You're the same. We work together all week and live next door to each other, and I know nothing except things like that you don't like mushrooms on your pizza."

Riley shrugged. It wasn't just relationships she kept easy-breezy. Friendships ended up that way, too. It was one of the downsides of being a nomad. But the upside was the next beautiful place she got to see. "There's nothing much to know. I'm shallow like that." Riley nudged Starla toward the s'more station. "Almost time for guests to start arriving."

She did another scan of the patio. Knowing Ms. Aguilar, she'd probably be stopping by to check on things. Sometimes it seemed like the manager didn't have a home. She was always here. But let her come. Now that Starla was in place, everything was ready. Satisfied, Riley stealthily pulled out her phone and did a quick search for other animal adoption options. She found a site called SmoochiePoochie, where she could make a listing for the pup. Perfect. It shouldn't take long to find him a good home. He was little and cute, and that's what people liked.

Daniel sat on the floor, leaning against the couch as the puppy took another lap around the room, scrambling under the armchair, around the coffee table, over Daniel's legs. The pup started on a fifth lap, then suddenly veered to the left for a surprise attack on the pizza squeaky. He pounced on it, and with the highest, tiniest, most ridiculous growl, which he probably thought sounded ferocious, gave the toy a vicious shake. "My dude, pizza doesn't have a neck to break."

At the sound of Daniel's voice, the puppy spun toward him, ran over, and launched an attack on one of Daniel's shoelaces, already wet with slobber from a previous bout. Then with astonishing suddenness, the puppy's body went limp. This had happened once before, and that first time, Daniel had been alarmed. But a little googling told him it was normal for puppies to fall asleep practically mid-play, because they were growing so fast and it took a lot of energy.

He'd followed link after link, doing a deep dive into puppy development. He was a research kind of guy. He liked to feel as prepared as possible for whatever might come up.

Daniel leaned forward and ran his hand lightly down the puppy's back. "You're a good boy." He'd been through so much, being out in the desert for who knew how long all alone, getting stuck with the cactus spines, but it's like he'd forgotten it all. Or if not forgotten, all that mattered was the fun of the current moment. Daniel envied that ability. He leaned his head back against the sofa cushion, his thoughts drifting to his parents, the way they so often did lately. They'd sounded so worried when he'd called them to give them a Sam update, not that he had anything to tell other than that Sam was checked in, plus the reassurances he'd gotten from Ben. Maybe they should get a puppy. They took a lot of looking after, a lot of attention, which meant a lot of distraction. Watching this one had given Daniel a few in-the-moment stretches.

Daniel returned his attention to the TV. He'd moved on to a Nate Bargatze stand-up special, needing something he could pay off-and-on attention to. Bargatze was like comfort food. He never said anything controversial, and it felt like the world he lived in was basically a good place, where a spat with his wife was the worst that happened. Daniel liked to visit that world. When the special wrapped up, he started it again. Might as well catch the stuff the puppy wrangling had made him miss.

About ten minutes later, the puppy's head jerked up, ears pricking. Then he was running as fast as his little legs would carry him toward the sliding door leading to the patio. He put on the brakes too late and bonked his nose on the glass, leaving a little smudge. Didn't faze him. He started hopping from side to side, yipping like crazy. It was a good thing Ben had been so generous. If Daniel had a regular room instead of the casita, he'd definitely get busted for puppy possession. "Calm down, my dude." Daniel pushed himself to his feet and walked over to the door. "What do you see out there?" When he looked at the patio, he didn't see anything that would have gotten the puppy so agitated. But a couple seconds later, the woman—he couldn't believe he hadn't gotten her name—appeared. Daniel hadn't thought the puppy had a higher setting, but he somehow took it up to eleven, jumping even faster. Daniel scooped him up, and he struggled to free himself as Daniel slid open the door.

The woman stepped inside and quickly shut the door behind her. The puppy's yips turned to high squeaks of excitement. "Are you ready for his welcome?"

"I don't think I have a choice." She knelt down as Daniel returned the puppy to the floor, and the pup was instantly on her, climbing onto her thigh and putting his paws on her chest as he tried to lick her face. She let out a surprisingly loud whoop of laughter, one of those laughs that makes anyone who hears it laugh, too. "Hi! Hi to you, silly." She gave the puppy a few pats and an ear ruffle, then stood, trying to ignore him as he danced around her.

"I wanted to give you this as a little thank-you for taking care of him today." She pulled a gift card out of her pocket and held it out to Daniel. "This will give you any treatment at the spa. They're all incredible, but I recommend the Perfect Balance massage, which is back, neck, and shoulder, followed by a half hour of foot reflexology. Or if you want something that's more classic Sedona, try the Change of Heart treatment, which uses healing crystals, essential oils, and native rattles to balance the chakras."

Daniel was thrown. It's like she was reciting something

she'd memorized. "You don't have to thank me. I enjoyed the company." He tried to hand her the card back, but she refused to take it. "I'm not so much of a massage guy." At least he didn't think he was. He'd never had one, but was pretty sure it would make him stressed out instead of relaxing him.

This time when he held out the card, she took it—reluctantly. "Okay, I'll leave a gift certificate for Mecca, our gift shop, at reception for you instead. There are some lovely things from local artists—if not for you, perhaps a start on holiday shopping."

That was definitely a canned response. No human spoke like that. But she was clearly determined to give him something. "Sure. That's great. I appreciate it. Want something to drink? I don't know what I have, but I know I have something. And our friend isn't going to be happy until he has well and truly defeated the nefarious shoelace." The puppy had started a fresh attack and had almost managed to bite through it.

"No, thanks. I'll get out of your way. I'll get both of us out of your way. We've taken up way too much of your time already. You're a guest. You're here to relax. I was just desperate, and—" She gave a helpless shrug. "Where's the crate?"

Daniel felt a pang at the idea of her leaving. Well, probably at the idea of the dog leaving, he told himself. Not the woman, the woman with the long legs and all-in laugh. Just the puppy. It had been a good distraction, having someone to take care of. "I realized after you left that I didn't get your name. I'm Daniel."

"Riley."

He held out his hand, and when she shook it, he got a whiff of that green scent again, and something sweeter. "You smell like cotton candy."

She took a step back. Maybe he shouldn't have mentioned how she smelled, not when they barely knew each other. "Marshmallows. We had a s'more station on the patio. I should have brought you some of the chocolate."

"I'm still recovering from all the junk I ate on the road."

"It's not a road trip without junk."

Finally he'd gotten something out of her that didn't sound like it came from the High Sky brochure. "Exactly. Do you really think it would have been that bad if your manager found out about the puppy?" he asked, stalling their departure. He wasn't looking forward to being alone with his thoughts. "She wouldn't have expected you to leave him out in the desert, right? He wouldn't have survived."

"She always says her rules have no exceptions. She fired someone once for being three minutes late. There was an accident on his way to work, but Ms. Aguilar said that it was his responsibility to leave early enough for any delaying contingencies. That's actually how she talks."

"Yikes."

Riley nodded. "Guess somebody has to be tightly wound to make the experience so Zen for the guests." She sounded doubtful. "So, crate?"

She really wanted out of there. Well, why wouldn't she? She'd had a long day, and probably a lot of it was making chitchat with strangers like him. "Crate, yeah." Daniel was about to head to the bedroom, when he remembered the puppy was attached to his foot. He bent down, grabbed the closest toy—a Squidward with ropy arms—and gave it a squeak, then tossed it. The puppy was on it in a second.

"You bought all this for him?" Riley's eyes widened as she took in the toys scattered across the living room floor. She sounded horrified.

"We might have gotten a little out of control at the pet store. I wanted to get him some food, and—" Daniel shrugged.

"How much did it cost? I'll pay you back."

"No, no. I wanted to get it. Seeing him in the store was worth it. He lost his little mind. He wanted everything." The puppy gave one of his baby growls, vigorously shaking Squidward by the arm, which didn't do much because Squidward was about twice as long as he was.

"So, how much?"

Okay, clearly, she was going to insist on giving him money. But she shouldn't have to pay for the shopping madness. "The food was about thirteen dollars." And the bag was very small. The clerk had convinced Daniel that "his baby" needed the mix of chicken, brown rice, fruits, and vegetables.

"And the rest?"

Squidward had been about twenty bucks. The puppy had grabbed the largest one and done some serious damage to the long, droopy nose before Daniel could intervene. There were a couple—well, four—rubber squeakies, say twenty-five dollars. Then eight dollars for the rawhide bone the puppy grabbed, even though Daniel had to throw it away because it could hurt "his baby's" developing jaws and teeth. Some treats, soft-baked, which added about fourteen dollars. So around eighty bucks total. "It was about thirty-five."

"Bullcrap. The harness alone was probably fifteen."

Damn, he'd forgotten about the harness. It had been closer, a lot closer, to thirty. He'd also forgotten about the bowls, wipes, toothbrush and toothpaste, and poop bags. Only the best for "his baby." "I'm not sticking you with the whole bill. You didn't have any say in how much I spent. I didn't have to buy him all this stuff. I just wanted to."

"I can just look it up." She pulled out her cell. "Or I can just check the receipt." She strode over to the coffee table and started rooting around in the Pet City bags. A few seconds later, she pulled the long receipt free. "A hundred and thirty-three seventy-two." She sounded dismayed, but didn't comment on the total. "You have Venmo?"

"Yup." He gave her his info. He knew a no-win situation when he saw it. "But only half, okay?"

She nodded, then grabbed one of the bags and started packing up the toys scattered around the room. "I'll get the bowls and food." Daniel stopped on the way to the kitchen to give Squidward a couple gentle tugs, winding the puppy up.

Riley had everything but Squidward packed away by the time he returned to the living room. "Can you get the crate?"

"Yep." He fetched it and put it on the ground near her feet. "I messed up one of the casita towels. I wanted to give him something to lie on, and a few drops of blood got on it."

Riley laughed. "You sound so guilty. It's no problem." She turned to the puppy. "Okay, you. Time to go." She tried to scoop him up, but he thought she was going for the toy and backed away from her, dragging Squidward. He was clearly ready for a game. Daniel managed to snag him and held him cradled against his chest. "You think he remembers anything about this afternoon, out in the desert? I don't know how dog memories work. Maybe all that is already gone." Another delaying gambit. He should let her go, but it felt too good to have her with him. And the puppy.

"Even if he doesn't remember-remember, it's still in there. It's part of him."

"But so is the rest, then. You rescuing him."

"The shopping spree." Her lips slowly curved into a teasing smile. She hadn't been happy about him spending so much, but it seemed like he was forgiven.

The puppy started trying to climb Daniel like a tree. "What are you doing, crazy, huh?"

Her smile widened, and he realized she had a dimple by the left corner of her mouth. "You don't want a dog, do you?" she asked. "I happen to know of one looking for a home."

He scratched the puppy behind one ear. "Can't. I'm going to be here for a month, and I know you don't want to risk having him at the casita. What about you? You should have seen him when he realized you were coming. It was like Santa Claus for a five-year-old."

"I get room and board here. No pets anywhere on the premises." She shoved her fingers through her wavy blond hair—dark cadmium yellow, he decided, with so many other shades mixed in, streaks of mango and sizzling sunset, for starters. "And I'm not really a pet person."

"Can I ask what you're going to do with him?" Daniel held the puppy a little closer, the animal's warmth soaking through his shirt into his body.

"I found an adoption site where I can list him, Smoochie-Poochie."

"You should put in how you found him, the cactus and everything. That would pull the heartstrings, right? Poor little puppy, abandoned, injured." It got to Daniel. But even if he was leaving tomorrow, he wouldn't be able to take the dog. Once Sam was out of rehab, Daniel would have to put in a lot of time helping his brother get his life back in order. And Daniel couldn't have a dog near Sam—Sam was allergic. Daniel put the puppy down.

"I bet his cute little face is all it's going to take to get him adopted.

"You want me to help you take some pictures? He's pretty squirmy."

"Squirmy?" Riley stared at the puppy as he spun around three times, then launched himself at an end table and brought it crashing down. "It looks more like demonic possession."

Daniel righted the end table. "That was actually a pretty impressive takedown. The table probably outweighs him by at least five pounds."

She hesitated. "If you're sure you're up for helping."

"You want to be photographer or wrangler?"

She pulled out her phone. Guess he was the wrangler. He

was going to need an assist getting the pup to slow down enough for Riley to get a picture. He pulled a biscuit out of one of the shopping bags. "Hey, you!" He held it out, and the puppy bounded over—then snatched it away and took his booty under the closest chair. "That didn't go as planned."

Riley shook her head. "Clearly he doesn't allow himself to be photographed without hair and makeup. Let's do the profile first. First off, what kind of dog do we think he is?"

She brushed her thumb across her bottom lip as she stared down at the screen, distracting Daniel. If she wanted him to pay attention, she shouldn't be playing with her lip—Venetian red, which wasn't red, but more of a deep, dusty pink. She also shouldn't be smelling so good.

"What kind," she repeated. "I'm not much of a dog person. Not that I don't like them. I just haven't been around them much."

"I wanted one, but my brother's allergic. One of my friends had a greyhound. I can say definitively he's not a greyhound."

"Wait, let me put that in. 'Not a greyhound.'"

She'd definitely loosened up. Daniel pulled out his phone and did a search for dog breeds. "Jack Russell, maybe?" He tilted the phone toward her. "Looks a lot like him."

"It says they are fearless, feisty, smart, stubborn, and super friendly." She leaned down, trying to get a glimpse of the puppy. "You know him better than I do. Does that sound like him?"

"He's definitely friendly. And I think Squidward and my shoelace would say he's feisty."

"He managed to con you into buying him an astonishing amount of toys." That dimple of hers appeared again. "So *smart*, too." The puppy, having finished off his treat, reappeared, stubby tail vibrating with happiness. "Are you a Jack Russell, cutie?" The puppy tilted his head. Riley caught it and showed the pic to him.

"That's it. That's the money shot."

"Pretty irresistible. We can use the *smart* and *super friendly* in his profile, but I think we should go with *playful* instead of *feisty*."

"What did you think about telling how you found him, poor little injured pup?"

"Injured might make somebody think of vet bills. When I review social media for the resort, I try to think about the kind of person I'm trying to attract. Who are we trying to get to adopt the puppy?"

"Someone patient, with strong shoelaces." The puppy was once again gnawing on one of his.

"We don't want him to sound like work. Maybe something like, 'If you're looking for a buddy who's up for anything, this guy's for you.' That's kind of saying he's full of energy, but in a fun way."

"You're good at this."

"I should be. I've been handling social for years now at various jobs. When I'm off work, I can't stand to look at Instagram or any of the others."

"How about saying he comes with a free leash and a week's supply of food?"

"Not a bad strategy. Though I want someone who wants him for him, not because he's a bargain."

The puppy gave a huge yawn, and Riley moved fast enough to catch it. "I'm going to put this one up, too. Yawning makes him seem cuddly, like he'd curl up on the couch with you. I could put something like, 'He's also down for a quiet night at home.'"

"I like it."

"There's a space for a name."

"We can come up with something."

"I'm not sure I want to. I name him, he'll start feeling like mine, and that'll make it harder to let him go. But it's not going to let me submit his profile without one." She tilted her head as she studied the pup, the head-tilt almost as cute on her as it had been on the pup. "John Doe. You can't get attached to John Doe."

"That doesn't sound like a pick-me name. How about shortening it? J.D."

"J.D." She nodded, and typed it in. "It's submitted. Now we really should get out of here. It's late. You've got to be tired. You had the drive and then the puppy-sitting."

"I'm actually feeling kind of wired." Even if he wasn't, he knew he wouldn't be able to sleep. But he'd already offered her a drink, and he couldn't think of another way to get her to keep him company a little longer.

Riley scooped up the puppy, put him in the crate. "Thanks again." She started toward the door, then hesitated and turned back to him. "I've already asked you for so much. . . ."

"What do you need?"

"A ride. I was forgetting I walked to work."

Another problem with a nice, clear solution. "I'll get my keys."

CHAPTER 3

J.D. gave one of his ridiculously tiny growls, grabbed the tip of Riley's sock, and yanked. "Hey! Just so you know, you bit my toe! And I can get undressed by myself, thank you very much." The pup shook his head and managed to get another couple inches of her sock off while giving her another nip. Three more nips and one torn pajama-bottom hem later, she was ready for bed. So was J.D., judging by his double yawn. He'd had a long, hard day.

Riley moved the crate as close to the edge of her bed as she could get it, then plopped J.D. inside. He immediately started whining the way he had when she left for work. He probably needed company. He was little. Not too long ago, he had to be sleeping with his mom and brothers and sisters in a warm, cozy pile. "On it," she told him, and started for the living room.

Before she reached the door, J.D.'s whimpering turned into a howl. "Okay, okay." She hurried over and picked him up, then together, they retrieved his Squidward. She put the pup and his new bestie in the crate, gave J.D. a kiss on the head, tweaked Squidward's nose, then climbed into bed. As soon as she turned off the light, J.D. started to whimper again. Could he be afraid of the dark? She used to be afraid of the dark. Actually, it was more that she was afraid of falling asleep. Sleep meant nightmares. A lot of nights, she had to page through *Beautiful America* again and again, straining to see the pages, until exhaustion overtook her.

Riley clicked the light back on, sat up, and looked down at the puppy. "You're okay. I'm right here. And we both need to get some sleep." He'd stopped crying at the sound of her voice, but was staring at her with the biggest, saddest brown eyes she'd ever seen.

He'd probably feel better if he could sleep with her. She wasn't his family, but she was warm, with a beating heart. Was that okay, though? She was clueless about how to take care of a puppy. But there was any easy fix for that. She grabbed her phone off the nightstand and did a search on sleeping with a puppy. "Okay, this says you are basically disgusting with poop in the obvious place, but also on your back legs and tail, plus germs in your saliva. You might have parasites, which you could give to me. And it's possible you'll wet the bed." He continued to stare at her. Didn't he ever have to blink? "Come on, would you want to sleep with you after what you just heard?" He kept staring.

Riley found two more sites that also said sharing a bed with a puppy wasn't the best choice. "You won't learn to self-pacify and be okay spending time alone. Also, you might become territorial, and growl to protect your spot on the bed."

She looked down at J.D. Still staring with those big, sad eyes. He must have blinked when she was reading. It wasn't possible to go that long without a blink. "I'm not going to have you very long. You probably won't get too many bad habits from a night or two. . . ." She clicked to a new site. "And this one actually says you might get so traumatized by being alone that you'll develop separation anxiety. It says you're used to having brothers and sisters around, and if you sleep next to me, it will feel familiar and you'll go right to sleep. Which is exactly what I thought." This puppy thing wasn't so hard. She leaned down and scooped him up, then climbed back in bed and shut off the light. J.D. tromped around a little, managing to scramble up and over her, before curling up on the pillow right above her head.

"You're lucky you're cute," she told him, thinking of the poop and germs. He gave a sigh of contentment and within seconds was letting out adorable little wheezy snores. Riley expected to fall asleep immediately. Sleep didn't scare her anymore. She'd outgrown the nightmares long ago. Mostly. But her brain wouldn't stop spinning. She subtracted $133.72 from her bank balance, which she knew down to the penny, then did some calculations.

She definitely needed a new catalytic converter, but the mechanic had said she might also need to replace the O2 sensor. She'd done some research, and that could run her about $350. But the part was only around a hundred, and she'd figured she could ask Garret to put it in for her. There was nothing mechanical he couldn't handle, and she'd been confident her budget could take a hundred-dollar hit. But the payback for the puppy stuff was $133.73. And she had to find the puppy a home. It shouldn't take long, but she always liked to have a margin for error when she made plans.

She wasn't going to be able to give notice on schedule. She'd need an extra week to get the extra cash and deal with the pup. All those statistics from Chloe Campbell—who knew everything, or thought she did—came rushing back into her already spinning brain. Twenty-five percent of girls like Riley didn't graduate from high school. Before age twenty-one, ten percent of former foster kids ended up dead. Fifty percent of them developed a substance abuse dependence. Twenty-five percent became homeless. Twenty-five percent were incarcerated. Seventy percent of the female ones get pregnant. Less than five percent ever get a college degree. Ten percent dead. Fifty percent develop a substance abuse dependence. Seventy percent pregnant. Less than five percent—

Stop. Okay, stop. Usually when her brain went crazy on her, Riley would get up and go outside. Staring at the stars, especially here where they were so bright and felt so close, got her calmed down. But she didn't want to disturb the sleeping puppy.

Damage control. She'd add a week onto her departure date so she could earn another paycheck and make sure the pup had a home. She'd been planning to take her time on the drive, six days, with stops to ride the Sandia Peak Tramway, check out the St. Louis Arch, and visit the Rock and Roll Hall of Fame and Museum. She'd also built in a week in Stowe before her job started. She always liked to scope out a new place, and it gave her a chance to come up with the perfect suggestions for guests.

But she could make it work. She'd skip the side trips and cut back on the days to explore her new hometown. Riley didn't love changing her itinerary, but the travel specifics weren't part of T.U.P. All she needed was to get to the Summit Mountain resort in time to start the job. The Ultimate Plan was still on track.

But the stats kept coming. Fifty percent develop a substance abuse dependence. Seventy percent pregnant. Less than five percent—*Stop. Stop.* She remembered Ms. Owen's advice. Mary's, she corrected herself. Now that she was an adult, Riley called her Mary, but it still felt weird to call her social worker, her *third* social worker, by her first name. Mary would say stop and focus on your senses.

Riley could feel the band of satin at the top of her blanket brushing her chin and the warmth of J.D.'s body soaking into her head. He really was warm, like a mini space heater. How could one furry little creature give off so much cozy heat? And she could hear the puppy's baby snores, just adorable tiny little snores of contentment. Her chest loosened. The words of Chloe, who knew everything or thought she did, faded away, and Riley drifted into sleep.

Was Sam staring up at the ceiling in a strange bed the way Daniel was? His brother's bed definitely wouldn't be as big as this one, and the thread count on his sheets wouldn't be as high. Daniel didn't really understand thread count, but figured the sheets he was lying under had to have a good one. They were the softest he'd ever felt. Although Ben had raved about Ironwood to Daniel's parents, it wouldn't have sheets like this.

Sam would get a kick out of the crazy luxury of the resort, but he'd probably get bored with the place fast. He had a low boredom threshold. But for a day or two, he'd be loving it, and if he'd been offered a free spa treatment, he'd be there.

Daniel rolled over on his side, grabbed his phone from the bedside table, and checked the time, although that was pointless. It definitely wasn't close to morning. Only a little after two. He just couldn't shut off his brain enough to sleep. Maybe he should stop trying. It's not like he had to get up at any particular time. As long as he got his work done, nobody cared when he did it, and he'd gotten through almost all his assignments after Riley and the puppy left.

He skimmed a couple articles on Gizmodo, went down the YouTube rabbit hole for a while, played some Solitaire, but his thoughts kept returning to Sam. Did enforced rehab ever work? Didn't the person actually have to want to make a change? Sam was a good bullshit artist. Daniel was sure he could figure out what the counselors or whoever at the rehab wanted to hear, but it seemed pretty likely that when Sam's twenty-eight days were up, nothing much would be different. He'd have detoxed, yeah, but he'd probably have no interest in trying to keep it up.

Their parents thought different. They seemed convinced this

is what it would take for Sam to "turn his life around." He'd almost gone to prison. That would have woken him up. They were delusional. Daniel got it. He wanted to believe rehab would be a new beginning for his brother, too, but he couldn't find his parents' optimism. Or maybe it was desperation.

He started to google "family member in rehab," then put the phone down. It wasn't going to help. He'd already read dozens of articles, too many. They'd started getting repetitive almost immediately, but being as prepared as possible lowered his stress. He knew he was supposed to learn about Sam's addiction; be available—couldn't be much more available than he was; communicate honestly—not looking forward to that, but he'd show up for family therapy if it would help. He was also supposed to take care of himself, which meant exercise; eat right—all he had to do was open the stocked fridge; get enough sleep—none of the articles said how to actually accomplish that; get therapy for "codependency issues"—he'd do the family therapy, but he didn't need the other; explore his own interests— whatever they were.

He rolled onto his stomach and heard a long, wheezing squeak. He dug around and found the pizza toy he'd bought for the pup. He turned onto his back and gave the squeaky a couple squeezes. He wished he still had the puppy. Taking care of it had felt like taking care of ten puppies, not one, which had kept his brain occupied. Without the dog, his thoughts kept returning to Sam. According to all those articles, Sam would be needing a lot of support when he got out of rehab. Daniel should encourage Sam to find new interests—Daniel had no idea what those could be; encourage him to keep getting treatment—with the limited influence Daniel as Little Brother had; include him in social activities—Daniel probably needed to get more of those himself. He didn't know what he'd been doing with his time. Not drawing. Not going out much. That's actually why his last relationship had tanked. Mila had wanted to go out a lot more than Daniel had. He just hardly ever felt like it. After work, he was tired. Wasn't everyone? But he'd have to make an effort as part of keeping Sam clean.

And while he was doing all that, the articles again emphasized, he should take care of himself, by exercising, et cetera. Definitely not the time to add a puppy, which Daniel now knew would feel like ten puppies, into the mix, even if Sam wasn't allergic, which he was.

He squeaked the pizza again. It made a good fidget toy. He wondered how Riley was doing with little J.D.

CHAPTER 4

Riley clipped the leash onto J.D.'s hearts-and-dog-bones-printed harness, planning to lead him outside, but as soon as she opened the door, he bolted through and, if he weighed more, would have dragged her behind him. Daniel had gone nuts at the pet store—one toy would have been enough—but the harness and leash were definitely coming in handy. She could have let him pay for everything, he'd practically begged her to, but it didn't feel right. She was the one who'd rescued the puppy and that meant he was her responsibility, bills included. Riley always paid her own way. She always took care of herself. That was one of Mary's many life lessons—if you take care of yourself, you'll never have to worry. Usually Riley would never have let a stranger, even an incredibly sweet stranger who knew how to wear a towel, help her out with something that had the potential to get her fired. But she hadn't seen any other choice.

This was the third time Riley had taken J.D. out to pee. The first time, she'd done some more research, which told her he needed to pee every two hours. Not that she needed that info.

J.D. just pawed the top of her head when he wanted out. But research made her feel prepared. Before she'd aged out of the system, Mary had had Riley take the Casey Life Skills Assessment, and together they'd come up with a learning plan to fill in Riley's gaps, the things most kids learned from the families that she never had. It took a ton of research on everything from putting together a basic first aid kit, to resetting a circuit breaker, to being aware of basic etiquette. And so much more. Even now, she'd occasionally come across a gap she hadn't even realized she had. Not often anymore. She tried to remember the last time and was surprised to find she couldn't. Maybe she could finally walk around without thinking everybody else knew something she didn't. It was a strange feeling.

Thank god for Mary. She'd made sure Riley knew how to handle anything that came at her so she'd be okay on her own. In a way, Mary was responsible for The Ultimate Plan. She'd noticed that Riley always went for the big coffee-table book in the battered bookcase in the human services waiting area, and on Riley's ninth birthday, Mary told her to take *Beautiful America* home. It was one of the few things that really felt like hers. Back then, all her stuff had fit in one of those big black garbage bags that she lugged from place to place.

Even now, Mary hadn't forgotten her. A couple times a year, an email from her would show up, just a few lines describing her latest home decorating project or something like that. And asking how Riley was. Always. It was something Riley had incorporated into her own hospitality training, the way she worked with guests at all her jobs—always ask people how they are, and really listen to the answer.

Enough of that. Enough of thinking about the past, even the good parts. Riley pulled up the SmoochiePoochie app. Two messages already. Nice. She noticed she also had a message from Ms. Aguilar, who never seemed to sleep, and read it first. The group of scientists who were going to be studying the vortex were arriving earlier than expected and wanted to make a trip out tomorrow morning. No biggie, even though her manager seemed to feel it necessary to give her extensive instructions.

"A puppy!"

Riley turned toward the voice and saw Starla running toward her, wearing an oversized T-shirt as a nightgown that said YOU ARE ON MY TO-DO LIST. Had to be a present from Bumper, whose car was still in front of Starla's cabin. They'd managed to make it through the night without breaking up. Unless they'd broken up and already made up, which was a possibility.

Starla dropped to her knees in front of J.D., who tangled himself in the leash in his excitement to greet her. "Where did you get him?" Riley gave her the rundown. "Who could possibly do that to this sweet little baby?" Starla crooned, freeing J.D.'s legs for the fourth time. Her voice sounded a little husky, and when Riley glanced at her, she saw Starla had tears in her eyes. The girl went through an exhausting number of emotions every day, but no one could say she didn't have a good heart. "We should keep him. Dogs are wonderful healers and teachers because of their huge capacity for unconditional love."

If it was unconditional, my bank account wouldn't be down $133.72, Riley thought wryly. "No pets at the resort, including employee housing. That means no telling anyone else."

"For sure."

Reminding Starla of the no-exceptions rule gave Riley a twinge of anxiety. She couldn't afford to lose this job. Without a few more paychecks, she'd never make it to Vermont on schedule. But J.D. wouldn't be there much longer, so no worries. "There are already people who want to adopt him. I knew there would be."

"Of course, because he's so, so, so cute." Starla gave the puppy a kiss on the nose between every "so," and J.D. gave Starla a lick in exchange for each, one landing right on her mouth, which just made her laugh. The pup was such an affectionate little goof, and so was Starla. At least from Riley's pee-break study sessions, she'd learned that most of the bacteria in dogs' mouths wasn't—word of the day—*zoonotic*, so it wouldn't make a human sick.

While Starla started a baby-talk conversation with J.D., Riley read the info from the potential adopters—a family with two other dogs, and a couple, Jen and Jason, with no pets or kids. She messaged the couple back, figuring J.D. would get more spoiling without competition, then managed to drag Starla's attention away from the pup. "Sorry for the late notice, but I have to switch up your schedule tomorrow morning. That group of scientists is starting work earlier than planned, and I need you to take them to the vortex. It'll be even easier than a regular tour. You don't have to give them the whole spiel. Just drive them, hand out drinks and snacks, and hang out while they do their thing."

"I'm in my pajamas," Starla protested. "You can't talk to me about work when I'm in my pajamas."

"You're right. Sorry." Riley grimaced. Was she turning into Ms. Aguilar now? "If I do that again, throw a box of wintergreen Tic Tacs at my head." Riley looked down at J.D. "Come on. Let's get you some breakfast."

"Happy adoption day, sweet puppy!" Starla called after them.

Riley shook her head as she measured out a cup of the food, which from the list of organic ingredients looked like it was probably the priciest they had at the pet store and definitely more nutritious than the contents of her fridge. Whoever was working there yesterday must have heard a big *ka-ching* when Daniel walked in. The bowls he'd chosen were pretty cute, though, not that the puppy knew who Mickey and Pluto were.

She figured she could take a few minutes to get dressed while J.D. ate, but she'd only taken a few steps when she heard him coming after her. Clearly, he didn't want to dine alone. She returned to the kitchen and sat on the hardwood floor next to him. He took a bite, looked at her, took another bite, looked at her, like he needed to keep confirming she was still right there.

Poor thing—he'd been abandoned, after all. Riley knew what it felt like to be all alone in the world at too young an age. Maybe a little conversation would ratchet down his anxiety. "Here's the deal. You're getting a new home today. A furever home, they call it. This thing with me was just temporary, and now you're getting your real family. Their names are Jen and Jason. Maybe they'll decide to keep calling you J.D., so you can all be *J*s together, which is a thing some humans seem to enjoy. They don't have kids or other pets, so it's all going to be about you, buddy. A little advice? Making a good first impression is key, so you might want to rethink your howls of doom. If you have to sleep alone, you'll be okay. Morning will come. It always does, even when it feels like it won't. Trust me." She kept chattering, giving reassurances that, okay, were completely for her, until he finished the food, then together they went to her room so she could change out of her PJ's.

Her phone pinged. A message from the SmoochiePoochie couple. They wanted to know if she could drop off J.D. that morning. "See, it's all going to be good. They're so excited to see you." She had a few hours before the first of the two photography adventure outings she was running, so she messaged back that she would be there in about forty minutes. Easy-breezy.

Riley gave J.D. a treat—organic, obviously—and he followed her as she packed up all his stuff. She got it and the pup loaded in the car, and they were off, bouncing along the dirt road leading down from the summit. She cracked the window, and the puppy tilted his chin toward the warm air blowing in, his little nose twitching. His open mouth made him look like he was grinning.

She hit *scan* on the radio and stopped it when she heard "Waterloo." It was one of her aural happy pills, and she had to listen to it every time it came on. Every time. One of her prized possessions as a kid, second only to the *Beautiful America* coffee-table book, was a beat-up Walkman that some foster kid before her had left behind along with three cassettes—*Abba's Greatest Hits*, *Bat Out of Hell II*, and *Super Hits of 1995*. She knew every word to every song on all three. Her last boyfriend had died laughing every time she broke out "Pickup Man," but she loved it unironically, loved them all.

Riley started singing. J.D. stared at her. Maybe he'd never heard anyone sing before. He let out a little *awwooo*, like he'd decided to harmonize. It even sounded a bit like he was saying "Waterloo." Who could have decided to leave this little guy out in the desert? It had been so easy to find him a home. People sucked sometimes.

She glanced over at J.D. again when they were about to cross onto the paved part of Schnebly Hill Road. This was right about where she'd seen him, make that almost hit him. Was his nose good enough to identify the location? She'd read dog noses could be 10,000 to even 100,000 times better than human ones, and odors were supposed to be powerful memory stimulants. Definitely were for her. Whenever she smelled Coco Crush perfume, she thought of her mom. That was one of the few memories she had, that smell. She didn't even have something like that for her dad. She should have been old enough to remember more. She was six when they died. Probably memories were still there somewhere in her brain, but she'd never been able to reach them.

The GPS directed her to one of those classic Sedona houses that had a Mission style—adobe; small, square windows; flat roof with wooden beams sticking out. "Lucky you. Your backyard is pretty much the National Forest."

J.D. yipped with excitement when she let him out of the car.

He immediately peed on the driveway. "What did I say about first impressions?" she asked under her breath. Well, it would dry fast. She opened the wrought-iron gate and headed toward the front door. It swung open before she reached it, and a thirtysomething with perfect no-makeup-looking makeup and chunky blond streaks in her longer-in-the-back bob stepped out. She clapped her hands when she saw the puppy. "He's even more adorable in person! I'm positive he's a purebred Jack Russell."

She hurried over and knelt in front of J.D., who wriggled with excitement. Whatever had happened to him in his short life hadn't made him afraid of people. He seemed to assume everyone was his friend. Finally, she stood back up. "I'm Jen. Obviously."

"Riley. Hi. Like I said on the app, I just found him yesterday, so I don't have any medical records. You should bring him to a vet and get him checked out. It's doubtful he's gotten any of his shots." If whoever had him had cared enough to get vaccinations started, he wouldn't have been dumped. She handed the woman the leash. "He's a great dog. Here are a few things to get you started. Some food and toys." She held out the Pet City bags. She needed to get out of there. It was better to do hard things fast, and even though she'd had J.D. less than a day, leaving him was a hard thing.

J.D. gave a jump of delight when Jen pulled out Squidward, pinching one arm between two of her expertly manicured fingers. He managed to catch one of the toy's legs and refused to release it, hanging in the air by his teeth. Riley grabbed him, gently tugged him free, and put him back on the ground. Jen dropped the toy and he went into attack mode, giving his silly little growl. "That one's his favorite."

Jen looked through the bags and handed one back to Riley. "You can keep the bowls. They don't go with my kitchen." *Kind of rude*, Riley thought, then told herself not to be judgy.

She tended to size people up fast, and that didn't always make for accuracy. Although, really, she got it right a lot more than she got it wrong.

"You don't want to keep them just until you get your own?"

Jen's nose wrinkled. "No thanks."

Whatever. It wasn't like J.D. would care what bowl he ate out of. "Okay. Well, I guess I'll go." She bent down and gave J.D. a fast pat on the head, not letting herself look into those big brown eyes. "Be a good dog." She knew the puppy was trying to follow her as she started for the gate. She could hear his little nails scrabbling on the pavers, and he was yipping frantically.

"No, no. You're staying here," Jen told him. The puppy's yips turned into howls.

Riley's chest tightened. More than tightened. It felt like her ribs were pushing together, preventing her lungs from pulling in a deep breath. She ignored the sensation and didn't look back.

She'd rescued J.D. from the desert and found him a home. It was all she could do. T.U.P. couldn't accommodate a puppy. "Have a good life," she murmured as she shut the gate behind her.

Daniel's eyes were burning, and his brain felt like it was wrapped in a weighted blanket. The sleep deprivation was getting to him. He tried to remember the last time he'd gotten a solid eight. Before Sam was arrested, probably.

He needed some air. Riley had said she'd leave a gift certificate for him at reception. He decided to head over, just to give himself a destination. He took a shower. Didn't need one, but it gave him something to do. Threw on some clothes. Did the pickup. That killed about twenty minutes altogether. But he now had a new destination—the gift shop. Unfortunately, it was only on the other side of the lobby. He'd been hoping to waste a little more time finding it.

The air in the shop smelled woodsy. Pine, he thought, and maybe juniper, but with something sweet mixed in. Lavender? He wandered over to take a closer look at the astonishing range of essential oils surrounding a diffuser on a nearby table. A lot of the oils were familiar—clove, sage, gardenia—but there were a few he'd never heard of, like osmanthus and ravansara and vetiver. He picked up the little bottle of osmanthus. Almost a hundred bucks for a third of an ounce. The certificate Riley had left him was for fifty. Not that he was considering buying the oil. A hundred bucks? No matter how good it smelled, it wasn't worth it. He hoped she got an employee discount. Fifty dollars was a lot of money, especially on top of what she'd paid him back for the puppy supplies. But what could he do? She was one stubborn woman.

"If you have any questions, just let me know," the twenty-ish woman behind the blue-painted wooden buffet that served as the shop's counter called. The piece had the same vibe as the furniture in his casita, artfully weathered, color that echoed the local landscape.

Daniel twirled the little bottle between his fingers. "What's osmanthus?" He didn't add *And why does it cost so much?*, but that's what he was curious about.

"It's a flower. Same family as jasmine and forsythia," a man in khakis smeared with red earth answered before the clerk could. "From China."

"Here, let me let you smell it." The woman walked over and took the bottle from him, then put a drop of the oil on a little slip of paper. She waved it through the air and handed it to Daniel. He took a sniff.

"It smells like apricots with a little pepper mixed in."

"Good nose," the man said. He carried a wooden contraption—that's all Daniel could think to call it—that clicked and clacked as he joined them.

"Not to be rude, but why this instead of apricot oil? That

would have to be a lot less expensive." Daniel took another sniff.

The man checked the price and gave a low whistle. "I guess the amount of blossoms it takes for an ounce accounts for the price. You wouldn't need nearly as many apricots."

"Even though they smell similar, they have a billion and two different properties," the clerk told them. "Apricot oil, which we also have, is great for your hair and skin. Osmanthus oil is used for headaches and muscle pain, and it's also amazing for dealing with anxiety and depression."

If it worked, worked well enough to shut down Daniel's brain and let him sleep, it would be worth it. But he didn't think anything in one of these little bottles was the solution to his insomnia.

"Is there anything else you'd like to sample? We have some super wonderful blends. The one in the diffuser is Sedona Song." She adjusted the reeds, and the woodsy smell intensified. "Or you could try Sedona Morning. One sniff and absolutely instantaneous enlightenment."

"Not right now, but thanks." He wouldn't mind a little more conversation, though. He had a lot of day to fill. Maybe he should have gone home and come back when he could see Sam, but his parents wanted him here, even though there was nothing useful he could do. "Can I ask what you got there?" he asked the man. The doohickey—he'd come up with another word to describe the thing—had a piece shaped like a hand, a cord with a knob on it, a curved section. Daniel couldn't figure out what it was for.

"Something I've been tinkering with. I wanted to see if Cari here might want to sell it in the shop."

"Garret is our head gardener, but he's also a part-time inventor," Cari told Daniel. "Part-time, with full-time output. He gives birth to a hundred and a quarter brainchildren every day."

"I need someone to demonstrate my latest on." Garret looked

over at Daniel. "Are you up for it? You look like somebody who could use a pat on the back."

"Sure. Why not."

Garret placed the curved part of the device over Daniel's shoulder with the hand hanging down his back and the cord with the knob dangling over his chest. "Give it a pull." He flicked the knob, and Daniel obediently tugged it. When he did, the hand tapped his back.

"The way I see it, everybody has times when they need a pat on the back, an 'attaboy.' That's what I call it, The Attaboy. Say you finished a big job, but there's no one around to tell, no one to say 'good job.' You just stick on The Attaboy, and—" Garret nodded at Daniel, and Daniel tugged the cord a few times, getting a couple pats on the back. "Doesn't that feel satisfying?"

"Yeah." He actually did feel a little better than when he'd walked in, but he thought it was more talking to the cheerful, eccentric guy than the effects of his invention. "I'd buy it." Or at least he'd use a gift certificate to buy it.

"What do you say, Cari? Should I make up a couple dozen?" Garret slid The Attaboy off Daniel's shoulder.

"You know I can't add new merchandise without Ms. Aguilar's absolute approval." Cari sounded just the tiniest bit put upon. Daniel wondered how many times the two of them had had a similar conversation. "If you want to leave it, I'll show it to her."

"I'll do it next time I see her." He started toward the door, then veered over to the counter. "The eucalyptus needs to be moved to a spot with more light. That's why it's losing leaves close to the base of the branches." He adjusted the plant's position, then leaned close to it and started singing "Uptown Funk," his whole body rocking to the beat, The Attaboy clicking and clacking. He paused and looked over his shoulder at Cari. "Kitaro is well and good. I listen to him myself on occasion, and I get that his music suits the shop. But this beauty"—he gently ran a finger across one of the eucalyptus leaves—"likes boogie. You gotta give it a little Tower of Power, Ray Parker, Jr., like that, even just for half an hour a day." He returned to the song.

"Are you unconditionally okay with this?" Cari softly asked Daniel. "He shouldn't keep it up too long. I try to choose music that forms a bridge between the material world and the metaphysical, but . . ." She shrugged.

"It's all good." He waited until Garret finished up the song, then joined him in front of the plant. "How'd you conclude that it's a Bruno Mars fan?"

"Trial and error. You should have seen it a few days after I hit it with some Mark Atkins on the didgeridoo. I thought it might appeal to its Australian roots. Its roots," he repeated, laughing at his own joke, which made Daniel laugh. "But it broke out in pustules."

"Not a fan."

"Definitely not. Then I remembered almost all didgeridoos are made out of eucalyptus. A bit macabre for our friend, perhaps." Garret scratched the back of his neck. "Although there's an instrument made out of a human femur, usually from a criminal, that's played in a Tibetan ritual. It's called a kangling and is supposed to give angry spirits peace in the afterlife, so playing it is an act of compassion." He gave one of the eucalyptus's leaves a friendly pat. "This one didn't see the didgeridoo in that vein, though I meant well. It took a few tries, but I eventually found its grove." He winked at Daniel. "I mean groove."

"Fascinating." He could listen to this guy all day, but Garret pulled a High Sky baseball cap out of his back pocket and stuck it on.

"Gotta get back out there. Enjoy your stay, and thanks for letting me demonstrate The Attaboy. You deserved it. I can tell." He clapped Daniel on the back before heading off, invention in hand.

Daniel was horrified to feel tears sting his eyes at the man's kind words. The sleep deprivation was seriously getting to him. He blinked a couple times as he moved on to another display table, this one covered with rocks and crystals in a huge array of colors and textures. He spotted one that reminded him of the sugared green gumdrops Sam loved, even though they were disgusting. Impulsively, he picked it up and brought it to the register. He'd find a place that sold the disgusting gumdrops and bring the crystal and candy over to Ironwood. He couldn't see Sam, but at least his brother would know Daniel was thinking about him.

"This one is a powerful spiritual cleanser." Cari rang him up. "It's perfectly phenomenal for releasing any feelings of anger." Sam probably had quite a few of those. She reached for a bag.

"Do you by any chance gift wrap?" Sam loved getting presents. He always tore off the paper like an excited little kid on Christmas morning. He had a thing against gift bags, saying they just weren't the same as the real deal.

"Of course." She put the crystal in a box, wrapped it in navy paper covered with stars, and added a bow. Daniel left and started on his new mission, the candy. It took two stops to find the gumdrops. Bonus. That used an hour out of the endless stretch of time Daniel had to fill. He considered picking out all the green ones as kind of a joke, but in all the reading he'd done, he'd found out that a lot of people in rehab craved sugar. Sam would probably rather have all the flavors. Daniel decided to get a jumbo bag of mini candy bars, too, making sure it was one that had Twix, another, non-disgusting, favorite of Sam's. Sam would want to share with his roommate and whoever else was around. He was that kind of guy.

Daniel spent another fifteen minutes driving from the store to the rehab. There were a few people in the waiting area, and they all looked as stressed as Daniel felt. The research he'd done was supposed to help with the anxiety, but it wasn't working. Or maybe it was, and he'd be feeling a lot worse if he hadn't done all the prep. He wished he'd brought candy for everyone waiting. Or one of those Attaboy back-slappers.

He walked over to reception, skirting around the tree growing right out of the ground in the center of the room. "Hi. I'm Daniel Acker. Sam Acker's brother."

"Hey. I remember from when he checked in."

The man didn't look familiar, even with the deep red "2%" tat that covered most of his throat. "Sorry. I forgot your name."

"Trevor. And no worries. The brain can only handle so much input."

"I brought Sam a care package. I hope that's okay." Daniel set the grocery bag on the frosted glass counter.

"One of the counselors will need to go through it, and unfortunately unwrap the present, but if it's given the all clear, he should have it in the next couple hours. I'm sure he'll appreciate it. Not everybody has the support."

"Can I ask how he's doing?" Daniel was hoping for more than the brief reassurances he'd been given when he called yesterday, but after Trevor clicked a few keys on the computer, he said almost exactly what Daniel had been told on the phone. No complications with detox, settling in.

"I know it's not that satisfying. But as soon as Sam's team thinks he's ready, you'll be able to visit." He glanced at the screen. "And he's got phone privileges starting tomorrow, although only for a few hours in the morning and a few in the evening. A lot of his time will be scheduled—therapy, activities, cleaning, meals."

"Is there a number I can use?"

"He has to call you."

Daniel nodded, shuffling his feet. Being here made him feel itchy and antsy, even with the soft lighting, the cool blues and greens of the comfy-looking chairs and sofas, and the tree, but he was having trouble making himself turn around and leave. Like if he just kept standing here, he'd see Sam walking by.

Trevor seemed to get it. "Know what this tattoo means?"

"Huh-uh."

"Two percent of meth addicts survive. Or at least that's a statistic I read right before I got this." Trevor ran a hand down his throat. "I think it's actually better than that, at least marginally better. But whatever. The point is the odds are bad, but I made it. A buddy did the tat for me when I was ten years clean. He developed the ink himself. It's colored with earth from all the local vortexes. It's supposed to hold their energy." He laughed. "He's a complete Sedona-head. I grew up here. I think that makes me immune to the woo-woo. But it's a good reminder, and it was a cool gesture on his part."

"You've just given me something to tell my parents. I want to give them an update every day, and all I can tell them is what you told me—Sam's doing okay, getting settled in. But hearing about somebody who made it ten years—"

"Closer to twenty now."

"That'll give them some hope. If you don't mind."

Trevor grinned. "I live to inspire." He picked up the plastic bag. "You want to put a note in here?"

Daniel hadn't even thought of that. "Definitely." Trevor handed him a piece of paper and a pen, and Daniel took them over to one of the chairs next to a low coffee table. He hunched over it, trying to come up with something to write. Finally, he just scribbled *see you soon* and signed his name. That's the best he had. Another one of those times when his best sucked.

CHAPTER 5

Starla felt like she'd been eating mounds of Lori's sublime chocolates, that's how wide open her heart was. She had complete faith that getting back with Bumper was a decision the universe supported. She couldn't wait to get out to the vortex. It amplified everything, and with the way she was feeling right now . . . the vortex would bring her to a state of bliss.

She pulled the van up in front of reception and climbed out, spotting two guys and a girl, all around her age, weaving around the groupings of sofas, tables, and chairs artfully arranged on the front patio. One of the guys was carrying what looked almost like a bright yellow leaf-blower, but maybe twice as long, with the handle in the middle instead of one end, and some extra science-y stuff. The other two people carried bulky metal suitcases, probably filled with more science-y equipment.

"Hi, I'm Starla. I'll be taking you out to the Juniper Vortex." The guy with the leaf-blower thingy introduced himself. Adam. *Adam, Adam, Adam*, she repeated to herself, trying to come up with a way to remember it. Riley was all about entertainment staff remembering names. Got it. Uh, damn, Adam was cute. Maybe not everyone would think so, but Starla found geeky guys so adorable, and Adam was checking all the boxes—T-shirt with the pi symbol inside a pumpkin; curly, messy brown hair falling over his forehead; wire-rimmed glasses. With her geek attraction, it was kind of surprising she'd ended up with Bumper, whose look was more frat-boy chic, but Bumper made her feel electrically alive. Even when they fought—maybe especially then, well, then and when they were having sex—all her senses felt cranked up.

Not the time to be thinking about Bumper. She had a habit of letting her attention drift when she was supposed to be working. "Can I ask what that thing is?" Starla asked, nodding at the yellow thingy.

"A magnetometer." Adam shoved his curls off his forehead, and they immediately fell back in place. "We're going to get real-time measurements of the magnetic energies at the vortex site, and, if possible, find a way to amplify them."

Starla didn't think the essence of the vortex was something that could be captured with machines or even understood by the brain. It could only be experienced. She kept that to herself and continued the introductions. The girl's name was Rissa. *Rissa, Rissa, Rissa.* That was an easy one. Rissa meant sea nymph, and the girl had gorgeous butt-length red hair, just like Ariel's.

The last guy was Miles. *Miles, Miles, Miles.* Miles Smiles—that would work. He had a great smile.

"Love your hair," she told him, and that smile of his widened. His bleached tips set off his springy short dreads perfectly. Starla had almost gone with bleached bangs last time she changed up her hair, but then she fell in love with bubblegum blue and decided to do that for half her hair and keep the rest her natural black. "Isn't there supposed to be one more in your group?"

"Our boss will be here in a sec," Miles answered.

"Great. Let's go ahead and get your gear stowed." Starla

walked around to the back of the van and opened the door. Rissa handed her one of the metal suitcases, which was lighter than Starla was expecting. "Can I ask what's in these? I'm incredibly curious about everything. Some people call it nosy."

"Curiosity is the basis of science," Adam said.

"It's EEG equipment," Rissa explained. "We're going to see how our brain waves are affected by the vortex."

Maybe part of the vortex's power *could* be measured. Starla had had moments of deep insight while at the site. Could that show in brain waves?

"*If* our brain waves are affected at all." Miles shook his head. "Don't forget the part where scientists don't bring any expectations to the experiment."

"You're the one bringing the expectations. You keep saying the whole experiment is ridiculous." Rissa gave her beautiful red hair a toss.

"I might have said it once, because there's no evidence that there are any magnetic abnormalities around the vortexes, so building a study around the site's magnetism seems . . . I just think there are better ways to spend the university's research dollars." Miles pointed at Rissa. "If you repeat that in front of the boss, I'm going to call 'liar.'"

"There have been reports of sudden magnetic events," Rissa insisted. "Sudden, as in not constantly happening, which means readings that didn't show anything might not have been taken at the right time."

"In the almost two hundred years since the magnetometer was invented, there's never been a reading at the right time?" Miles shot back, but he still had his smile.

Rissa kept her smile, too. "You're forgetting our magnetometer was adapted to boost the magnetic energies, not just record them."

There was some heat there, some chemistry. Starla wondered if they were a couple. They argued like a couple. "Any of you want some prickly pear sparkling lemonade? Or water?" she asked as the science crew got settled in the back seats of the van. "There's some in that cooler on the floor."

Rissa slapped Miles's shoulder. "Have some. It's supposed to be great for a hangover. Although, I'm sure, as a scientist, you wouldn't have been drinking the night before you're doing research with very expensive equipment."

"You can be such a—"

"Here comes Dorothea," Adam said.

"Sorry, sorry. Lost track of time," a fortyish woman with her hair in two pigtails said as she took the shotgun seat. She was wearing red Converse high-tops, which made remembering her name easy. Red shoes equaled Dorothy equaled Dorothea. *Dorothea, Dorothea, Dorothea.*

"Not a problem." Starla pointed out the cooler again, and they were off. "The lemonade is antiviral and anti-inflammatory. It takes twenty-five pounds of prickly pear to make one gallon of nectar. We make it from cactus on the property." Riley always encouraged the entertainment staff to provide interesting tidbits.

Adam took a bottle. "I'll give one a try."

"The cactus is covered with tiny needles." Starla met his gaze in the rearview mirror. His eyes were almost as blue as the Sedona sky. "Getting to the pulp is quite the process, so know that what you're drinking was made with love."

"How can I resist?" Rissa took one. "Too bad that the only way we can get access to the Juniper Vortex is by staying at Sedona's most exclusive resort and drinking handmade love juice."

"Tragic," Dorothea agreed. "I tried to arrange for access without the stay, but no go. Still, it's not like we're the Royal Society of Chemistry spending god knows how much on the process of making the perfect cup of tea." She took a swig of her lemonade. "Does anyone want a Pop-Tart?"

"We also have homemade energy bars in that basket next to the cooler. Our chef's special recipe. They have amaranth, mesquite flour and syrup, piñon pine nuts, and dates."

"Cold Pop-Tarts?" Adam raised his eyebrows as he looked over at Dorothea. "A Pop-Tart needs the Maillard reaction to reach peak flavor."

What did ducks have to do with Pop-Tarts? Adam must have noticed Starla's confusion. "It's a chemical reaction between amino acids and reducing sugars that creates melanoidins." He could clearly see that didn't help. "The change creates different flavor compounds. It's what happens when you brown onions or meat or when you toast marshmallows."

Starla should tell Riley that. It could make a fun trivia fact for the next s'more night. "Thanks for explaining it." Starla hated it when people refused to explain things. People like Bumper. Riley's theory was that he liked feeling superior. Starla just thought he found explanations boring, but it was still irritating.

"I don't eat Pop-Tarts. They killed John Travolta," Miles said matter-of-factly, like it was common knowledge. He took one of the energy bars.

"John Travolta is dead?" Dorothea exclaimed. "I love him."

"He's alive," Adam answered.

"I'm confused." Dorothea took a sip of her water.

"Me too," Starla admitted.

Rissa sighed. "It's his *Pulp Fiction* obsession. For me, if a guy likes *Pulp Fiction*, *Fight Club*, or especially *American Psycho*, it's a deal-breaker."

"*American Psycho* is a brilliant repudiation of excess consumerism," Miles protested.

Rissa frowned at him. "It's a disgusting—"

"Can we go back to the Pop-Tarts and John Travolta?" Dorothea tore open a package of the Tarts.

"If you don't know, you don't deserve to know," Miles said.

"Don't ask me." Rissa took one of the Tarts. "All I've ever gotten out of him is that it has to do with his beloved *Pulp Fiction*, which I only watched fifteen minutes of once, because it's disgusting."

Adam was shaking his head again. "How long is the movie?"

"Two hours and forty-three minutes," Miles answered.

"Of course, he knows the exact length." Rissa waved a Pop-Tart in Miles's face, making him give an exaggerated flinch.

"As a scientist, you shouldn't judge something by observing approximately nine-point-seven percent of it." Adam took a Pop-Tart, pulled out a pocket knife, and began cutting it in half.

Miles stared at him. "You're eating it cold after all that Maillard reaction talk?"

"It might be useful for my Oreo system." Adam cut the Pop-Tart into quarters.

Starla glanced over her shoulder at him. "Have you seen the whole thing? Can you unconfuse us?"

Adam seemed happy to explain this, too. "In the movie, John Travolta's character goes to Bruce Willis's apartment to kill him. He puts some Pop-Tarts in the toaster and goes into the bathroom."

"Leaving his gun in the kitchen. Because somehow he hasn't put it together that every time he goes to the bathroom, something bad happens, which means he should always take his gun with him." Miles took a bite of the energy bar.

"Willis gets home, and when Travolta comes out of the bathroom, he's pointing Travolta's own gun at him." Adam folded his knife.

Miles jumped in again. "He's trying to decide whether or not shoot him. I say he was just going to maybe shoot him in the knee. But then the Pop-Tarts pop up, making that toaster popping sound, and instinctively Willis squeezes the trigger, and so—"

"Pop-Tarts killed John Travolta," Starla, Rissa, and Dorothea said together.

Adam pried one of the quarters of his Pop-Tart apart. Rissa caught Starla watching in the rearview mirror. "I know you're wondering what this freak is doing." She gave Adam an affectionate shoulder bump. "He's been trying to develop a way to pull an Oreo apart while leaving exactly half the cream on each side, but hasn't perfected it. He practices whenever he can, although clearly research on a Pop-Tart can't be accurate."

"You never know how a breakthrough will arrive." Adam popped one of the pieces into his mouth.

"He has a system for everything. It's one of the reasons I hired him," Dorothea said.

"A system gives you the most efficient way to do an action. It reduces the number of mundane decisions in a day, which frees up brain space." Adam ate another piece of Pop-Tart. He was definitely the geekiest of the team. How cute was he? Starla would love to see the systems he had for other things.

"Here we are." Starla guided the van onto the small dirt lot near the vortex and parked. "Right up ahead, you can see the three junipers the vortex is named for. The vortex is believed to emanate from the spot that is equidistant from the trees." Oops. Starla forgot that Riley said Starla didn't need to give the science crew the usual spiel, but since she'd started, she kept going. "Look at the trunks of the junipers. See how twisted they are? They grow that way because they are constantly hit by the powerful energy of the vortex. If you look at junipers in other locations, their trunks are perfectly straight."

"But that doesn't—" Miles began.

Dorothea cut him off. "I'd like to hear the lore."

"It's possible that you'll feel physical sensations as the energy swirls around you. Your skin might tingle, you might even feel dizzy. It's completely normal, and nothing to worry about." Starla got out of the van and slid open the side door to let the group out. "Let's approach with an open mind and heart." That line wasn't part of the High Sky tour narration she'd memorized, but she always added it. "Is there anything I can do, anything I can help with?" she asked as the scientists began unloading their gear.

"Having untrained people participating could interfere with the results." Adam smiled at her. He didn't have the toothpaste-commercial grin of Miles Smiles. Adam's was more shy, starting with completely closed lips, then widening just enough to show that one of his front teeth had a little chip.

"I'll be right here if you need me, then." Starla grabbed a camp chair, a beach umbrella, and a bottle of water, got settled next to the van, then watched the crew get to work. Adam was fiddling with controls on the magnetometer, while Dorothea, Rissa, and Miles opened one of the equipment suitcases and pulled on tight caps of what looked like latex, studded with dozens of electrodes.

It was clear they had everything in hand, so Starla shut her eyes and opened her senses to the vortex. She pressed her feet firmly into the ground, and felt the slight vibrations of the earth. She wondered if the scientists could feel it. Some people couldn't, which Starla attributed to a chakra blockage, possibly caused by actions in a past life or an ancestor's physical or mental pain. She wished everyone could feel what she was feeling as the vibrations moved from her feet all the way to the top of her head until it felt like every cell was glowing. The bliss she'd felt ever since she and Bumper had had that amazing makeup sex was amplified until it consumed her and she lost awareness of everything else.

"Starla. Starla!"

It took a few moments for the sound to penetrate her brain and become translated into words, then another few seconds for her brain to send the signal to her eyelids to cause them to open. When they did, she saw Adam, Uh-Damn-He's-Cute

Adam. She sat up fast. Or she intended to sit up fast, but actually sat up in a slow, languid motion.

"We're almost ready to head out."

Starla realized the rest of the group had almost finished packing up their equipment. Uh-oh. She must have blissed out so completely, she'd completely lost track of time. That had happened the first time she'd visited the Juniper Vortex, but usually she was able to keep at least partial awareness of what was going on around her. Maybe she let her guard down since she knew the group wouldn't be needing her. "How'd it go?" she asked Adam.

He glanced over his shoulder at the others. "The equipment worked fine. We took all the readings we had planned for the day, and that should count as success. This is exploratory research, not confirmatory research. Any outcome gives more knowledge. Whether a hypothesis is proved or disproved shouldn't matter, but Dorothea seemed . . . to me it seemed as if she were disappointed that there were no magnetic or brain wave abnormalities, but I'm not always the best at reading people."

Starla looked over at Dorothea and could almost feel the woman's disappointment and frustration. Her shoulders were rolled forward, and she was moving with a stiffness that usually meant unaligned chakras. "I think you're definitely right this time."

"Was the magnetometer adapted to my exact specifications?" Dorothea demanded when she reached them, sounding like a completely different woman from the one who'd been chatting about Pop-Tarts and John Travolta.

Adam stood up a little straighter. "All five elements of calibration standard were met."

Dorothea only snorted in response and slammed the door after she got in the passenger seat. Her negative emotional state permeated the van on the ride back to High Sky, and there was none of the fun of the ride out. Starla didn't like returning a group in worse shape than when they'd started. "Do you have any plans for the rest of the day?" she asked as she parked in front of reception. "We have several activities coming up— glass bead making at one of the local studios this afternoon, live music by the fire pits tonight. I can set you up with mountain biking or a hike, but you might not want more sun so soon."

Dorothea answered for the whole group. "We're not here for vacation. We need to get the gear unloaded and go over the readings again. We might have missed something."

"I reviewed everything twice and—"

Rissa put her hand on Adam's arm, stopping him. "Sure thing, boss."

Starla opened the van's back doors. Adam, Miles, and Rissa quickly got everything out and followed Dorothea inside, Adam taking time to give Starla a wave over his shoulder. She hoped Ms. Aguilar didn't run into them right now. She would not be happy to see guests so obviously unhappy. Well, Starla was assigned to the lunch buffet, just to be around to give suggestions for activities and spa treatments, basically make sure everyone had what they needed. Maybe they'd be there, and she'd have another chance to cheer them up.

After she parked the van in the employee lot, she scanned the area for Ms. Aguilar, then took her cell out of the glove compartment. She always left it there so she wouldn't be tempted to peek at it while she was supposed to have all her attention on guests. Although today, the vortex had clearly distracted her more than the phone ever would.

She smiled when she saw Bumper had texted her five times. She clicked the most recent one:

I am really sick of this and sick of you. Forget tonight. It's over.

What? Where did that come from? Fingers trembling, she quickly read through the rest of the texts. The earliest one was a simple *Hey, baby, can't wait to see you tonight.* In the one after that, he sounded irritated she hadn't texted him back. And the next two moved from irritation to out-and-out anger. Why did he do this? He knew she wasn't allowed to use her cell on the job.

The deep bliss Starla experienced at the vortex felt like it was rushing out of her body, the glow in her cells blinking out, leaving her feeling chilled.

Riley checked her watch. Two minutes 'til five. She waited until it was five straight up, then knocked on Ms. Aguilar's door. Punctuality was one of her manager's many requirements, but Riley didn't want to be early. She might end up having to make chitchat until Lori and Garret showed up. Riley could do chitchat. It was part of the job, a part she usually enjoyed. But Ms. Aguilar didn't make it easy.

"Enter." The words weren't quite distinct, probably because Ms. Aguilar had just popped half a dozen of her beloved wintergreen Tic Tacs.

Even though Riley had stalled, she was still the first one there, but Lori dashed in a moment later, a smudge of pesto on one cheek. As they took seats in front of the desk, Riley caught Lori's eye and rubbed the spot on her own cheek. Lori wiped the pesto away, but not before Ms. Aguilar saw it, her lips pressing into a disapproving line. She was a woman who never had a hair out of place, a stain on her shirt, or a wrinkle in her skirt, and she expected the same from the staff.

"Hola, everyone." Garret strolled in, a smear of dirt on his forehead, more dirt on the knees of his khakis. He plopped down into the empty chair next to Lori. Ms. Aguilar's tight lips twisted into a frown. Her posture was always perfect, shoulders back, back straight. Riley was sure she didn't approve of plopping and was definitely hating the dirt. But although Ms. Aguilar easily intimidated almost everyone, Garret was impervious. Riley wasn't sure if he didn't notice the manager's disapproval or just didn't care. Either way, he got away with it, because he was a truly genius gardener and it showed in every plant on the place. Lori was just as genius in the kitchen, but didn't seem to realize how valuable she was to High Sky and so to their manager. Lori followed every rule to the letter.

"Let's begin." Ms. Aguilar flipped open the small notebook she always carried. "I had a complaint that the creosote bushes are 'too pungent.'"

Garret laughed. "Where I grew up, we called it *hediondilla*. That means *smelly*. You can't change a thing's nature."

"Perhaps we should consider replacing it."

Lori surprised Riley by coming to Garret's defense. The chef usually liked to stay under Ms. Aguilar's radar. "Some complaints are just silly. The other night, someone complained because the pasta in the artichoke and blue cheese fettuccine was too short." She blinked rapidly, as if she'd surprised herself as much as she had Riley.

"I wasn't informed of that. I'm to be informed of all complaints." Ms. Aguilar shook the three wintergreen Tic Tacs remaining in the box into her mouth.

Riley glanced at Lori, whose eyes were lowered, clearly stung by Ms. Aguilar's criticism. "At one of the vortex tours, a guest said that creosote 'evoked the essence of the Southwestern desert,'" Riley put in, to pull Ms. Aguilar's attention away from the chef. It was a total lie. But it could be true, and "essence of the Southwestern desert" was a phrase the manager tossed around a lot.

"There's something to be said for highlighting our unique landscape," Ms. Aguilar conceded. Riley struggled not to smile. She had a gift for manipulation, at least according to one of her foster parents. What that really meant, she'd come to realize, was that she had a gift for understanding people, one of the things that made her good at her job. "Moving on."

"Anyone want to meet up at Rocky's later?" Garret asked

when Ms. Aguilar released them. "Ten-dollar wine night." His eyes lingered on Lori. Maybe Starla was right. Maybe there was some liking going on there.

"Can't." Lori didn't offer an explanation, and her eyes stayed off Garret.

"I think I need an early night." Riley hadn't slept well, even though she hadn't had to deal with puppy pee breaks every two hours. She'd found herself missing that warm spot J.D. made on the top of her head. "See you two tomorrow." Knowing Ms. Aguilar was safely in her office, Riley pulled out her phone and checked messages as she headed out of the reception building.

"What the—" she muttered, stopping to give her full attention to a text from Jen. She and Jason wanted to give J.D. back. They'd had him less than two days. Two days. And they'd decided it "wasn't working out." What did that even mean? That had happened to her once. She'd been placed in a new home, and a couple weeks later, bye-bye, Riley. She'd asked Mary why, and her social worker had just given a hopeless shrug. Riley had gone over every move she'd made, every word she'd spoken, and couldn't come up with anything.

Well, she wasn't going to let her puppy—*the* puppy—stay with people who didn't want him, who didn't see he was everything a puppy should be. She immediately texted back, asking if they were home. When Jen said yes, Riley texted that she was on her way. At least she was off that night. She hurried outside, then paused again.

Uh-oh. Daniel sat at one of the little patio tables with Starla, which would be fine, except for two things. Since Starla was part of the entertainment team, chatting with guests was part of her job, but Starla wasn't on the clock right now. And—much bigger problem—she had clearly been crying. Riley rushed over. If Ms. Aguilar came out of her office and saw this little scene, she would not be happy. Crying in front of a guest wasn't on the list of no-exception rules, but only because it had probably never occurred to Ms. Aguilar that one of her employees would shatter the resort's serene vibe with tears.

"Hi, what are you two up to?" Riley tried to keep her voice light while sending Starla a this-is-completely-unacceptable look.

Starla sniffled. "Bumper thinks I don't love him."

"Maybe think more about how you feel about him than how he feels about you," Daniel suggested. "How'd you really feel when you got those texts?" His eyes, the same dark brown as the puppy's, were warm and concerned.

Clearly, Starla had dragged Daniel deep into her drama. Now it was up to Riley to drag him back out. Damage control. Starla opened her mouth to launch into a description of her emotional state, but Riley cut her off.

"It's too beautiful out for such depressing talk! We have a great local band who'll be playing by the fire pits tonight. Unlucky Devils. They have a fun, folksy feel. Do you have dinner plans?" She was talking way too fast, trying to get control of the situation and then get to her poor puppy. *The* poor puppy.

She took a deep breath and slowed down. "Our chef is awesome, but if you're thinking you'd rather go into town, Starla and I can recommend a ton of places. All you have to do is tell us what you're craving." Riley gave Starla another pointed look, hoping that hearing her in work mode would remind Starla that she also worked here, whether she was officially on the clock or not.

Instead they both looked at her like she was crazy. Riley kept her entertainment director smile on her face, feeling a little crazy. Then Starla seemed to get it. She grinned at Daniel, a little too widely for it to be natural. "Right. My relationship drama is definitely not part of the evening's entertainment. You'll love Unlucky Devils. The fiddle player is phenomenal." She stood up quickly, almost knocking her chair over. "I should go . . . somewhere." She hesitated, glancing around for a destination.

Daniel stood up, too. "It was nice to meet you. I enjoyed talking to you."

"So, restaurant suggestions?" Riley asked.

"Can I ask how . . . our friend is doing?"

The way he phrased it let her know he wasn't going to out her in front of Starla. "She knows about the dog." Riley was tempted to do one of those lies of omission, tell him she'd found J.D. a home and leave out the part where J.D. was being returned. He'd want to know the truth, though, after spending all that time with the puppy, not to mention spending all that cash without knowing he was going to get it back. "I don't know exactly what happened, but the people who took him changed their minds. I'm going to get him back now."

"Oh, no! How could they give up that sweetie?" Starla exclaimed.

"Exactly!" Riley's outrage made her voice come out a little too loud.

"Can I go with you to get him?" When she hesitated, Daniel lightly touched her arm. "I'd like to see him again. I didn't get a chance to say goodbye."

"I want to go, too! I have to do something, or I'll lose it completely."

"You can come," Riley said quickly, to stop Starla from losing it then and there.

Daniel pulled out his keys. "I could drive."

"That'd be great. Riley's car smells like rotten eggs every time she starts it up, and mine is a complete mess." Starla's voice was trembling a little, but she was holding it together.

Riley's head was spinning. She'd come over here to stop Starla from inappropriately fraternizing with a guest, and now she was about to go off on a puppy-retrieval adventure with the two of them? This was not keeping her eyes on the prize. Still, getting the chance to spend more time with Daniel would be great. She'd been hoping she'd run into him. But how could she let go of the fact that he was a guest at one of the highest-ranked resorts in Sedona? The High Sky entertainment director part of her wanted to make sure he was enjoying himself. That was her job. And being good at her job was vital to T.U.P. It's what gave her the résumé to keep getting the next job in the next beautiful place. Did this friend-of-the-owner guest really want to spend his time on Starla's boyfriend crisis and Riley's puppy situation?

She was good at reading people, and her read on Daniel was Boy Scout. Even his face seemed to say, *hey, trust me*, with its wide-set eyes and snub nose. He even had a few freckles. His lips didn't quite match the rest of him, though. Too sexy. The only word for them was *cushy*. She realized she was staring at them, and it took her a second to remember what she'd been thinking before she started thinking about what it would feel like to kiss those lips.

Right—she'd been trying to decide if he was offering to go with her because he felt like it was kind of his duty to always step in and help, the way he had when she'd barged into his casita with the pup. Definite possibility. "You sure you wouldn't rather hear the band?"

"I'm sure."

Riley wasn't going to ask him twice.

CHAPTER 6

Jen and Jason stared down at the little puddle of puppy pee, identical expressions of disgust on their faces. Daniel laughed. How could you not laugh at a puppy so joyful, he couldn't control his bladder? The second the pup had seen Riley, he'd flung himself on his back and let fly, tail wagging hard enough to create a breeze, flinging pee everywhere.

Starla was giggling, and Riley was giving a throaty chuckle. Jen and Jason were not amused. Anybody who adopted a puppy should have expected to deal with a little pee. Daniel spotted the bags of dog accoutrements he'd bought at the pet store. "There are some wipes with his stuff that are supposed to neutralize urine smells. If you get me one, I'll clean this up." Riley elbowed him in the side, hard, clearly not pleased he'd offered to deal with the mess.

"Are you also going to replace my duvet, because it chewed it to shreds," Jen said, as Jason went for the wipes.

Daniel reached for his wallet, but Riley elbowed him again, hard enough to leave a bruise, and said, "Absolutely not. He's a puppy. Puppies chew."

"I told him *no*," Jen informed them. "I said 'bad dog.'"

"You think he was born understanding English? That's ridiculous." Riley scooped up J.D., even though Daniel hadn't had the chance to clean him off. "And he's not bad."

Starla put her hands on her hips. "Yeah, he's just a baby."

Jason threw the wipes to Daniel, harder than necessary. Dick move. But Daniel had already figured out he was a dick. While Daniel cleaned the floor, Riley gathered the bags with her free hand, J.D. trying to lick her face and giving high whines of excitement. Without another word, she started for the car, moving fast with those long legs of hers. "If there's a way to rank people on SmoochiePoochie, they are getting zeros." Riley rubbed her cheek against J.D.'s head and got all those kisses he'd been struggling to give.

"Where to now?" Starla asked when they were settled inside.

"I'm sure Daniel's ready to get back to the resort."

"I'm in no hurry." He'd be happy to circle the block a few hundred times, just to have the company.

"Bumper is texting me, apologizing again. If I go home, I'll end up telling him that everything is fine and that I overreacted. I'm weak, I tell you." Starla tilted her head from side to side. "Neck stretches are supposed to help when your throat chakra is unbalanced, which mine definitely is. I'm not accessing my true voice, because my true voice would not be wanting to speak to Bumper."

And if Daniel went home, he'd start reading about someone whose addict brother cleaned out their parents' life savings and someone whose brother left rehab and was high less than an hour later and someone whose brother OD'd. And if he managed to stop doomscrolling, he'd be checking his phone to make sure he hadn't missed a call from Sam. Trevor had said Sam would have phone privileges starting today, so why hadn't his brother called? Had he done something to get the privilege revoked? Or was he pissed at Daniel for bringing him to rehab, even though it was court-ordered? Basically, if Daniel went home, he'd be driving himself nuts. "Is there a park around? J.D. could probably use some playtime."

"Oooh. The dog bar on Navajo Drive. It looks so fun. Even without a dog, I've always wanted to go there." Starla bounced up and down in excitement like a little kid.

"Is that okay?" he asked Riley.

"Riley is always up for anything," Starla assured him.

Looking at Riley's face, he wasn't sure that was true, but she nodded. "I'll buy you a drink. Pay you back for the ride." Payback was clearly a big thing to her. She didn't know she was doing him a favor just by giving him something to occupy his brain other than Sam, Sam and his parents.

"Just tell me where." He put the key in the ignition.

"I wish I loved anything as much as that dog loves water." Daniel nodded toward a golden retriever, who had two feet in one of the water bowls, joyfully splashing. J.D. nipped playfully at the retriever's wagging tail.

"Dogs naturally practice mindfulness. That dog isn't thinking about anything but the feel of water between his toesies." Starla toyed with the golden moons, all different stages, that hung from her necklace. "I need to do that. I need to be thinking about warmth from the fire pit sinking into my skin and the slide of the celery juice down my throat. But inside my head it's all Bumper, Bumper, Bumper."

Riley put her fingertips in her water glass and flicked a few drops at Starla. "Just trying to help you get in retriever mode," she said when Starla gave a jerk of surprise.

"It actually helped. For a second."

"Maybe I should try it," Daniel said.

Riley flicked some water at him. "You going through a breakup, too?" She'd been wondering if he had a girlfriend—

not that it mattered, when her departure date was so close. This wasn't the time to be starting something up. It was the time to be closing things down, getting ready to move on. Probably there'd be someone at Spruce Summit who caught her fancy, preferably someone who could teach her to ski. Part of T.U.P. was experiencing everything the current destination had to offer. You lived in Stowe, you had to ski. You lived in Sedona, you had to hike Devil's Bridge and get a psychic reading of some variety at the deep purple Center for the New Age, both of which she'd done her first week in town.

Daniel shook his head as he wiped the droplets off his face. He had a little scruff going tonight. It looked good on him. For a second, Riley imagined the bristly feel of it under her fingertips, under her lips. Maybe it had been a bit too long since her last boyfriend. She hadn't had one since she moved to Arizona five months ago. Her guy back in Cape Elizabeth had actually volunteered to move out here with her, but she suspected it was more because he was bored than because of her. In either case, a traveling companion was not part of The Ultimate Plan. Keeping to her schedule meant keeping her eyes on the prize, and eyes on the prize meant every decision made by her. No distractions, nothing that could trip her up.

"You're not in a breakup, but you're not here with anyone, right? Or they'd be here." Starla shot a look, an obvious look, at Riley. She hoped Daniel didn't catch it and misinterpret, think Riley had asked Starla to scope him out for her.

"Nope, just here by myself."

Starla shook her head. "See, I can't do that. I don't even like to eat by myself. I'd starve if I went on vacation alone."

Riley raised her eyebrows. "Come on. What about fast food? People go to fast food places by themselves all the time." Riley for sure did, although a lot of times, she'd end up chatting to whoever was at the next table. That was part of the fun of the road, meeting people from everywhere, hearing their stories.

"I get it. Mostly I'd rather not eat alone out in public, either. The exception is popcorn, because I shove huge handfuls in my mouth. If I'm at the movies with someone, I have to restrain myself." Daniel scooped some guac onto a chip. A chunk of it fell on his chin before it reached his mouth.

Riley had the crazy impulse to reach over and lick it off. She'd definitely let her dry spell go on a little too long. Or else Daniel was just especially lickable. And especially likable. Listening to Star, buying all that stuff for J.D.—undeniably likable.

Daniel grabbed a napkin and wiped his chin. "And I'm a slob. Eating in front of a woman at any time probably isn't a good idea. Sorry." He took another swipe at his chin, although he'd gotten all the guacamole the first time.

"We won't judge. Well, I won't. I'm not sure about Riley. Once I said 'no problem' when a guest asked for another napkin, and she gave me a look that almost turned me into a popsicle."

"Just trying to keep you safe from Ms. Aguilar." Riley considered protecting her people from the wrath of their manager to be one of the most important parts of the job.

"Yeah, you're right. You just gave me one of your looks. Ms. Aguilar probably would have kicked me out, especially because she'd already *spoken* to me about it once, although *spoken* isn't the word for it."

"What's wrong with 'no problem'?" Daniel took a swig of his beer.

"'No problem' can come off like you think whatever the guest asked for is an inconvenience. Saying 'my pleasure' gives a nicer vibe."

"That's kind of ridiculous," Daniel said.

Riley laughed. "Well, that's why I'm in hospitality and you're not. People notice things like that subconsciously, and it impacts how they feel about a place."

"The subconscious mind has a huge effect on your experience," Starla agreed.

Daniel scratched his chin, looking thoughtful. "Guess I should pay more attention to my subconscious."

Watching his hand brought her mind right back to the feel of his stubble. She needed a distraction. Riley picked a dog biscuit out of the basket in the middle of the table. "Come and get it, J.D." The puppy trotted over, snatched the biscuit, then put both paws on Riley's calf, staring at her with those big brown eyes, clearly waiting to be picked up. She scooped him into her lap, and he gave her chin a lick. "Maybe I should give him to you, Daniel. You wouldn't need a napkin."

"Hand him over." Daniel reached for the puppy.

"He's already settled." She curled one arm around the dog. "I can't believe those people decided to give him up after two days." She raised the pitch of her voice and imitated Jen. "'I told him *no.*'"

Daniel leaned close and gave J.D.'s head a pat, and the pup wriggled happily in her lap. "Everyone knows puppies chew stuff up and pee. If they didn't want to deal with that, they should have gotten one of those robot dogs."

"A lady brought one of those to the resort once," Starla said. "It made Ms. Aguilar crazy, even though it didn't look real or anything. It could recognize over a hundred different people. It didn't walk very well, though. Its little feeties only lifted up about half an inch. It tripped a lot."

"If I ran High Sky, I'd let people bring their real dogs," Riley mused. "I read an article about the Sunburst Resort's 'Love That Pup' campaign, announcing they welcomed dogs. It added more than a hundred and fifty thousand to their yearly profits."

"It would be like bringing a little bit of home on vacation with you." Daniel leaned close again to stroke the sleepy puppy's head.

"Before I let anyone else have J.D., I'm going to have some questions. Starting with 'You do understand he's a puppy, right? *Pup-py.*'"

"Yeah. He needs someone who's going to love him even when he messes up a little. Or a lot," Daniel added.

"That guest really loved the robot dog." Starla rested her chin in her hand. "I could tell. But I think I'd always have it in my head that a robot one was just pretending to love me back. Programmed to, I mean."

J.D. shook his head, and one of his ears flipped inside out. Daniel reached over and flipped it back into place. "Maybe everyone should be forced to start with a robot, and then if they proved they could take care of it, they'd get permission to have a real one."

Riley nodded. "Babies, too."

"And girlfriends," Starla added. "Not like a sex robot! But if Bumper had to—I don't know, ask a robot how its day was and give it compliments before he was allowed to date me—that might have been good."

"Be right back." Daniel stood, and as soon as he took a step away from the table, J.D. freaked and half-jumped, half-tumbled to the ground.

"He's coming with you," Riley called after him. Daniel immediately turned and scooped the puppy up. Another of his lickable moves. *Likable,* she corrected herself. *Likable.*

Once Daniel and J.D. disappeared inside, Starla sing-songed, "He likes you."

Riley shook her head. "It's like you've done a body-switch with a hormone-crazed thirteen-year-old." Although Riley was the one who kept thinking about licking Daniel.

"What's wrong with that? I think it's awesome he likes you. Daniel's a good guy."

"You met him, what, three hours ago?" As soon as the

words were out of her mouth, Riley realized she'd made the good-guy call about Daniel within about three minutes.

"I can sense his chakras. That's all it takes." Starla reached across the table and put one hand over Riley's. "Right now, your heart chakra is beating at a low frequency. His is beating at high frequency. That's why he'd be so good for you, why you'd be good for each other. You know how people say opposites attract? That's why. Opposite chakras want to balance each other. And also, he's cute."

Riley shrugged. She'd already decided it wasn't the right time to start something up, even short-term.

Starla imitated her shrug. "What is that supposed to mean? That you don't see it?"

"No, I see it. Obviously, he's cute. But lots of guys are cute. The one over there with the pug—cute. The one wiping down the bar—cute. That one coming through the gate—is Bumper. You told Bumper where you are?" Unbelievable. No, completely believable. This was Starla and Bumper she was dealing with.

"I had to. I know you don't understand, but I had to." Starla gave a squeal of laughter as Bumper scooped her out of her chair and swung her around, almost stepping on a low-slung dog wearing a baseball cap.

With Starla's legs wrapped around his waist, Bumper backed toward the bar, then laid her down on it and went in for a kiss. A couple guys started to cheer, and Bumper pumped one fist, his other hand on Starla's breast.

"Hey, there are puppies present." Daniel returned to his seat and let J.D. down so he could play with a Saint Bernard.

"Don't let him sit on you," Riley cautioned J.D. The Saint Bernard was a puppy, but it still had to outweigh her puppy by fifty pounds. No, no, no. She had to stop thinking like that. J.D. was not her puppy. She couldn't get attached. More attached. She'd only be keeping him long enough to find—and thoroughly vet—an owner for him. She could definitely accomplish that before she left town.

Daniel glanced over at the bar. Bumper had maneuvered himself onto a barstool with Starla on his lap, all without breaking the kiss. "I'm assuming Bumper."

"Yeah. They have an on-again-off-again relationship, if you add in about a dozen more ons and offs."

"Get a room!" a guy in a SERVICE HUMAN shirt yelled, and, still kissing, Bumper carried Starla off the patio.

"Good thing you went to the bathroom when you did. I think it's going to be occupied for a while."

Daniel raised his eyebrows. "What do you think of him? From the way Starla described his reaction when she didn't return his texts fast enough, he sounded really possessive. Should I be worried?"

Yeah, she'd called it right when she decided he was the Boy Scout type. It was kind of nice having one around. "I've never seen things get physically violent between them, and Starla's never said anything like that. I think she would have. She's a sharer."

Daniel didn't look entirely convinced. Should Riley be worried? Her gut told her no, and her gut almost always knew what's what.

"Do you think he has a tracking app on her phone?"

J.D. returned to them, thoroughly covered in slobber. That Saint Bernard's tongue was probably as big as her puppy's whole head. Damn it. Not *her* puppy, *the* puppy—*the* puppy she'd be leaving behind with some very nice people. She grabbed a napkin and tried to scrape off some of the slime. Gross. "Nope. She told him she was here."

"I thought coming here was supposed to distract her from thinking about him."

"Welcome to the wacky world of Starla and Bumper. I think they kind of enjoy the drama."

"Not me. Drama makes my stomach hurt."

Riley wasn't much for drama, either. Easy-breezy, that's the way she liked it. "Drama's a waste of time when there's all this to explore." She threw one arm wide, indicating the red rock cliffs, visible from almost every place in town, and the way the sunset had turned the thin sweep of clouds pink and purple.

"Good point." A waitress used a pitcher to refill the water bowls, and the golden retriever immediately ran over and put his paws in one. His red paisley bandana was still wet from the last time. "Do you think I should have bought J.D. an outfit? Our boy is almost the only one naked."

Our boy. He was as bad as she was.

"Did you see the one in a hood that makes it look like a frog?" Daniel continued. "That just seems so wrong. Why dress something warm and furry up as something cold and clammy?"

"Maybe I could make J.D. a little bow tie. He could wear it in his SmoochiePoochie pic. Which reminds me. I need to activate his profile again." She started to pull out her phone but froze when she heard a man shouting.

"You are always pulling this crap." Pretty sure it was Bumper.

"What crap, exactly? All I want is for you to admit you were looking at her. I don't care if you did, but I want you to tell the truth about it." And that was definitely Starla.

"A new land speed makeup-breakup record." Riley grabbed a chip. "At least I think we're almost to breakup."

"Do you think I should go in there?" Daniel half-stood.

He might be a Boy Scout, but she wasn't going to let him handle this alone. Before Riley could stand up, Bumper burst out onto the patio, fumbled with the first of the two-gate system that kept the dogs safely inside, and was gone. A moment later, Starla appeared, face flushed, eyes teary, one of her two buns—the one on the blue side of her head—coming down. She repaired it as she slumped down in her seat. "I need tequila. Celery water is not going to do it."

Riley didn't remind Starla that she always said alcohol created holes in your aura. Tequila seemed appropriate to the situation.

Daniel stood. "Got it. Riley?" She shook her head, still working on her first beer. She didn't like to drink enough to make her thinking fuzzy. Ethan from Cape Elizabeth had called her a control freak, like control was a bad thing.

Starla pinched her left nostril closed, breathed in, released the left nostril and pinched the right, breathed out. "I am not letting this happen again." She did another of the funky breaths— Nadi Shodhana breathing, she called it. "Bumper and I are done."

Riley didn't express any doubts, although, of course, she had them. That's not what Starla needed from her right now.

"I am not doing that again," Starla told Daniel when he returned with her shot. She downed it. "I clearly have a love addiction. So, no more love." She plopped her head into her hands. "But that will leave a horrible, aching hole here." She lifted her head and pressed her hands against her heart.

"Don't say that," Daniel protested. "So Bumper's not the right guy for you. That doesn't mean the right one isn't out there."

Riley's Boy Scout was a romantic. No! Not hers. What was with her? Not her dog. Not her guy.

"Nope, just nope. Love is bad for me. I'm stopping cold turkey. Okay. I can do this. A couple years ago, I'd gained about twenty pounds—bad breakup, don't ask—and I created a diet for myself. Every day, I only ate one color of food. And it worked. I think a lot of it was because of Blue Food Tuesdays. There are only so many blueberries you can eat, right? The first Tuesday, I ate a lot of blue raspberry Airheads. A lot. But that actually killed my cravings for them. Picking out all the blue M&M's took a long time, and I would have had to buy a ton to make it worthwhile."

Daniel shot Riley a questioning look, and she shook her head. When Starla got on a roll, it was best to just let her keep going.

"I need something like that now. I know I should just get my chakras balanced or do a fast to cleanse my soul, or practice my breathing techniques, but I just—no. This is going to take more tequila." Starla stood and headed for the bar.

Daniel stared after her. "Uh . . . not exactly sure what I'm supposed to do here."

"Me either." Riley frowned. Starla thinking a problem was too big for her usual spiritual woo-woo? That was concerning. "I think all we can do right now is keep her company."

"I'm brilliant," Starla announced when she rejoined them. She downed her new shot and slammed the glass onto the table. "I've already figured it out. I'm going to get a new addiction to replace the love addiction, so even though I'll be going cold turkey, it won't really be cold."

"Lukewarm turkey," Daniel offered.

Starla pointed at him. "Exactly. But I don't want to really get addicted to whatever my new addiction is, so I'm going to switch addictions every week. That won't be enough time to get addicted-addicted or to do any real damage. Even if I drink all the time"—she glanced at Riley—"when I'm not working, of course, I won't ruin my liver or anything. Not in a week. Same with lungs, if I smoke for a week." She stood. "Right back." She headed for the bar.

"It's a twisted kind of genius," Daniel said.

"Emphasis on the *twisted*." Riley finished her beer. "When she gets back, I'm going to tell her I'm ready to go. I don't know how many shots she thinks will qualify for addiction, and I don't want to find out."

"Good call. She's switched to double-fisting."

Yep, Starla was coming back with a shot in each hand. Time to go.

On the ride home, Starla insisted they list every addiction they could think of. "Exercising," Riley suggested. She was going to at least attempt to keep Starla from self-destructing. Possibly she'd forget about the whole thing by tomorrow. She didn't have the longest attention span.

"Social media," Daniel offered. He'd clearly picked up on Riley's strategy.

"Food." Riley knew that could get serious, but she was trying to think of things that weren't drugs. "You're halfway to being a chocoholic. If you choose that, you could get a new addiction and improve your heart chakra at the same time."

"Addictions shouldn't have an upside." Starla pressed her hand against her mouth and squeezed her eyes shut. Riley hoped she wasn't about to puke in Daniel's car.

"Pornography," he suggested.

Starla rolled down the window and stuck her head out. At least if she puked, it would land outside. Riley had to tighten her grip on J.D. It seemed like he wanted to stick his head out, too, but the window was open wide enough for him to tumble through.

"Pornography?" Riley repeated.

Daniel shrugged. "Did you want me to say meth?"

"Point taken."

Starla kept her head hanging outside until they got back. When Daniel parked, she didn't move. Riley handed the puppy to Daniel and climbed out of the car. "Starla, we're home." She didn't answer, so Riley slowly, cautiously opened the door, then used both hands to prop Starla up so she wouldn't slide onto the ground.

Daniel hurried over, J.D.'s leash wrapped around one wrist. Together, he and Riley managed to get Starla out of the car and started walking her to the cabin. She almost went down when

J.D. dashed from Daniel to Riley, then back around to Daniel, wrapping his leash around all their legs, but they executed a circle that detangled them and continued inside.

"Couch is good." Riley didn't want to try to negotiate the narrow hallway. It wasn't designed for three people and a dog. They helped Starla lie down, then stood there side by side for a moment, staring at her.

Daniel turned toward Riley. "I think she's already out." He was close enough that she could feel the warmth of his body, even through her linen shirt. She was so tempted to lean into him, just for a minute, soak up more of that warmth.

Starla jerked bolt upright. "Did Bumper text me?"

"No," Riley answered, without checking. She pulled off Starla's sandals and covered her with the throw that was spread across the back of the couch. "Good night, Princess."

" 'Night." Starla's eyes were already closed, her breathing deepening.

"Thanks for the assist getting her in the house," Riley said, shaking off the crazy impulse to snuggle up to him as they stepped outside.

"No problem." Daniel let J.D. tow him from bush to bush as they headed toward her cabin, the puppy giving each a squirt of pee. "I mean, my pleasure!"

Riley snorted. "That trick doesn't work if you're being sarcastic."

Daniel grinned down at her. "What, you think I didn't truly enjoy helping you haul a heartbroken drunk girl home? Joke's on you. I loved it."

Looking into his deep brown eyes, Riley almost believed him. She'd never seen him look so relaxed.

She found herself smiling back. "Well, I owe you one."

"You can just give me another gift certificate."

"Oh. Of course." Riley flushed. He probably thought she had a supply to give out to guests who needed appeasing, but she'd paid for the last one out of her own money, further depleting her catalytic converter fund.

"Kidding. I didn't want the first one, but I was afraid you'd wrestle me to the ground and shove it in my pocket if I didn't take it." He moved a step closer. "Which could have been fun."

Riley took a step away. Kidding. Of course he was kidding. And he was right, it could have been fun. It still could be. But she'd decided not to go there, and she had a policy: she decided something, it stayed decided. That's how you made a plan work. Eyes on the prize. "It's just that it was a big ask for you to watch J.D."

The puppy gave a little yip. Daniel stared at him. "Hey, I think he's learning his name. Let me try it. J.D." The puppy yipped again.

"Our boy is smart." Dang. She was doing it again. *Our*.

"Our boy is brilliant." He was doing it again, too.

They both had to stop. They were standing here cooing over J.D. like a couple of proud parents. It had hurt her heart a little when she'd walked away from the puppy the first time. If she wasn't careful, the next time she had to do it, her heart might actually crack.

J.D. lifted his leg on the clump of creosote growing beside her porch steps. Nothing. "I think he's finally tapped out." Riley took the leash from Daniel, ignoring the little thrill that shot up her spine when her hand brushed his.

"What are you doing with J.D. tomorrow?"

Riley hadn't even thought about that. How could she not have thought about it? Jen called to say they didn't want J.D., then there was Starla drama, then picking up J.D., then more Starla drama. It had been crazy. But that was no excuse. She wasn't keeping her eyes on the prize.

Damage control. She needed damage control. She could call out sick. But her schedule was packed: a picnic, the candle-making workshop at Blessed Flame, a reading from a local author. But if she was sick, she was sick. Ms. Aguilar didn't have a no-exception rule about being sick. But she wouldn't like it, and Riley would be leaving her team in the lurch. Dog daycare was a thing. But how much did they cost? A day probably wouldn't break her. But more than—

Daniel touched her arm. "I can practically see your brain spinning. I can watch J.D. while you're at work, no problem. That's why I asked."

She could feel her pulse in her wrists and fingertips and ears. This was a risky situation. She could end up getting fired if things went bad. There should be a way she could handle this herself. You take care of yourself, you don't have to worry. "I don't get what you're doing. Why aren't you going for a hike? Or renting an ATV?" Riley could hear the sharp edge in her voice, but she couldn't stop herself. "Why aren't you taking a ride on the Verde Canyon Railroad? Or going on a winery tour? There's one that takes you around in a stretch limo. I can set you up."

"Wow, okay." He held up both hands. "I thought we were past entertainment director mode. I had fun tonight. I thought you did, too."

"I did, really," Riley said softly. "Sorry I snapped at you. I just . . . I don't handle it well when I mess up my plan, and my plan was to find a home for the puppy."

"It's not your fault that those people couldn't tell J.D. is the brilliantest, bestest, handsomest puppy in the world. And it's really my pleasure, no sarcasm, to take care of the brilliantest, bestest, handsomest dog in the world."

He was such a good guy. And he'd already proven she could trust him. But it was too much to ask. "You're a guest, Daniel. And I don't mean that in an entertainment director way. I mean, this is your vacation. You're staying in a gorgeous place. I want you to be able to enjoy it."

"This isn't a vacation. My brother is at Ironwood—you

know, the rehab," Daniel admitted. "When his counselors give the okay, I can see him. Until then, I'm working. I always work remotely, but since I haven't been sleeping, I'm getting most of my work done at night. So I have nothing to do all day. I guess I could do the touristy stuff, but it doesn't feel right, and anyway, I don't want to blow hundreds of dollars a day."

That was a lot. Daniel had as much spinning around in his head as she did. More, even. She sat down on the bottom step leading to her porch, feeling her body relax. "I'm sorry about your brother. Oh, no! And we ended up talking about addictions for half the night, thanks to Starla's drunken rant."

Daniel sat down next to her, shoulder lightly touching hers. "That didn't matter. It's not like part of my brain isn't thinking about him pretty much all the time, anyway." Daniel picked up J.D. "But this guy keeps me on my toes. No time for too much thinking."

"I was considering calling out sick tomorrow, which is also not sticking to the plan. I never do that. If you're really up for—"

Daniel interrupted. "You'd be doing me a favor."

"He can be noisy. It was risky to keep him in your casita that first day, but every other option I could think of was more risky. Do you think you could stay with him here?" The cabins were more than a mile away from the main grounds, and Ms. Aguilar had her own separate house over on the other side of the resort, near Ben Osborne's.

"Sure. Honestly, I feel kind of like an intruder in the casita. It's not a *me* kind of place. Not that I don't appreciate Ben letting me stay there. He's an old friend of my parents'." He handed J.D. to her and stood. "I should head out. You've had a long day. What time should I get here in the morning?"

"Does eleven work? Unfortunately, I have an event tomorrow night, and I won't be back until nine at the earliest."

"I'll be here."

And she knew with absolute certainty he would.

* * *

Daniel checked the phone for what felt like the hundredth time. 7:02. Almost two hours since he'd last checked. That was the longest stretch of sleep he'd had all night. He kept thinking about Sam, which was ridiculous, because there was absolutely nothing he could do for Sam right now and, for once, he knew Sam was safe. He went over those obvious points a few more times until his brain started to quiet. But the Sam thoughts had only been part of his problem. Daniel's body was messed up— queasy stomach, tight chest, and was his heart beating faster? Or was he just freaking himself out, imagining it was beating faster?

With a groan of frustration, he got out of bed. Day four. Sam should have had phone privileges yesterday, but nothing. He better call Daniel today. Or, even better, call their parents. Sam had to know they'd be stressing, but when Daniel had talked to them yesterday, it had been clear Sam hadn't been in touch. They just assumed Sam had used his phone time on Daniel, and Daniel had let them keep on thinking that, giving them generic reassurances about how Sam had sounded. There was nothing wrong with protecting them a little. It's not as if their worry could make anything better. If it could, Sam would be . . . happy.

Daniel marched himself into the shower and played around with the controls, trying to convince himself he was enjoying the luxury, then he got dressed and checked the time. Not even 7:30. It was hours before he was supposed to be at Riley's. Of course, he still had a job. But at one point last night, he'd gotten so sick of lying in bed, not sleeping, that he got up and did pretty much everything on his to-do list. He'd have to wait for something new to come in before he could use work as distraction.

So, breakfast. The fridge had plenty of food, but he needed to get out, even if it meant eating in the resort dining room by himself. At least the walk over would get rid of some of his restless energy. He picked up his pace when he saw one of the few people he knew heading in the same direction. "Starla!" She turned, shading her eyes, and gave a half smile, half grimace. "You have an early start this morning?" he asked when he reached her.

"I'm taking some guests to the Amitabha Stupa in about an hour, then I'm working the picnic with Riley." She scrubbed her forehead with her fingers. "But first I need a seriously greasy egg sandwich. It will hurt the chef to make it as greasy as I need it, but she'll do it for me. The body knows what's best for it, and that's what mine wants."

"Feeling last night pretty bad?"

"Big yes. I feel like I'm dying. I'm not sure alcohol is going to work as my substitute addiction."

"Probably not the best idea." Sam had almost died once after a drinking binge—well, pills and drinking. That's how he ended up in rehab the first time, when he was nineteen. Their parents had panicked, and Sam had been in such bad shape that they'd convinced him to go. He'd checked himself out less than a week later, and managed to hold it together—or at least keep whatever he was doing out of sight of Daniel and their parents—for a while.

"I hope I didn't do anything too stupid. Did I puke in your car or anything? My mouth isn't tasting good, but it doesn't feel like it was puked out of."

"No worries."

"No worries yes, or no worries no? Because you seem like you'd say no worries either way."

Probably true. He let some of Sam's behavior slide, because it seemed pointless to make him feel bad over something he didn't even remember. "No worries no."

"That's something, at least." Her phone pinged. "Bumper again. He's already texted me a couple times this morning, still apologizing. He gives good apology. But I can't take him back." She swallowed hard. "I need that grease. See you later. And thanks again." She gave him a little wave and headed to what he figured was the back entrance of the dining room. He went in the front and had the best frittata he'd ever tasted. He'd almost passed on it. He wasn't sure he'd like the artichoke and mint combo, but, yeah, it worked.

He lingered over coffee as long as he could, then wandered around the grounds, where he ran into Garret. Fortunately, the guy liked to talk, so that ate up some time. Then he went back to the casita and checked his work email, handled the two little things that had come through. Finally it was time to go to Riley's. She opened the door before he could knock, and it was obvious she was stressing as she freed her hair from its ponytail, started to twist it into a bun, then let it fall free before putting it back in a ponytail.

"Should I come in, or. . . ."

"Sorry." She stepped back and gestured him inside. Daniel heard a frantic scrabbling on the bedroom door, then a string of barks, surprisingly loud for such a little guy.

"Get ready. I'm about to release the hound. I shut him in there so he wouldn't bolt out the door when you got here. I knew he'd be crazy happy to see you." As soon as she opened the door a crack, J.D. shoved through, Squidward in his mouth. He ran over and dropped the toy at Daniel's feet.

"I guess it's playtime." He hurled Squidward across the room. J.D. returned it to him in seconds.

"I gotta go, but make yourself at home. I don't have a lot in the fridge, but whatever's there is up for grabs. I'm sure it would be okay to leave J.D."—the pup barked at the sound of his name—"alone long enough to go to the dining room or into town. Just know he has to pee at least every two hours."

"If I want a food run, I'll just bring him with me, go to a drive-thru."

"Okay. That'd be better." Riley stood anxiously for a moment, looking at the two of them as J.D. pawed at Daniel's leg.

"It'll be fine," Daniel told her. "Go."

She gave J.D. a kiss on the head, then a kiss on the nose, then another kiss on the head. "Be good," she told him. She took one step toward the door, but didn't seem to be able to make herself go any farther.

"Riley, go."

"I'm gone!" She grabbed her backpack from a hook by the door and hurried out. J.D. gave a pathetic whine, then he noticed Squidward, snatched him up, shook him, tossed him into the air and caught him, then managed to hurl him halfway across the room.

Daniel sat down on the denim-covered sofa to watch the puppy show. He felt more comfortable than he had since he arrived at the resort. The small living room's haphazard mix of furniture styles, with its mishmash of colors and patterns, somehow worked. There wasn't a TV in the room. Maybe Riley just watched on her phone. He thought about pulling up something on his, but wasn't in the mood. Instead, he picked up the large book on her coffee table—*Beautiful America*.

He flipped through the pages, soft with wear. Each chapter featured what the photographer had decided was the most beautiful spot in each state. There was a spread on Sedona, and Riley had almost the same view from her cabin's small porch, just big enough to hold two rockers. In the margin, someone had written, *I will see these red rocks*. Riley?

There were similar notes throughout, all in the same rounded writing. *I will climb to the top of this lighthouse. I will drive down the crookedest street.* Each letter was written with such force that it had caused an indentation in the page. Looking closer, he realized that they had been written over and over, layered on top of each other, sometimes with little bits of different ink showing. He ran his finger lightly over a few words, and it was almost like he could feel the emotion, the determination, being transferred from the ink into his skin.

When he'd looked at every page, he returned the book to the table and stretched out on the couch. As soon as his head touched the pillow, he got a whiff of that green scent of Riley's. He still couldn't quite identify it. Moss? Ferns?

J.D. came over and whined, so Daniel picked him up and set the puppy on his stomach. The pup turned around three times, then curled up and settled in for a nap. Daniel closed his own eyes and almost immediately felt himself begin to drift off, sleep coming easily for the first time in days.

CHAPTER 7

Starla's phone chirped. Another text from Bumper. That made eleven in the three days since their breakup at the bar. She'd told him it was really and truly over, but he wouldn't accept it. Which was probably her fault. She'd told him the same thing so many times and then taken him back. Should she give it one more try? He wouldn't be so persistent if he didn't really love her.

No, no, nope. Not this time. She had a plan. She would stick to the plan. She looked over at the bottle of tequila on her kitchen counter. Her plan was to be an alcohol addict for a week, but her body hadn't let her choke down a single drink, still recovering after the big drunk. She wished she was scheduled to work, but she was off until tonight, when she was scheduled to take the science crew out to the vortex. For some reason, they wanted to do some experiments after dark.

Maybe it would be good to meet up with Bumper so they could talk face-to-face. Maybe that way, she'd be able to convince him to stop contacting her. But face-to-face was dangerous. Face-to-face was a little too close to lips-to-lips, and once that happened, forget it. With a groan of irritation, she shoved herself off the couch and walked into the kitchen. She screwed off the top of the tequila, determined to take a swig, but just the smell made her stomach try to climb out of her mouth.

She wasn't going to spend the day vomiting. She'd just move on to another addiction a little ahead of schedule. Shopping, she decided. The only problem was, she didn't have much money until payday. She thought for a moment, then decided she'd go to the ATM, get a hundred dollars, and blow it all, but not on one big thing. Picking out a fab blouse wouldn't give her enough Bumper-avoidance time. But spending a hundred at garage sales, that should do it.

Starla put on her sunglasses and her favorite floppy hat and started for town. On the way to the ATM, she spotted a sign for a garage sale, and looped back as soon as she had her cash. The front yard was covered with goodies. Two picnic tables, a card table, and three makeshift tables made of sawhorses and plywood were all loaded, and a couple blankets spread out on the driveway held even more. A woman was wheeling out a dented metal clothes rack as Starla found a parking place. The Shopping Goddess was smiling on her!

The sale was organized, which was a little disappointing. Part of the fun was finding a bag of assorted mini shampoos from assorted hotels next to a pair of Ninja Turtle basketball shoes—did the Ninja Turtles even play basketball?—next to a garden statue of a rooster with a baby head. But it was early. She had lots of sales to hit. Maybe the next one would be a complete mess!

Starla decided to start with the closest picnic table, determined to take her time and examine each item. This one was all kitchen stuff, and she instantly found something she wanted— Mr. Salt, Mrs. Pepper, and Paprika shakers, just like the ones on *Blue's Clues*. She loved that show. Sometimes she still streamed it when she had a cold and just wanted to curl up under the comforter and veg. She gathered the shakers in one hand, struggling to keep a grip on them, as she picked up a chicken lamp, where the lightbulb was the egg coming out of her butt. Whoever arranged the table clearly thought it was a kitchen item, but it would make a super cute night-light. She turned it over, looking for a price tag, and almost lost her grip on Paprika.

"You didn't come prepared."

She looked up and saw one of the science guys—Uh-Damn-He's-Cute Adam, wearing his pumpkin pi T-shirt again. He'd been wearing it every time she'd seen him, but must wash it constantly, because he always smelled like the resort's shea butter soap, sometimes with just the tiniest whiff of sweat, that yummy sweat some guys had that smelled almost like vanilla.

Adam popped open a collapsible storage cube and tilted it toward her. "You always have to bring a container."

She put the shaker family and the chicken lamp—only six dollars—inside. "Thanks."

"It's a garage-sale essential. You also need hand sanitizer, a tape measure, batteries, paint chips if you're looking for home décor, and of course, a shopping list." He looked at the items she'd put in the box and raised one eyebrow, a talent Starla had always wished she had. "I'm thinking you don't have a list."

"I didn't even know the chicken-egg butt lamp existed. How could I put it on a list?"

"I never considered that. I might need to come up with a metric for evaluating whether a new item is worthwhile that I can use in the moment. Something that contrasts its usefulness with the amount of upkeep it requires. Price should be a factor, too, but for me time is a human's most precious commodity, and I've found there is an inverse correlation between free time and the number of objects I own."

His expression was so serious as he straightened his silly T-shirt. Adorable. No, wait. She wasn't just trying to get over a Bumper addiction. She was trying to get over a love addiction, and she had a plan to follow. She forced herself to study Adam and pick out something non-adorable. It was a little hard. His ears were a little sticky-outy. There. Not adorable. Except it kind of was. She took another look, trying to keep it quick. She didn't want to be staring like a freaky starer. There was that chipped tooth . . . but that was part of his shy smile's charm. Okay, there. He had a small strawberry birthmark that looked a little like a bullfrog on the side of his neck. Frogs were adorable, but bullfrogs, not so much. If she thought she was getting into a dangerous love-addiction area, she'd just focus on the bullfrog.

"My initial hypothesis is if you didn't know it existed, and never wondered why it didn't exist, then it's not essential."

"But who shops at garage sales for essentials?"

"I do. Today I'm looking for Lego."

"How are Lego essential?" Was he one of those guys who was making something like an enormous Death Star? Because that was a little adorable. *Bullfrog*, she reminded herself.

"I use them to design research tools."

"Wow. Cool. I would never have thought of that."

"I'm working on a device to amp up the magnetism, if it exists, at the vortex site. I'm thinking along the lines of a conducting cylindrical shell oriented vertically." His eyes seemed to lose focus, all his attention on the apparatus he was imagining.

"Gathering data doesn't feel like the right way to explore the vortex. It's a *here* thing"—Starla pressed her hand over her heart—"not a *here* thing." She tapped his head, his curls bouncing under her fingers.

"Can't it be both? Or if not, can't there be two methods that lead to discovery of the same truth?"

Starla considered for a moment. "Emotions definitely affect the body. Like right now, I'm feeling like my throat chakra is out of line." She didn't mention that her head and stomach were in distress, too, although the cause of the nausea, headache, and weak throat chakra was the same—Bumper, at least if you blamed Bumper for the drinking that caused the nausea and headache, which she definitely did.

"I don't know anything about chakras." He pulled a small notebook out of the back pocket of his jeans and plucked one of those little golf pencils from behind his ear. His wildly curly hair had completely hidden it. He made a note, then returned the notebook and pencil to their places. "I always make a note if I encounter something I don't know anything about. I like to fill in my gaps."

Starla hadn't thought a science-y guy would consider chakras a gap. She smiled at him. "We have an awesome spa treatment—and I mean *awesome* in the truest meaning of the word, as in inspiring awe—that uses massage and essential oils and energetic techniques to find any blockages in your chakras. Oh, and crystals, too. If you want to fill in that gap, that's what I'd do." Out came the pencil and notebook again. "The treatment is called Balanced Touch." Adam wrote it down.

She took another look at the kitchen items and decided there was nothing else that called to her. "That card table by the clothes rack has toys. Want to check for Lego?"

"Sure." He led the way over. It was comfy being with him, so even though he had a lot of adorableness, and nice arms—maybe from carrying around that heavy, not-a-leaf-blower thingie—she could relax. She didn't feel any of that tight, twangy feeling that she always got around a guy she like-liked, which meant Adam was the perfect companion while she worked on her love addiction.

Her phone vibrated, and she took a quick glance. Bumper. *Don't read it, just don't read it*, she told herself. She squeezed her eyes shut and took a deep breath, getting just the tiniest whiff of vanilla-esque sweat. She felt the temptation to open the text fade enough that it felt safe to open her eyes. She focused her attention on the toy table. She didn't see any Lego, but half-hidden behind an Elmo sitting on a potty, diaper around his furry ankles, she spotted a familiar face. "Mr. Wonderful!" She pulled him free. "My mom had one of these. Her BFF gave it to her after she had a blow-out with my dad. Then my dad threw him away, leading to another blow-out. Then they paid for me and my BFF to go to pizza and the movies, which I now know meant they were ready for some truly epic makeup sex, which is the best sex, right?"

"Uh—I haven't studied that question."

Color surged up Adam's throat, making that little red birthmark almost impossible to see. She wanted to run her fingers over it to feel how warm the blush had made it, but, hello, inappropriate. She gave Mr. Wonderful a squeeze to give her hands something else to do. "I have to get it. I can send it to my mom next time she starts complaining about my dad." She put the doll into the box.

Adam pulled it back out and turned it over, examining it. He gave the left hand a squeeze. He frowned and squeezed it again. "It says 'Press Me,' but nothing happens."

"Oh, yeah. That was the best part. It would say things like 'Here, honey, you take the remote.' "

Adam pulled up the doll's shirt, unzipped the back, and took out the batteries. "Hold these, please." He took fresh batteries out of his fanny pack and slid them into the doll. "A lot of times, batteries in old toys are corroded. That's why you always need to bring new ones." He squeezed the doll's hand again.

"You're going shopping by yourself?" the doll asked in a voice that was a little staticky, but still easy to understand. "How about if I tag along and carry your bags?"

Starla laughed. "Adam, do you know what this means?" He shook his head. "You're Mr. Wonderful! Look at you, carrying my stuff. You even provided the bag. Well, it's a box, but it still counts."

His neck had almost returned to normal color, but now it reddened again. "I would have thought the probability of being called Mr. Wonderful by a beautiful girl was under one percent."

"Guys really have no concept about what women consider wonderful, at least in my experience." Starla gave Mr. Wonderful's head a pat. "I can't believe it's only twenty dollars. I haven't seen one since I was a kid. It has to be a collector's item."

"You aren't going to pay the price on the tag, are you? That's a violation of the garage-sale code. Bargaining is expected. Only a complete novice would put the price they actually wanted on an item."

"I'm not that worried about it."

"It's a good idea to do a quick internet search to see what the going rate is." He pulled out his phone. "I see one on eBay for twenty-two, but it's still in the box. Taking shipping cost into account, I'd make an offer of thirteen fifty, which is a little on the low side, because the seller will want to haggle. Now the shaker set is a bargain. There's one on Etsy for thirty-four ninety-nine, and it's in thirteen people's carts." He did another search. "I'd offer two less than the sticker. You could point out that little chip."

Starla did a quick calculation. "I have sixty-two fifty to go. But I don't have to get everything here. Do you see anything you want? I can buy you a little present for helping me."

His brow furrowed. "I feel that I'm missing something, which is not unusual."

He'd think she was silly if she explained. Riley and Daniel had. They hadn't said anything, but she could tell. Oh, well. It didn't matter. She wasn't trying to get him to like her. Right now, she wasn't trying to get anyone to like her. "Here's the thing. I'm trying to break an addiction I have, a love addiction. So I'm substituting a shopping addiction. But I'm not going to do it long-term. A week, tops. Then I'll switch to something else, so I won't get addicted to the new addiction." She'd blurted all that out without taking a breath, so she had to pull one in before she added, "You probably think that's ridiculous."

"Not ridiculous at all. It's scientifically sound. According to the most recent research, it takes between nineteen and two hundred and fifty-four days to form a new habit. Switching negative habits in seven days or less allows you to weaken the neural pathway associated with the behavior you're trying to eliminate without giving enough time for the substitution behavior to form a new neural pathway."

Starla beamed at him. "You get me!"

Riley hurried up the path to her cabin. Not because she was eager to see J.D. and Daniel, although coming home to them instead of a dark, empty house the last three nights had been a nice change. It's just that it had been a long day, she was kind of thirsty and needed a drink of water, and she kind of needed to pee, that kind of thing. Yeah, that was why she especially wanted to get home tonight.

The door flew open, and J.D. raced toward her, spraying pee as he went. Joyfulness expressed with urine. Riley backed away to give him time to empty his tank, then knelt down so he could give her a dozen wet kisses. When he'd calmed down, she headed up to the porch, where Daniel was waiting for her, J.D. trotting beside her. He didn't really need a leash. He liked to stay close.

"How was your day, dear?" Daniel was wearing one of the aprons, green with tiny blue flowers, that had been in a kitchen drawer when she moved in. He looked ridiculous. And adorable. Ridiculously adorable.

"Did you cook?" Oh, man. If he'd cooked, she might really want to keep him. Where did that come from? No guy was a keeper. Part of the plan was traveling solo, every decision hers. That's how you did eyes on the prize.

"No. I just thought this made me look cute."

He hadn't cooked, but he *was* flirting, which was almost as bad. She should probably tell him she was going to be leaving soon. What did it matter, though? He was leaving, too. Which made him perfect for a fling.

Nope. She had too much to do before she left town. She decided she'd tell Daniel she was going when she gave notice, which she couldn't do until she got J.D. settled in the perfect home. She was almost positive she could get him situated in the two weeks she'd have after she told Ms. A she was leaving, but she didn't want to risk it, so new home first, then notice. That meant pushing back her departure date again. Her realization made her stomach tighten, and she took another look at the spectacle of that sturdy body in that dainty apron to distract herself. It helped.

"I should check the SmoochiePoochie app." She'd been planning to do it when she'd had a break before leading the shopping expedition to Tlaquepaque Village, but had completely forgotten.

Daniel untied the apron and sat down in one of the rockers. When J.D. yipped, he pulled the pup into his lap. "Anything?"

"A few responses." She clicked past the one from a family in an apartment. J.D. needed more room. "This one might be a possibility." She looked at the picture of a man and woman in front of a house with a lawn big enough for a small dog. The house looked nice, but not too nice. Riley thought that was one of the problems with the Js. They cared more about their stuff than a living, breathing animal that wouldn't just sit where they put it until they were ready to take an Instagram pic. She opened the bio. "There's a couple with a baby on the way. They want the puppy and the baby to grow up together."

"I bet J.D. would like being around a kid."

"A kid, yes. But a baby . . . they take a lot of attention. How would they have time for a puppy? J.D. would probably end up starving." She moved on to the last response. "And this guy already has three dogs. It seems like he really loves them. He gave each of them their own bio. But I wouldn't want J.D. to get lost in the shuffle."

"Agreed. I'm sure more people are going to want him."

True. It was going to be okay. It wasn't going to take long to find J.D. the perfect home he deserved. She'd just drive a few more hours every day on the way to Vermont, maybe have a day less to explore Stowe before she started her job. T.U.P. wasn't at risk.

Daniel leaned back and stretched, his T-shirt riding up, giving Riley a little more distraction from her worries. "I had an amazing nap again. Your couch is magic. For three days in a row, I actually napped. Sleep when you haven't been sleeping is better than anything."

Had it only been three days since he started puppy-sitting? She was already used to having him and J.D. waiting for her when she got home. "Nice." Riley sat down in the rocker next to his. "I brought you something." She handed over a High Sky tote. "A local artist was doing a class for us this morning, and I snagged some extra supplies. I saw that little doodle you did of J.D."

Daniel pulled out the sketch pad and colored pencil set. "This is fantastic. Just the other day, I was trying to remember the last time I'd broken out the colored pencils. They've been stuck in the back of my closet for"—he shook his head—"so long I have no idea."

"You should go back to it. You really captured J.D."

"I wonder if Sam would like some drawing stuff. He's never been into it, but I read an article that said craft supplies were a good gift idea for someone in rehab—that, and 'self-care items.' Sam would bust a gut if I sent him some fuzzy socks or shower gel. I'm sure the only 'self-care' he's interested in is a bottle of scotch."

It's like everything made him think about his brother. If she'd grown up in a normal family, is that how she'd have turned out? Would she have loved somebody enough to put her whole life on hold if they needed her? "I'll grab another set tomorrow. I always try to order enough for five more than I'm expecting."

"I wasn't saying you should—"

"I know you weren't. But my boss would love it if she knew. She'd have art supplies delivered to your door, probably with a fruit basket, if she knew you wanted them. She lives to suck up to the owner. She went vegan, just to show how super committed she is to the High Sky healthy lifestyle, even though the resort is only vegetarian."

Daniel laughed. "I don't know him very well, but I'm almost positive Ben isn't the kind of guy who cares about anyone kissing his ass."

"That's what I suspected. None of the employees are even expected to give up meat, as long as we don't eat it in front of guests."

"Speaking of eating, you want to take our guy to a drive-thru?"

"Sure." They'd gone out the last two nights, too. But she didn't have to worry that he'd be thinking of something starting up between them. He didn't know she was leaving, but he was leaving himself in a few weeks. "There's a food truck festival at Posse Grounds Park tonight. We should have a pick of six or seven. You up for it? There's a DJ, too."

"Sounds perfect." He looked down at J.D. "Want to go for a ride?" The pup gave a high yip. "He's starting to learn English." Daniel clipped on his leash, and they headed to the car. His phone chirped just as he put the key in the ignition. "Let me check this real quick." He read the text, and Riley could almost hear the gears in his brain turning.

"Everything okay?"

He started the car and pulled onto the dirt road that led down from the mesa where the resort sat. "Yeah, fine. Just Sam's landlord sending me a link so I could pay his rent online. I'm not even sure if he'll be going back there once he's out. He has no job, something I found out when I tracked down his boss to let him know about the rehab situation. Sam hasn't worked there for almost two months, even though he let me think he was. I have no idea how much savings he has, but I doubt it's much. He's not a planning-ahead kind of guy. I can't pay two rents. I guess my parents could cover it for a while, maybe until he gets a new job." He glanced over at her. "Sorry. Just thinking out loud. I'll pay this month, and see what happens. From what I've read, the counselors will help him make a plan for when he leaves."

That was the second time he'd referenced what he'd read about rehab. She got it. She liked to have as much info as possible about any situation she found herself in. But no wonder he was having trouble sleeping. Those brain gears must be constantly cranking, throwing out scenarios and trying to come up with solutions. "Maybe for the rest of tonight, at least, try not to think about it. Give yourself a break."

He gave a snort of laughter, like it was a ridiculous suggestion. "No, you're right. I'll try."

Riley pulled up the food truck festival info on her phone. "Maybe this will help. You can think about what food you want. We'll start with my fave—The Cheese Stop, which is exactly what you'd think, just cheesy goodness. In my humble opinion, the best combo is bacon jalapeño, which you can have in a grilled cheese, mac and cheese, or cheese nachos. If for some reason you aren't in the mood for cheese . . . well, first, what's wrong with you? Cheese is the ultimate goodness. But there is also Down by the Bayou, amazing catfish po'boys. Old Crow, which is barbeque." She glanced over at him. Her patter seemed to be distracting, so she kept going. "There's also a whole truck for Dippin' Dots. You may ask, why do Dippin' Dots still exist, at least for non-astronauts? Which I wonder, as well. But they do have a flavor inspired by Blue Razz Icees, and I am a fan of the Icee, so maybe I'll have to reconsider."

"There was one summer when Sam had a Blue Razz Icee every day. He'd just gotten his license, and most of the time he'd take me with. He's eight years older, so any time he took me with was a big deal."

And they were back to Sam. Sounded like maybe there was a little bit of hero worship going on there. Maybe that explained how devoted Daniel was to him. "Eight years. That's kind of a big difference. Any other sibs?" Clearly distraction hadn't been the right strategy. Maybe Daniel needed to talk about his family.

"No. Well. No."

Riley nodded. Obviously there was some kind of story, but if he wanted to go there, he'd have gone there. She wasn't going to push. There was lots of stuff she preferred not to talk about, too.

Daniel raked his fingers through his hair. "Before I was born, I had another brother, which always sounds weird to say, because obviously I never knew him. He was just a little more than a year younger than Sam. He died when he was six."

Riley did some quick mental math. She thought Daniel was around her age, which meant he was born pretty fast after the death. His family must have still been reeling. "I'm so sorry."

"It's not like it happened to me. Sometimes growing up, it felt like this earthquake had happened, and a big, gaping crack opened up in the earth, and my parents and Sam were on one side, and I was on the other."

"Sounds lonely." Something she knew something about. But not something she wanted to share.

"I didn't mean it like that. It's just that they went through something so huge, and I can't ever fully understand what it did to them. We never talked about it. Well, obviously, I was told it happened, but that was it. There were no pictures up of Kevin. No one ever brought up a memory that involved him. Once Sam told me he put it all in the closet and shut the door." Daniel sighed, a sigh that sounded like it came from deep in a cave. "Gotta take a lot of effort to keep that door shut. I can't help but wonder how much his . . . extracurricular activities were a way of trying to keep it locked."

Riley tried to think of something to say in response. Nothing felt right. "I'm sorry," she said again. It was the best she could do, and she knew it wasn't enough. She knew it better than anybody.

"No, I'm sorry. Didn't we say I wasn't going to think about Sam for the night?"

"It's okay. It was just a suggestion. But if you want to talk about him, that's fine. I'm here." If it would help, she would listen. Sometimes it was nice to be reminded that hers wasn't the only sad story in the world. When she was a kid, she'd gotten used to not talking about her family situation, because it seemed to freak everyone else out. They never knew what to say, and a lot of them dealt with that by avoiding her entirely. Not the best way to make friends. So she'd stopped telling anyone about the accident, about that scary time when the social worker came to explain that she had no other family, that she'd be going to a foster family, which wasn't a family at all. Mary was the only one she talked about it with, other than the short answers she'd given the other two social workers. Now that she was an adult, it probably wouldn't freak anyone out like it did back then, but she'd never done it.

Sometimes she could still feel that old fear of the way Chloe and the other girls looked at her, which was ridiculous. She'd figured out her own life plan, and she'd gone out and done it. Not everyone could say that. She was fine. She was strong enough to listen to Daniel's pain.

She reached over and took his hand, giving it a squeeze.

Daniel gave his head a shake, a shake-it-off kind of shake. "Let's have some fun, starting with eating a disgusting amount of cheese."

Riley laughed. "That's going to take a lot. I have a very high tolerance for cheese."

"I haven't ever reached my limit. Maybe tonight's the night. I could do an appetizer of nachos, with a grilled cheese, plus mac and cheese on the side. The only downside is that cheese makes me fart."

"Me too."

"Problem solved, then. Two people's farts cancel each other out."

"I think it's more like double."

"We'll just keep the windows down on the way back."

"Deal. The turn for the park's coming up, where that line of cars is."

Daniel found a parking spot near the back of the lot. When she climbed out of the car, Riley pulled in a deep breath. Even at this distance, the air smelled delicious. It was impossible to pick out all the individual scents, but there was definitely barbeque sauce, cotton candy, and smoked meat.

J.D. obviously liked the smell, too. He pulled on the leash so hard he started to choke. Daniel scooped him up. "Seems like instinct would kick in, and when you start to choke, you'd stop pulling like a maniac." The puppy wriggled in his arms, trying to get down—and started choking again.

"It's why puppies are so cute. So someone will keep them alive until they develop common sense."

The first truck they passed was the Dippin' Dots one. "I'm definitely coming back for the Icee flavor. I wish I could bring some to Sam, but I'd probably need dry ice to keep them frozen."

That mental break didn't last long. Riley wasn't going to call him on it. "There's the cheese one." She and Sam got in line and decided to split all three varieties of cheese, jalapeño, and bacon, then added a few sides of chips, and a couple sodas.

They found a spot on the grass, eating as they watched the sun slowly set behind the buttes. It was hard to believe life could get better than this, but you never knew what would be down the road. Every once in a while, she had a moment that made her want to settle down, toss The Ultimate Plan, and this was one of them. But if you settled down, what about all those other moments in all those other places that you'd miss?

She pulled a little piece of bacon out of her mac and cheese and tossed it to J.D. He caught it in the air with a snap. She bet this was one of his moments. In the distance, the DJ started up some electro house, and Riley stretched out on the grass so she could get the best possible view of the sunset. Daniel lay down, too, his shoulder just touching hers, the warmth of his body soaking into her, warmer than the sun. J.D. snuggled down between them and fell into one of what she called his puppy-coma naps. Yeah, this was definitely one of her moments, probably the best of her entire trip so far, her endless beautiful trip.

She'd spent so many nights under the covers with her *Beautiful America* book and a little flashlight she'd liberated from a CVS. She hadn't stolen much, but every once in a while, she'd nabbed something essential that she couldn't get any other way, and some nights it had been essential to see the book. She'd stare at the pictures, planning and replanning her route, imagining every stop, but her imagination hadn't been good enough. Reality was even better.

"What are you smiling about over there?"

She turned her head so she could look at Daniel. "Isn't it obvious?" She circled both hands, trying to encompass the sunset and the blend of food smells, and the music, and the puppy, and him.

"Yeah. I actually forgot why I was even in Sedona for a minute."

"It's good to forget sometimes."

"Yeah."

"Yeah."

She held his gaze for a moment, then looked back at the sky. The buttes were glowing gold and orange, as if they were the source of the light. They watched in silence until the stars began to appear.

Riley pushed herself up. "I think it's dessert time. You still want the Dots?"

"I'll come, too." He started to stand, but she put her hand on his arm.

"You save our spot, but I'll take the beastie, since he's awake." She picked the puppy up and carried him. The lawn had gotten crowded, and there was way too much food in grabbing range.

"Anybody want a rabbit? Free rabbit over here!" she heard someone call as she approached the Dippin' Dots truck. A little boy, probably around eight or nine, leaned against the side, a large cardboard box clutched in his arms. It looked like he'd been crying. "Rabbit. Free rabbit!" he yelled again.

Riley, you do not want a rabbit, free or not, you know you absolutely do not want a rabbit. No animals on the road. That decision was made a long time ago. That means just keep walking. She ignored herself. A crying kid was her kryptonite. The boy held the box out in front of her. When she glanced down, she immediately saw that he was going to have a hard time finding the bunny a home. One of its eyes was swollen and squinty with a yellow crust around the edge.

"Do you want her? She's really great, but my mom says I can't keep her because we're about to move to Utah, and she doesn't want to ride all the way there in a car that smells like rabbit poop."

This boy wasn't exactly a born salesman. "Sorry. I'm not allowed to have pets where I live. What's going on with her eye?" Why had she started this conversation? She felt for the kid, she did. But she already had a puppy that she had to deal with before she left town. She couldn't take on another animal.

The kid stared down into the box, his eyes and mouth opening with exaggerated surprise. "Wow. That's weird! It wasn't like that at home."

An obvious lie, but Riley didn't call him on it. There was no point.

"Mom says we have to go now!" A kid who looked like a slightly aged-down version of the boy in front of her announced as he trotted up to them. "Now, Matty. Now, now, now!"

Matty's eyes welled up with tears. He angrily wiped them away with the back of his hand, then gently ran his fingers down one of the rabbit's ears.

"Just leave him. Someone will take him. Come on!" When Matty didn't obey, his brother tried to wrestle the box away from him. The rabbit began stomping its back feet and whimpering. Riley hadn't even known rabbits could make that sound.

She didn't want a rabbit. She didn't. She was leaving. She didn't have time to find the rabbit equivalent of Smoochie-Poochie, HuggyBunny or whatever. Even if one existed and she did find it, no one was going to want an obviously sick, possibly infectious, rabbit. But her hands were already reaching for the box, already gently tugging it away from Matty. "I'll take care of her."

"Her name's Petunia."

"I'll take good care of Petunia."

Matty nodded, then turned and walked away fast, his shoulders shaking, as he either started crying or struggled not to cry. His brother trailed after him.

Riley turned around and walked back to Daniel, holding J.D. under one arm and bracing the rabbit's box against her body with the other. "Don't even say it. I'm a soft-hearted dumbass." She put the box down next to him. "There are a couple hundred people here. You think we can find one who would want a free pet rabbit?"

He gaped at her, then looked into the box. "Uh, the eye might be a problem."

Understatement of the decade. "My mouth and hands got possessed by . . . some rabbit-loving demon." She dropped down onto the grass and groaned. "There was a crying little kid looking for somebody to take care of his bunny because he had to leave her behind. Why couldn't somebody else have gotten this one? I got the dog in the desert!"

Daniel looked at Riley, looked at the rabbit, looked at Riley again. "I say we get dessert to go and eat it in the parking lot of an animal urgent care."

Ka-ching, Riley thought. And she was right. The visit was a hundred and fifty. The antibiotic to treat the infection was twenty-two. Then there was the banana-apple flavored gel—sixteen dollars—and syringe—seven dollars—to feed the rabbit. The vet explained rabbits lose their appetite when they're sick and can only go about twenty-four hours without food, because their digestive systems slow down and they could get blockages, which could then lead to painful death. How could she say no? She'd told the kid she'd take care of Petunia. Good care.

She crossed the parking lot to the strip of patchy grass where Daniel was letting the puppy sniff around. As usual, her Boy Scout jumped in to help as soon as she started telling him what the vet said. "J.D. and I will watch her while you're at work, handle the midday drops."

"She's going to need them for ten days." Ten days. Riley would have to push back her arrival date in Vermont. There was no way around it. She couldn't get Petunia a new home until her eye infection was clear, and she couldn't give notice until she had the rabbit settled—the rabbit and J.D.

She could probably accomplish everything in the two weeks she'd have after she gave notice—it wasn't fair to leave without notice—but she couldn't risk it. What if there was another Jason and Jen situation?

There was no way in hell she was going to make her Spruce Summit start date. If she mainlined NoDoz and didn't sleep until she got there, she wouldn't make it. A dull thud started up in her ears. . . . *Dead, addicted, homeless, pregnant, jail.* The words came with every beat of her heart. *Dead, addicted, homeless, pregnant, jail.*

She'd message her new manager and explain the situation without giving too many details. She wasn't going to tell him she'd be delayed because she had to rabbit-sit. But what if that lost her the job? What if—

Stop. Just stop. Focus on your senses. The hard asphalt under her sneaks. The sound of her heart in her ears. The feel of it beating, heavy in her chest, squeezing the air out of her lungs. *Not helping.* Daniel's lips. The sight of Daniel's lips. And J.D. She scooped him up, pressing him against her cheek, feeling his warm fur.

The combination of man and puppy did it. Her heart began beating easier. She was able to breathe again.

CHAPTER 8

Daniel leaned close to Riley, as close as he could with J.D. lying between them on the couch, so he could see the video on her phone. Had it really only been a week since they'd done pretty much this, her showing him the vid about dealing with a hurt animal? It felt like he'd known her a lot longer.

J.D. let out a breath that was half wheeze, half snore and shifted position, resting his head on Daniel's knee. Daniel scratched the puppy's head as he watched the woman on the screen put drops into a rabbit's eye. It looked simple, but the woman, in her bunny-patterned scrubs, was clearly a professional.

Riley stood when the video ended. "I'll get a towel. You get the rabbit."

"Yes, ma'am."

Riley paused on the way to the bathroom and looked back at him. "Am I being bossy?" She held up one hand. "Don't answer that. Obviously, I was being bossy. Sorry."

"There are times where I enjoy being told what to do." She gave that whoop of laughter he loved as he took Petunia out of the crate. Her eye was still looking really messed up, but she'd only had one dose of the drops, the one the vet had given her last night.

Riley spread the towel out on the coffee table, and Daniel set the rabbit down on it. He lightly ran his hand over Petunia's soft fur, trying to keep her calm, while Riley quickly folded one end of the towel and both sides over the rabbit's back, making a bunny burrito. J.D. put his front feet on the table, wanting to get in on the action. Daniel quickly scooped Petunia up out of puppy range, and Riley pulled the eye drops out of her pocket and unscrewed the top.

Petunia started to struggle, her back legs kicking against the towel, loosening it. Riley stepped closer so they could hold the rabbit lightly pressed between their bodies, preventing her escape. Daniel could feel Riley's breath on his cheek, smell that green scent—light, fresh, and somehow cool.

"Got it." She stepped back.

"I brought her some carrots. I read that usually you shouldn't give bunnies too many, but since she probably doesn't have much appetite, it's good to tempt her and let her have as many as she wants."

"Yeah, I read that, too."

He'd figured out that Riley liked to be as prepared as possible, just like him. He put a few carrot pieces next to Petunia, and they watched with satisfaction as she took a little nibble from one.

"I gave her some of the liquid food first thing this morning. She should have more in three or four hours." Riley glanced at the clock, the face that cactus green used in so much of the resort's décor. "I gotta go." She took another look at the clock, but didn't move.

"I've got it covered."

"I know. I just—"

"When are you going to accept that I want to do this?"

She laughed. "Never. I've worked at a lot of resorts, and I've never subjected a guest to so much pet-sitting before. Or any pet-sitting."

"I hope I'm beyond just 'guest' status at this point."

Riley looked him up and down, and his heart rate sped up. "Mmm," she replied, which could mean anything. She grabbed her backpack off the hook by the door. "Call if something goes wrong."

"Nothing is going to go wrong. I can handle one little puppy and one recovering rabbit."

One half of Riley's mouth curved up in a teasing smile, bringing out that dimple of hers. "Boy Scout," she said.

J.D. started to whine when she left, so Daniel grabbed the canvas tote she used as a toy box and dumped everything in a pile on the floor, which almost made J.D.'s head explode with joy as he tried to decide what to play with first. He picked up the squeaky pizza, then spotted the squeaky mail carrier and managed to cram it into his mouth, too. He picked up the squeaky cat by the tail and began to take a victory lap, but after only three prancing steps, he couldn't keep his grip, and all three toys tumbled to the floor.

Trying not to think about what this afternoon held—the stress of seeing Sam again—Daniel stretched out on the couch to watch the show as J.D. started round two, this time grabbing the cat by the head before going for the pizza. He didn't even get to the mail carrier before he dropped everything again, but didn't even pause before making another attempt.

At some point, Riley's house or the puppy or both must've worked its magic and sent him off to sleep, because Daniel found himself waking with a start, nearly dumping the sleeping puppy off his stomach. He glanced at the time on his cell. Nearly two. He'd slept almost three hours. He should ask if he could sleep here at night. Except that would sound like he wanted to sleep with her. And, of course, he did want to sleep with her. But she was giving him no signals that said she was interested, or at least not clear ones. Although yesterday . . . that stretch of time at the park had been just about perfect. Who knew? Maybe things would have taken a turn toward the romantic, with the music, the sunset, but the rabbit had changed the mood.

"Thanks a lot, Petunia," he said. The rabbit ignored him.

When Daniel stood, J.D. dropped the pizza squeaky, now coated in slime, at his feet. Daniel picked it up with two fingers and flung it across the room, then prepped the rabbit's food syringe and fed her. Much easier than the eye drops. He couldn't put it off anymore. It was time to get to Ironwood.

"Ready for a ride?" he asked the puppy.

J.D. was always ready for anything. Maybe when things calmed down, Daniel *should* get a dog, somebody who'd be happy to see him no matter what, who wanted to be with him whenever possible. He hadn't had a dog growing up. He'd wanted one, but he'd never told his parents that. When he was little, they couldn't have one because Sam was allergic, and even after he moved out, Daniel hadn't asked. He knew his folks wouldn't have really wanted another thing to take care of—two sons, one of them as messed up as Sam, had been hard enough. Daniel was good at predicting their reactions and accommodating them. There was always part of him holding the knowledge that they'd already had enough pain in their lives. His job was to keep things smooth. Puppies were fun, but they weren't smooth.

Daniel had just started down the road leading into town when he realized he'd left the zucchini bread his mom had overnighted back at the casita. He could wait and drop it off for Sam tomorrow, but he knew on their nightly call, Mom would ask if he'd delivered it, and he wanted to be able to say yes. "You going to be a good dog?" he asked J.D.

J.D.'s big brown eyes seemed to say, *Me? I'm always a good, good dog. That's what you always tell me.*

"We'll only be there for a minute. Two, tops," he told the pup, knowing Riley would not be happy if she could see him driving up the resort's long, windy front drive. At least the casita had a private parking space. He pulled in, then zipped open the soft-sided pet carrier he'd bought yesterday. He hadn't mentioned it to Riley, because he knew she'd have insisted on paying him back. But he needed it. It was the only way he could bring J.D. to Ironwood. Trevor was going to keep him behind the counter.

Something else Daniel hadn't told Riley. If she'd known he had to go to Ironwood for family therapy, she'd have made herself nuts trying to figure out what to do with J.D. while he was gone. But he'd come up with a plan. No need to stress her out.

J.D. was not happy, loudly not happy, when Daniel tried to put him into the carrier. He made a mental note to have treats on hand next time. It was only a few feet from the driveway to the door. Should he risk it? Who knew how long it would take to get the pup in the carrier. The shortest amount of time on the resort grounds was safest. He picked up J.D., and the protests stopped. He dashed to the house. Yes! Made it! He grabbed the bread. Two more seconds, and they'd be out of there.

Daniel, J.D. under his arm, was halfway back to the car when he heard a plaintive rendition of "Every Little Thing She Does Is Magic" start up. Before he could decide if he should keep going or turn back, Garret came around the hedge, hose in hand.

Busted.

Riley might actually kill him. His one job was to keep J.D. out of sight. Well, and now being a bunny nursemaid. Maybe he could say he found the dog running around outside the casita and was trying to figure out who it belonged to. Except Garret might be required to call animal control. And, Daniel belatedly remembered, he had the carrier in his free hand. That wouldn't match the lie.

Garret sang a few *eee-oh*s as he approached. "The bushes like the Police?" Daniel asked, deciding to just play it off, like he didn't know he shouldn't have a dog. Maybe a guest of the owner actually could have one, not that Daniel wanted to take advantage of Ben's kindness.

"That one's just what came up from my heart. Sometimes I have to sing what I feel."

Daniel ran through the lyrics in his head. His mom was a fan. "Maybe you need to tell whoever it is about whatever those feelings in your heart are."

"When the time is right."

"How do you know it's not right now?"

"I'm waiting until I get a profile in *Invention Today*."

Daniel thought about The Attaboy. Creative. But not something with high demand. Probably not profile-worthy. "Why wait?"

"I haven't been having much luck with the lady in question as head gardener. But as a noted inventor—" He started singing some song Daniel had never heard before about love being in the air.

Daniel thought about saying that if this mystery lady would only be interested in Garret if he had a different job, maybe she wasn't the right person. But who was Daniel to give advice on romance? It had been almost two years since he'd broken up with Mila, and wow, coming up on—he flipped through a mental calendar—eight months since he'd had fun, meaningless sex.

J.D. tilted his head back and started howling along with Garret. Daniel had almost forgotten he was holding the puppy.

Garret stopped singing mid-line. "You must have done something doggone good for Riley to have trusted you with that puppy." He ruffled J.D.'s fur, then repeated "doggone," and laughed.

"She told you?"

"I saw her with him. And I saw her take him into your casita. I don't know what you said or did, but you got her to trust you, and my impression is that Riley doesn't trust easily."

Interesting. That wasn't his take on her. She was so outgoing and connected with people so naturally. He'd seen her turn a guest into a friend with a few words, and she'd come to that kid's rescue by taking Petunia. Daniel had felt comfortable enough to tell her about Sam being in rehab and about Kevin's death. But now he was realizing she'd told him almost nothing about herself. He knew she loved cheese, but not much else.

"It wasn't so much that she trusted me as that she was desperate."

"Maybe that first day, but if she didn't trust you now, you wouldn't be holding that dog."

J.D. started to scrabble frantically in his arms. Did he have to pee? He wriggled harder, and managed to jump to the ground. And then he was running. Fast. Heading straight toward a woman in a suit climbing out of a sedan across the street.

"Ms. Aguilar!" Garret yelled, taking off after the puppy.

Ms. Aguilar. Daniel froze. That was the name of the manager, the one Riley and Starla said was so uptight about rules. He stayed where he was, afraid chasing after J.D. would draw her attention to the puppy.

Garret's legs were longer than J.D.'s, and he reached the woman first. He skidded to a stop in front of her, grabbed her by the shoulders, and turned her halfway around so her back was to the puppy. "Ms. Aguilar, there's a crisis! I think the front lawn might have a white grub infestation!"

In one second, there was going to be a puppy/manager collision. Daniel let out a high squeak that he hoped sounded like one of J.D.'s toys. The puppy turned, then galloped back across the street, looking for the source of the sound. Daniel scooped him up and ran into the casita, slamming the door behind him. He dropped to his knees and crawled over to the nearest window, raising his head only high enough to bring his eyes above the sill. He watched as Garret towed the manager down the street, talking animatedly, wildly waving his free arm. Daniel stayed motionless until they rounded the corner and disappeared from sight.

"What did you do that for?" he asked J.D.

J.D. gave the I-have-no-idea-what-you're-talking-about head tilt.

"If you value your life—make that if you value mine—never do that again."

J.D. tilted his head in the other direction, giving him the I-*really*-have-no-idea-what-you're-talking-about look, big puppy eyes wide and innocent. Daniel shook his head. "You're going in that dog carrier on the way to Ironwood, my friend. That's just the way it's going to be."

"Sorry if he's whiny. He's just a puppy," Daniel said as he handed the carrier to Trevor. "I forgot to bring treats. Always be carrying treats. That's going to be my new motto."

Trevor smiled. "No worries, I'm a dog whisperer." He tucked the carrier under the desk, unzipping the top to get a glimpse in at J.D. "You go ahead. Down the hallway, follow the crowd."

Daniel fell in with the group of visitors as they headed down a long corridor lined with photos. He thought they were all taken in the desert, but each was an extreme close-up, so it was hard to tell for sure. He'd need more time to study them.

They trooped through double doors into a large room

soaked in sunlight. The inmates—that's the word that came into his head, although he knew it wasn't correct—were already sitting in the circle of mismatched—artfully mismatched—chairs.

Sam looked haggard, his usually wavy hair limp and oily. He jerked his chin in greeting as Daniel sat down next to him. Daniel could feel the spaces between his fingers getting sweaty, and his heart felt weighed down, like it was resting lower in his chest and struggling to beat. Sam leaned close so only Daniel would be able to hear. "Just go ahead and piss your pants. You'll feel better."

"I already did."

Sam laughed, and that laugh was exactly the same as it had always been. Making Sam laugh always made Daniel feel proud, probably a holdover from when they were kids. It's hard for a nine-year-old to make a seventeen-year-old laugh, at least on purpose. Daniel always wanted to be as old as Sam. He used to go next door and ask if Chris could come out and play, even though Chris was Sam's age, Sam's friend.

"What do we do?" Daniel had read as much as he could about family group therapy, trying to feel prepared. What he'd wanted was a list of questions, so he could formulate the correct answers in advance. But he hadn't found anything that concrete.

"They ask questions. We come up with bullshit."

Daniel realized he was bouncing his heel up and down, making one leg jerk, a habit he'd gotten rid of in high school. He had to get a grip. He glanced around the circle, trying to gauge if anyone else was as nervous as he was. The middle-aged woman across from him had a death grip on her purse, and he didn't think it was because she was worried someone was about to grab it. A teenage guy was doing the leg-bouncing thing Daniel had just stopped. *See? It's normal to be nervous,* he told himself. *And in a couple hours, it will be over. And in a few weeks, Sam will be out of here, and the whole thing will be over.*

Unless it wasn't. Unless this changed nothing. Daniel shoved that thought away, or at least to the way back of his brain, as a woman with green eyes and lots of black curly hair pulled two chairs into the middle of the circle. Daniel didn't like the look of that.

"Welcome to family day. I'm Sydney Grant, one of the counselors. Today we're going to explore the way addiction impacts everyone in a family. What I'd like is for us to come to the center in pairs and talk a little about that. We can all learn from hearing about other people's experiences. Is there anyone who'd like to go first?"

Daniel definitely didn't want to go first. He didn't want to go at all. He had nothing to say that would help Sam. If he did, he'd have said it before Sam got arrested. No, before that. Back to a year ago, a year or more, when he could see Sam spiraling down and down and down, all the while trying to convince everyone, most of all himself, that he was having fun, doing great.

But even if Daniel had come up with some insightful, Oprah-wise thing to say back then, it wouldn't have mattered. Little Brother was never going to be listened to, not on the big stuff. Sam could give him advice, but it couldn't go the other way.

"We'll go." The man next to the jittery-legged teen stood and strode to one of the chairs in the middle. After a brief hesitation, the kid followed and sat across from, Daniel assumed, his dad. There was some strong family resemblance between them, same widow's peak, same Roman nose. People wouldn't guess Sam and Daniel were brothers by looking at them. Sam's face was all angles, cut jawline and cheekbones. Daniel had a round baby face that he was still waiting to grow out of, although if it hadn't happened by age thirty-one, it probably wasn't going to. Mila had actually liked to pinch his cheeks the way you pinch a baby's. Not sexy. Nobody was going to pinch Sam's cheeks. He didn't have any of that pudge to grab.

Sydney got the introductions, first names only, out of the way, then got down to it, without much of a warm-up. She asked Timothy—Daniel had been right about him being the dad—to talk about a time when Eli's addiction had negatively affected him.

Daniel's brain started to churn. Was he going to have to answer that question? What was he supposed to say? He could immediately come up with ways Sam's substance abuse hurt his parents. Sam had moved back home for a while when Daniel was in high school, and there'd been a lot of nights when he'd found his mom sitting up, waiting for Sam to come home, and half the time he didn't. He'd say he was a "grown man," and he didn't need to tell Mommy and Daddy what he was doing. She never said anything, but Daniel knew those nights were an agony of wondering whether Sam had ended up driving drunk and getting hurt or hurting someone else. Or worse.

And his dad—his father felt like he'd broken his and Sam's relationship when he'd basically forced Sam into rehab the first time. Daniel didn't think it had been broken. If it was broken, would his dad be asking Daniel for daily updates on how Sam was doing? But it had changed things between Sam and his father, and he knew his dad walked around with deep regret. Even though he might manage to keep it buried most of the time, it was there.

"And here we go. Money. That's what it's always about with you, right? Money?"

The raised voice snapped Daniel away from his thoughts, and he realized he'd been so absorbed in trying to figure out what he was going to say when it was his turn in front of the group that he'd been paying no attention to Timothy and Eli.

Timothy crossed his legs. Unlike his son, he kept his voice

low and even. "I was simply trying to explain that your actions affect everyone in the family. Your sister will still be able to go to college, but she'll have to take out a loan. If things had been . . . different, that wouldn't have been necessary."

"What do you expect me to do about it? If I could get my job at Mr. C's back, which we both know isn't going to happen, I'd never be able to come close to the money she'd need even for a semester. Same for any other McJob I could get."

Daniel felt each beat of his heart resonating through his body. He didn't know these two people. Their experiences didn't match his. Sam hadn't caused financial hardship in his family that had interfered with Daniel's college plans. But even so, it was almost like Daniel was sitting up there, or like there were invisible wires connecting him to Timothy and Eli, pumping everything they were feeling into him. He felt that way a lot of times when people argued around him, even people across the room, people he'd never even seen before.

Timothy recrossed his legs. "I'm not saying I hold you responsible."

"Bullshit," Sam muttered in Daniel's ear. "That's exactly what he's saying."

Sydney held up one hand. "But aren't you saying that Eli's substance abuse was responsible?"

"You think it's my fault, too?" Eli demanded.

"Part of recovery is accepting the way we've hurt other people and making amends."

"I just explained that I can't make that kind of money."

"But say you gave your sister a portion of the money that you did make. How would you feel, do you suppose?" Sydney rested one hand on Eli's shoulder.

"She'd just laugh at it. She'd say what did I want her to do, buy a couple pencils and maybe a pen?"

"We've all talked about assuming we know what's in someone else's heart and mind. In any case, I'm talking about you.

How would you feel if you did what you could to make it up to your sister, no matter her reaction?"

Eli ran his hands roughly over his face. "I don't know. And like I said, no job, so pointless to talk about it."

"Making amends is a way of acknowledging the way your substance abuse hurt other people. That acknowledgment can be powerful. Something to think on and perhaps discuss in our next one-on-one." Sydney waved them back to their seats in the circle. "Who would like to go next?"

Sam stood up. "Let's get this over with," he muttered to Daniel.

Maybe that was the right idea. At least if they went now, he wouldn't have to be filled with dread for the rest of the session. Because that's what it was. His body felt so cold and so heavy that what he was feeling deserved to be called dread. As he sat down across from Sam, he felt like he was trembling underneath his skin. He hadn't been expecting this. He'd realized he was nervous, had been nervous since he'd known he was going to have to do the group therapy. But he hadn't been expecting his body to react like he was under attack.

Sydney did the introductions, then hit Daniel with basically the same question she'd asked Timothy. "Can you tell us about a time when Sam's substance abuse had an effect on your life?"

"I know my parents are terrified that Sam will go back to—"

Sydney held up a hand. "Let's stick with you, Daniel. Your life."

He resisted the urge to wipe his sweaty hands on his jeans as he frantically tried to come up with something to say. "Well, uh, I'm here. I'm staying here until Sam's released. That's a thing." *Wow, eloquent, Daniel.*

Sam gave a snort. "Poor Daniel. He has to stay in a four-star resort for a month free of charge. Sounds like my substance abuse"—he gave those two words a sarcastic spin—"wasn't completely negative for everyone."

Daniel felt anger rip through him, hot and sharp, then re-minded himself of what he'd read about detoxing. Sam had to be feeling like shit, nauseous, going from shivering to sweating, his whole body throbbing with pain. The articles said he could be paranoid and anxious and angry. It's like it wasn't even Sam sitting across from him, not really.

Sydney fingered one of her silver broccoli earrings. "Look-ing at Daniel, I don't see someone who is in the middle of a fun Sedona vacation."

"Minimizing," someone in the group called out.

"Good observation. But for now, let's keep the talk between Daniel and Sam."

"And you," Sam muttered.

"Yes, and me," Sydney agreed. "What do you think, Sam? Do you think because Daniel has a nice place to stay while you're in rehab that it isn't painful for him?"

"I didn't ask him to be here."

Not really Sam. Daniel had to remember that. Sam was the guy who'd driven him to get Icees. The guy who'd taught him how to throw a ball. The guy who'd told him his first dirty joke. Those things were a long time ago. But there'd been other things, too. . . . His mind went blank as he tried to come up with some.

"That wasn't my question. I want you to look at your brother and tell me if you think he's enjoying himself."

Sam, who'd been slouching in his chair, straightened up and made a show of looking at Daniel. "I guess not. But he's not big on enjoying himself in general."

"Do you hear how you're dismissing what Daniel is feeling?"

Daniel wanted out of there. And it wasn't like Sam wanted him there, at least not right now, other than to deliver candy. Fine. He'd rather be anyplace else. Except that he'd made a commitment to their parents. Maybe being here wasn't really making it much easier for them, but leaving would make it harder, and he wasn't going to do that.

Sydney turned to Daniel. "Can you tell your brother how you're feeling being here?"

Daniel flexed his hands, feeling the sweat between his fingers. "Nervous, anxious, uncomfortable. Worried that nothing is going to change."

"And what would that be like, if things didn't change?"

"Our parents would never be able to be at ease. They'd always be wondering what was happening with Sam, if he was okay. They've lived their entire lives that way, and they would keep doing that." Daniel stopped talking to Sydney and looked at his brother. "Forever, Sam."

Sam opened his mouth, but didn't say anything.

"For you, though? What would it be like for you if things didn't change?"

"Miserable." The word just came out. And it was the truth. Sam made him miserable.

CHAPTER 9

Riley's head pounded as she started gathering up the little vials of essential oil. The mix of all those strong scents had gotten to her, that and Marti and Andi, the mom and teen daughter duo who were at the resort for what Marti called "bonding time," and Andi called "boring bullshit."

"Jeez, I thought the rosemary camphor would have at least some effect on them." Cari took a whiff from one of the vials before adding it to a carrying case. "It definitely makes my outlook a ton and a quarter more positive, but they seemed in worse moods when they left." She shook her head. "I guess even the most powerful oils aren't a match for mom and daughter drama. My mother and I definitely had a few years when one of us ended up screaming or in tears or both every few days. I'd say something, and she'd lose it, or vice versa. I'm twenty-eight, and she can still make me crazy. Moms, right?"

Riley made a noncommittal sound. A lot of people, lucky people, didn't seem to realize how screwed up the world could be. Clearly, it didn't even occur to Cari that Riley might not have a mom to make her crazy.

"Hmmh." Cari imitated Riley's sound. "That's all I get? Usually when I say the word *mother* to a woman, I get at least an eighteen-minute rant, without pause for breath."

Cari tended to exaggerate, but in fact, Riley had heard a few good mom rants in her time. When she was younger, hearing complaints about someone's mother sent a fiery blast of anger through her, and she'd have to restrain herself from yelling, "At least you have a mother to whine about." It still happened, but not as often, and the blast wasn't quite so hot. She was maturing. All three of the therapists she saw before she turned eighteen would be so proud. If they remembered who she was, which they wouldn't, because there was a pretty much endless line of girls like Riley waiting to be seen.

Mary would remember, and she'd be proud, but Riley didn't want to think about that frightened kid she had been. Who cared about the past, when she'd created an amazing future for herself.

She realized Cari was still waiting for an answer. "The older I get, the less crazy she makes me."

"So there's hope."

"There's hope." Sometimes telling people what they wanted to hear was the best strategy. Right now, it was getting her out of this mom convo as fast as possible. "You going to go get dinner? Lori told me she's making creamy, dreamy enchiladas." Riley loaded the vials she'd gathered into the carrying case.

"I still have to put in a few hours at the shop, but I'll definitely stop by after that. I never miss the latest enchilada creation. Those sweet potato and black bean ones last time? My tongue melted. Literally."

Yeah, Cari was an exaggerator. Riley grabbed her backpack, checking her phone as she headed out of the dining room and into the hallway that ran alongside the kitchen. There was a message from Mitchell Benson, her new supervisor at Spruce

Summit. She read it and had to stop walking and brace one hand against the wall. It felt like the floor was breaking up under her feet.

She read it again, then again. The words didn't magically change. *Sorry, if you can't make it by the start date we agreed on, I'll have to give the job to someone else.* More words mixed in with them. The words of Chloe Campbell. Those statistics she'd looked up just so she could shove them in Riley's face. Twenty-five percent of girls like Riley didn't graduate from high school. Ten percent of former foster kids end up dead before age twenty-one. Fifty percent develop a substance abuse dependence. Twenty-five percent end up homeless. Twenty-five percent end up in prison. Seventy percent of the female ones get pregnant, and less than five percent ever get a college degree. Ten percent end up dead before age twenty-one. Fifty percent develop a substance abuse dependence. Twenty-five percent end up homeless. Twenty-five percent end up in prison. Seventy percent pregnant. Less than five percent—

Stop. Just stop.

But she couldn't stop. T.U.P. was falling apart. Ten percent end up dead before age twenty-one. Fifty percent develop a substance abuse dependence. Twenty-five percent end up homeless. Twenty-five percent end up incarcerated. Seventy percent pregnant. Less than five percent—

You have to get a grip, or Ms. Aguilar will see and you'll lose this job, too, she told herself. All she wanted to do was crawl under the covers with *Beautiful America* and a flashlight. And J.D. curled up on her head. But she was at work, where any moment somebody could see her having a meltdown. She pushed away from the wall, jammed her phone back in her pack, and focused on her senses, on the faint smell of Lori's cheesy, dreamy enchiladas.

Okay, she'd go to the staff dining room, sit down for a few, eat some enchiladas, act like a normal person, get a handle on her panic, and then go home, and if she still needed it, get in bed with the book. And the puppy.

She was in control of her life, she reminded herself as she continued down the hall. There were tons of resorts near Stowe. And if she couldn't get a job at one of them, she had a lot of restaurant experience. She'd shoot out a bunch more applications, and she'd get something. She didn't care what it was. The *what* didn't matter. The *where* was the important thing. Stowe was up next on The Ultimate Plan, and she was getting herself there.

Chin up, shoulders back, she headed into the small room, just big enough for a table that sat fifteen, a sideboard loaded down with food, and nothing else. She slid two of the enchiladas on her plate, added a dollop of *arroz rojo*.

Riley grabbed a seat at the table across from Garret. He didn't look up, writing in his inventor's notebook with one hand and forking enchilada into his mouth with the other. Good, if she still looked a little shell-shocked, he wouldn't notice. She took a bite of her rice, forcing herself to notice each flavor: cilantro, tomato, garlic, serrano pepper, onion. She was okay. She was okay because she was in charge. She was taking care of herself. Take care of yourself, and you don't have to worry.

The door swung open, and Lori walked in with a platter of chocolate cupcakes. Garret's head jerked up, and he dropped both his pen and his fork. "You're my muse, Lori. I smelled those baking, and the way you add that kick of sauerkraut to the batter made me think maybe those science kids should add mu-metal to their magnetometer—not an obvious combination, but I think it might give the magnetic energies at the vortex a boost, which would allow them to register. Starla said they were having trouble picking up the readings they needed."

Lori, usually happy to have a chat, just murmured, "Sounds

great," and scurried back out the door. Garret looked at the spot where she'd disappeared for a long moment before he retrieved his pen and fork. They ended up in the wrong hands, and he tried to spear a bite of his notebook, smearing enchilada sauce across the page.

Riley couldn't help smiling. This had been the right move. The food, Garret and Lori, the familiarity—they were all working for her, settling her down.

"The positioning will be tricky, but I think this could increase the sensitivity," Garret muttered. Riley picked up the water pitcher and filled her glass. He looked up. "When did you get here?"

"Couple minutes ago." He'd clearly been in what he called "the good place," his brain humming with ideas. Lori had somehow managed to penetrate his thoughts, but not Riley.

"I have something for you. Well, not you, your baby." He pulled J.D.'s pizza squeaky out of his pocket and set it in front of Riley's plate. "He dropped it during his little escapade."

"Escapade?" Riley didn't like the sound of that.

"He almost ran right into Ms. Aguilar, but I used some of the ol' razzle-dazzle to distract her." Garret did jazz hands, and almost dropped his pen and fork again.

Riley's stomach gave a twist, the panic starting to jangle through her again. "Where was this?"

"Over by the La Fonda casita."

Daniel's casita. Why had he had the puppy on the resort grounds? He knew about the rules. That's the reason he'd been staying at Riley's place.

"I had her out inspecting the lawn for grubs for almost half an hour."

Ms. Aguilar didn't see. But that wasn't the point. The point was, she could have, and she could have found out Riley was the one who'd brought the dog onto the property, and then

Riley would have been immediately fired, because that's how Ms. Aguilar operated, and then she wouldn't have the money for the catalytic converter or the O2 sensor if she needed it, and she wouldn't have a place to live, and her savings weren't going to go far even if she stayed in the cheapest motel. Homeless. That's how people ended up homeless. Twenty-five percent for former foster—

Riley was spiraling. Senses, she needed to focus on her senses. She cut one of her enchiladas with the side of her fork, but as she raised the bite to her mouth, she could tell her stomach wasn't having it. She shoved away from the table and started for home. Home and bed and book and dog. That's what she needed. When she took the last curve of the trail and her cabin came into sight, J.D. came hurtling toward her. Tears stung her eyes at the sight of him. She blinked them away as she hugged the puppy tight, tight, tight.

She straightened when Daniel walked over and joined them. "I heard you almost got J.D. caught by my boss."

"Uh." Daniel raked one hand through his hair. "Yeah. I was going to tell you about that. I was taking him with me to rehab. I'd just started down the road to town when I remembered I left the zucchini bread my mom made for Sam at the casita. I figured I could just duck in really fast with no one seeing us, but J.D. had a fit. He practically hurled himself out of my arms and took off. No one saw him, thanks to Garret."

Sam. Of course it would have to do with Sam. That's all Daniel thought about. "You knew I was worried about anyone seeing him. I told you about my boss. I told you about the no-exceptions. You could have gotten me fired."

"Like I said, I thought I'd only be there a minute, just in and out. Then he got away. I'm sorry. It was a bad call."

"Couldn't you have waited until tomorrow for the bread?"

"It's really important to my mom. I knew she'd ask about it

when I talked to her tonight. She wants to feel like she's doing something for Sam, and she knew I'd be seeing him in person for family therapy. I know it's just bread, but to her, it's big. You know how moms are."

Another mom thing, another person who could afford to just be thoughtless about it.

"Why couldn't you just tell Mommy you forgot?" As soon as the words were out of her mouth, she knew she'd gone too far. Daniel recoiled like she'd slapped him.

He'd made a stupid mistake, really stupid, but she'd made a mistake, too. She should have handled the puppy's care herself. She shouldn't have put herself in the position where someone else could screw it up. It was too important. "Sorry. I'm sorry. I shouldn't have said that. You were doing me a favor. Nothing happened. It's fine." She pulled in a deep breath. Damage control. "Sounded like Garret put on a show. Razzle-dazzle, he called it." She did the jazz hands Garret had used when telling her the story.

"Yeah. It was epic. He told her there was a grub infestation on the lawn, and he made it sound like those grubs were as big as the worms they ride in *Dune*." His voice didn't match the funny story he was trying to spin, kind of flat.

"Those worms, yeah." She forced a laugh, trying to show everything was good, that she wasn't panicking about her job situation, that T.U.P. was still on track, that she wasn't a crazy lady who yelled about people's mothers.

"Should we go eye-drop Petunia?"

She wanted him to just go away. She wanted her book and her bed and her puppy. But she couldn't say no. She didn't want him to think she was still angry, even though she was, but mostly at herself. "Sure. Great." She led the way into the cabin.

Daniel picked up the eye drops from the kitchen counter. Then put them back down. "You know what? Maybe I should just go; I feel like I'm in the way." His words came out so quickly that Riley wasn't even sure she heard him right. "Can you handle the drops on your own?"

"I—"

Daniel cut her off. "No, sorry, that's incredibly rude. I said I would help." He picked up the eye drops again and smiled, a smile that was obviously forced, and he wasn't quite meeting her eyes.

"What's going on?"

"Nothing. I think you're still mad I took J.D. to my casita, and honestly, I don't need anyone else being mad at me today."

Riley sighed. "I said I was sorry—"

"But you don't mean it."

"I do mean it!" She was surprised to realize how true that was. "I *am* sorry, I didn't mean to jump down your throat about your mom. I know you're worried about your parents with the whole Sam situation."

Usually, he'd be jumping in, accepting her apology, telling her it was okay, but he didn't reply.

"It's just . . . look, Cari was on me earlier about why I never complain about my mom, and that's a subject that always pisses me off. And then it was your mom with the bread that nearly got me fired. People make a lot of assumptions about mothers and how we all feel about them, when some of us just don't."

Daniel stared at her. "Don't?"

Riley felt a rush of tears, so humiliating. The last thing she needed today was to be crying in front of somebody. All she wanted was her bed, her book, and her puppy. But Daniel was a good guy, and he'd been amazing when she needed help.

Before she knew it, he was standing next to her with a box of tissues. See? Amazing.

"I'm okay," she told him. "It's been a long time."

"I'm confused," he admitted.

"I don't have a mom. Or a dad. They died in a car crash when I was little." Riley felt lightheaded as the words left her mouth. When was the last time she'd told anyone about her parents? When she was ten? Had to be before middle school, when Chloe Campbell somehow found out and began making fun of her for being a foster kid. "And then it turned out I had no other family, at least none that wanted to deal with me, so I went straight into foster care. Babies end up with adoptive families. People like little and cute, I guess. But older kids don't, usually. I bounced around a lot. I never had a real foster mom or anyone like that."

She didn't know when it had happened, but slowly she realized that Daniel had his arms around her, keeping her steady. "I don't tell people that, about my parents being dead," she said into the softness of his shirt. "It makes everyone treat me like I have a disease or something."

He nodded. "You looked woozy." He moved away, releasing her. "Want to sit?"

Riley sank onto the couch, missing the warmth of his arms. She was glad when J.D. clambered up next to her.

"Sorry to dump that on you. Usually, I just let people assume, like Cari. Nobody ever thinks, *Oh, maybe she has no mom, maybe she's a foster kid and wishes she had a mom to complain about.* It's better to keep quiet and blend in. Be normal, you know?"

He sat down next to her, and the puppy snuggled in between them. "I don't think it's a matter of normal, really. Plenty of people have lost family. I'm just sorry that you had to go through all this alone, especially as a little kid."

Riley blinked at him in surprise. He was right; of course a lot of people had lost family. He'd lost a brother, even though it was a brother he'd never known.

"That's not what the other kids said when it happened. They

just avoided me. It's like they thought it was contagious. 'Look out, it happened to her, and I don't want it to happen to me,'" she blurted out.

"Well . . . kids." He shrugged. "'Children are unformed little monsters who don't know how to behave properly in any situation, and that's why a good education is so important.' I'm quoting my last girlfriend, Mila. She was a sixth-grade teacher."

Riley snorted. "She knew what she was talking about. I met plenty of little monsters growing up in the system." She sighed, exhaustion seeping into every pore of her body. When was the last time she'd talked to someone about her life this way? Had she ever? Besides Mary, of course.

Daniel was watching her carefully. "I won't break," she assured him. "I just don't usually discuss my private life, so I'm . . . I don't know, panicky? I've had a panicky day."

He surprised her by laughing. "Me, too. What else happened? It's more than just Cari's mom talk and me letting J.D. loose, isn't it?"

"It's just that Ms. Aguilar could fire me, and that would be—" The words caught in her chest, the memory of losing her Vermont job bubbling back up. If she got fired from High Sky on top of not having the next job lined up, The Ultimate Plan would be so far off track that she might as well be eighteen again, working three minimum-wage jobs just trying to keep a roof over her head, nowhere near able to afford a car to get her started on T.U.P. She would have to begin all over again; everything she'd built up over the years would be for nothing.

Dead, homeless, addicted, in prison, pregnant. Dead, homeless, addicted, in prison, pregnant.

"I know the owner, you realize? I could probably explain the situation to Ben, and you wouldn't have to worry about keeping J.D. hidden," Daniel said, snapping her out of her thoughts.

"No way." It was an automatic response, sharp and hard. She couldn't let herself depend on help.

"Wow, Garret was right—you really don't trust people."

"He said that?" Riley frowned. "I don't think that's true." Was it?

"Until today, you haven't told me anything personal about yourself. And you've never been comfortable letting me help with J.D. and Petunia. Half the time, I still think you're about to whip out another gift card," Daniel teased gently. "And I mean it, Ben Osborne would probably step in if I told him it was my fault, that you were just turning a blind eye to me keeping a rescued puppy here. Why won't you let me take some of the stress off you?"

She chewed on her lip, thinking. "It's not because I don't trust you, not exactly. But when I'm the one taking care of myself, I don't have to worry. I'm the only one who's always been there for me. I'm the only one who always will be. I can't leave the plan to anyone else. It's already all messed up."

"You've lost me."

Riley pressed her hand against her mouth. Had she really just mentioned T.U.P. to a stranger? Nobody knew about T.U.P. except Mary. That wasn't anyone's business.

"Nothing—I just get panicked when things go wrong. Garret told me about Ms. Aguilar almost finding J.D., and I realized I should've been watching him myself, because that way I would know for sure that everything was under control. The idea of maybe losing my job . . . it makes me spiral. There was this girl when I was a kid, Chloe, and she used to quote all these statistics to me about foster kids. Like twenty-five percent of foster kids don't graduate from high school. And after they age out of the system? Before they're twenty-one, ten percent of former foster kids end up dead. Fifty percent develop a substance abuse dependence. Twenty-five percent end up in prison.

Seven out of ten girls get pregnant. All of that before they turn twenty-one. Less than five percent get a college degree. I didn't. I've spent my whole life focused on proving her wrong about the rest. It's not about trusting anyone or not. It's about making sure that I don't become one of those statistics."

"Riley." Daniel reached across the sleeping puppy and took her hand. "I think you can let go of that. You said all those horrible things happened before the kids turned twenty-one. You're at least ten years past that. And I'm assuming you graduated from high school?"

She nodded, surprised. Why hadn't she ever thought of that?

"Did you ever fact-check this girl, Chloe?" He waved his hand. "You know what? It doesn't matter. At this point, it's impossible for you to become one of those statistics. You've already made sure of that."

Riley gaped at him. His words made perfect sense, but they still sounded insane. She'd never thought about being older than the kids in those stats, or the whole thing just not making sense, or the possibility that Chloe Campbell, who knew everything or thought she did, was a liar. It never even occurred to her. But let go of it? Only someone like him, someone who hadn't had her life, could just say *let go of it*. Chloe had told her over and over that foster kids would never turn out to be as good as other people, and Riley had spent her life proving Chloe wrong.

"Anyway, I'm really sorry I let J.D. get away. He ran straight at your boss. I seriously didn't mean for anyone to see him. I was probably more stressed about seeing Sam than I realized, or I wouldn't have brought him to the casita." Daniel sat back and let out a deep breath. She looked at him, really looked at him, for the first time since she'd come home. He looked the way she felt: wrung-out, barely holding it together.

"Wait, you saw Sam? I thought you were just dropping off

the bread. How did I not know you were seeing Sam today?" Riley felt awful. "I would've figured out someplace else for the pup to stay."

"No, it's not your fault. I didn't tell you, because I came up with a plan to leave J.D. with the desk guy at Ironwood. I didn't want you to have to worry. I'm the one who messed up by getting the stupid bread—"

"Daniel," she cut him off. "I didn't realize you were seeing Sam face-to-face. Of course you wanted to bring your mom's bread. I'm sure he appreciated it."

Daniel gave a short bark of laughter. "No, he did not. He didn't appreciate anything I brought or anything I said."

She just waited, not sure what else to do.

"We had group therapy, and Sam . . . well, the goal was to make all the patients listen to how their addiction had impacted their loved ones, right? So when they got to us, I tried to talk about how worried my parents always are."

Of course he did. It seemed like Daniel was always thinking of other people—Sam, his parents, even her, who he barely knew, and J.D. "But they wanted to talk about you?" She'd been through enough therapy to know that.

"Yeah. Sam didn't want to hear it. Getting clean makes him mean. He didn't used to be like that. Even when he's using, he's actually kind of a fun guy." Riley nodded. "Anyway, the therapist asked how I felt, and I said miserable. Sam went off. He was furious, and I don't even know why I said it. I'm not miserable, he is. He's the one with the problem."

Riley shook her head. "You are too miserable." The expression on his face was almost comical, he was so astonished. "I know you want to argue, but it's true. You think you have to take care of everyone in your family because they went through this horrible tragedy and you didn't. You've let it take over your whole life. Daniel, ever since I met you, the only thing I've seen you do is worry about other people. You think about Sam all the time, Sam and your parents. And you worry about the puppy, you listen to Starla's romantic drama, you go out of your way to help me with everything, even giving a rabbit eye drops, and you don't even know me!"

"I know you."

"You do now," she agreed. "But that's only because you've spent so much time trying to help and so little time actually enjoying yourself here in this beautiful resort in Sedona."

"That's what Sam thinks I've been doing, living it up, so I should have nothing to complain about."

"Obviously he's wrong. Have you even gone to a vortex? You're an artist, right? I gave you those pencils. Have you even used them? When's the last time you did something for yourself?" she asked. Impulsively, she got off the couch and knelt in front of him so she could look directly into his face. "Even today, I snapped at you, and you just stayed here and listened to me and kept being so sweet. You didn't even tell me you'd gone to group therapy, not right away. You're always thinking about other people. What do *you* want?"

Daniel held her gaze for a long moment. "This. I want this." Then he leaned forward, threaded his hands in her hair, and pulled her to him for a kiss.

This is what she wanted, too. Right now, it was all she wanted. The sensation of his lips on her, his hands on her, made everything else, the whole horrible day, fade away.

CHAPTER 10

"Dorothea is so different in class than she is in the field. I had her for Physics and the Environment two semesters ago, and she was always so upbeat and funny. But out here." Rissa shook her head as she took a seat on the patio. "And it's getting worse. We've been here a week, and she's gotten more impatient and snappy every day."

"Yeah, I bet right now she's flossing to get pieces of my head out of her teeth." Miles grimaced.

"I don't get it." Which wasn't unusual. A lot of times, Adam didn't get jokes. Too literal-minded, his dad would say, as if that was a bad thing. Literal was logical. If everyone kept their conversation literal, there would be a lot fewer misunderstandings. Adam went back to trying to parse the flossing comment.

Rissa scooted her chair closer to the fire. "He means because she bit his head off back there when he messed up the VMS device setting."

"You are correct, sir."

And now Miles was calling Rissa *sir*. Adam didn't bother to ask why. It wasn't necessary to follow every nuance of the conversation. His strategies were all geared to keeping his brain free for the important things.

"Although I wouldn't say I messed up the reading," Miles added.

"What would you call it when you run the wrong slurry velocity?" Rissa didn't give Miles a chance to answer. "Let's let Adam decide if 'messed up' is the appropriate description."

"It's possible that a lower output reduces the possibility of blockage. A case can be made for lower slurry velocity."

"But that's not why Miles—"

"I hoped I'd find you out here," Starla called as she crossed the patio. "I brought you some snacks. Peggy told me you had a kind of frustrating time when she took you to the vortex. Seemed like you could use some happy." She set a tray on the table between them.

Miles half-moaned as he put one of the deep-fried mini tacos into his mouth. "I worship you."

"It's our chef you should worship. Try this one." She popped a charred-cauliflower taco with mango salsa into Adam's mouth. It felt like he'd grown extra taste buds.

"Gotta get to reception. I'm leading a shopping expedition." With a little wave, she headed off, then turned back and added, "The shirt looks good on you. I knew it would."

Adam wished she'd stayed. She had an unusual mind. That was something on his list of attributes he found attractive in a partner. An unusual mind was like a puzzle, and he liked puzzles. Miles also had an unusual mind. That comment about Dorothea flossing pieces of his head out of her teeth wasn't standard. But he'd never found himself attracted to a guy, so that data point wasn't relative to partner potential.

He glanced at Starla as she walked away. She had a nice butt, which was also on the list, although he knew it probably shouldn't be. It's not like he expected any woman to have all the attributes, though, and it's not as if he thought a nice butt was the most important. The list had forty-three items. He didn't ask a woman out unless she had a minimum seventy percent. He'd been collecting data since he asked Holly Zimmerman to the eighth-grade homecoming dance. He'd never had a successful date with anyone with less than seventy percent, but it wasn't impossible that he would be compatible with someone with a lower percentage, though he felt it was statistically unlikely.

"Were you checking out her ass?" Rissa demanded.

"Yes." He liked to answer questions truthfully, unless it seemed like he might hurt someone's feelings, something his grandmother had worked with him on. Along with literalness, truthfulness made for fewer misunderstandings.

"Do you like her?"

Adam shrugged. He couldn't answer that. He hadn't amassed enough information.

"I freaking love her." Miles tossed another mini taco into his mouth. "Anyone who delivered these snacks unasked, out of the goodness of her heart, deserves devotion."

Adam realized Starla had another quality on his list—thoughtfulness. She had been told they'd had a difficult day working at the vortex, and she'd done something to make them feel better. He pulled the golf pencil from behind his ear and noted his new observations. Starla now had 16.2 percent of the attributes.

"Let's back up to what she said about your shirt. She said she knew it would look good on you. Explain."

"Yeah, explain. Because you've worn the same shirt and pants every day since I met you, then, bam, this one shows up in the rotation." Miles took a third mini taco.

"Not the same shirt and pants. I have multiples of both." Adam took one of the little tacos. He wasn't quite ready for another, but at the rate Miles was eating them, there might not be one left when Adam was ready.

"Like Einstein." Rissa intercepted Miles's hand as he reached for another snack and took the cauliflower taco for herself.

"Exactly. Why waste brain space on unimportant decisions."

"So why this?" Rissa gestured at the shirt.

"Starla bought it for me at a garage sale. I ran into her when I was shopping for Lego." He realized he'd forgotten to recalculate after Starla'd insisted on buying him the LET'S CUDDLE AND TALK ABOUT SCIENCE T-shirt for helping her carry all her purchases, her random and probably unnecessary purchases. That was generous, another of the key qualities. So she was actually at 18.6 percent. He made another note.

She definitely required further study. Although she was trying to overcome a love addiction. He theorized that love would require at a minimum an eighty-five percentage, although he couldn't be sure, never having been in love. But love didn't have to be part of his calculations in this case. He was just thinking of possibly asking her out. And possibly sex.

Daniel felt like the ground was pushing up on his feet with each step, giving him a little bounce. Maybe it was because he'd finally gotten a good night's sleep. Make that three. Make that every time he'd slept in Riley's bed.

No, he decided. He did sleep great in Riley's bed, but it was the time they spent not sleeping that was giving him the bounce. Which meant it was Riley changing the physics of his world. Although in physics, the ground actually was pushing back on you with the reaction force. But it had never felt like this.

He sat down at what he'd started to think of as his usual table in the dining room, trying to come up with a plan for what to do with the hours until he could see Riley again. More drawing, maybe. Or grab a mountain bike—he had kind of an in with the activities director and had been loaned one for the rest of his stay—and do a short ride, less than the puppy's two-hour bladder limit. The Bell Rock Trail sounded like about his speed—beginner. He hadn't been on a bike in . . . in so long, he couldn't remember when. Or maybe he'd loop back to that shop he and Riley had wandered by a couple nights ago and pick up that cuff bracelet with the engraved flowers they'd seen in the window. He could tell she liked it, and he'd had zero expenses lately. He could afford it.

Wow, he was thinking like such a tourist. But why not? He might never come to Sedona again, and he was starting to love the place. He wanted to see it all, and there was nothing to stop him. He hadn't gotten a call from Sam asking him to run something over to Ironwood, so no Little Brother duties. Daniel hadn't heard from Sam at all since group therapy day. He wasn't surprised. They weren't the kind of family that liked to talk about things. Sam was probably as freaked out by that therapy session as he was. He probably needed recovery time as much as Daniel did. It had been days, but every time Daniel thought about the session, which he tried not to do, he felt a little queasy.

So should he grab the colored pencils Riley had bought him, or the bike she'd arranged for him to borrow, or—his phone pinged, and he saw he had a text. From his mom. She wanted him to pick up some cactus candy she'd seen on a Sedona website and take it over to Sam. He clicked the link and read the description. The texture was described as fluffy, and Daniel had never gone for that kind of candy. Didn't matter. It wasn't for him. And in a way, it wasn't even for Sam. It was for his mom. Picking out candy for Sam probably made her feel like she was taking care of him, even if just in a small way.

He got that. Dropping off care packages made him feel like he was doing something for his brother, too. He needed to get another one together. Maybe when he went to get the candy, he'd look for one of those weighted blankets. That had been on the list of good things to bring to someone in rehab. Probably he should just use this time to get some chores done. That way, he'd be free when Riley got off work. At least he could stick J.D. in the carrier and bring him along.

"You look like you're thinking way too hard for someone on vacation." A fiftysomething woman in chef's whites stopped at his table holding a plate of . . . breakfast appetizers, was all he could think to call them. "How would you like to try a new creation of mine? I call it 'omelet sushi.' It's basically an omelet rolled up with the fillings in the center. I've got one with a tuna melt filling. One southwestern, of course. And one with goat cheese, avocado, and microgreens. They're all yours if you're interested in being my guinea pig."

"Did you make that artichoke mint frittata the other day?"

She nodded, and Daniel said, "I'll happily eat anything you come up with. It was delicious."

The woman set the plate down in front of him. "I'm Lori."

"Daniel. Have you been the chef here long?"

"Getting close to twelve years now, just after the place got the new owner. Started out chopping, then line cook, then sous chef."

"And now coming up with omelet sushi." Daniel took a bite of the tuna melt one, creamy with some bits of toasted bread-crumbs to give it crunch. "I'm not sure I'll ever be able to eat my mother's tuna melt again." She thought of it as one of her specialties, but along with the zucchini bread, not so much.

"Awww, no. Nothing can replace Mom's."

"I'm sure your kids think that."

A flicker of sadness crossed her face, so fast that Daniel wasn't completely sure he'd seen it. "No kids. I'm one of the Sedona free spirits. No ties." That fleeting expression made him wonder if she wished she had at least a couple of ties. As much as his own ties weighed him down sometimes, he wouldn't want to be without them. He hated that that's how things had turned out for Riley. Although she had a kind of family here.

She took care of Starla like a little sister, and it had been clear Garret cared about her.

"Did you grow up here, then?"

"No, but I've been here more than half my life now." She gave a wry smile. "That's a crazy thought."

"Yeah, time goes faster and faster, right? When I was a kid, summer vacation lasted forever. Fourth grade lasted forever. Now, summer—" Daniel snapped his fingers.

"True." Lori's stomach growled, and she slapped both hands over it. "Sorry. I'm the chef, but I never take time to eat, except little test bites."

"Have a sushi." Daniel gestured toward the free chair.

"I guess I could take a minute, although the manager will want to slaughter me if she sees me sitting in the dining room."

"I've heard she's pretty strict."

Lori raised an eyebrow. "Someone's been gossiping?"

He definitely wasn't going to out Riley. "I just overheard her complaining to the gardener about the lawn outside reception. Something about grubs."

"Impossible. Garret practically gets down on his knees and combs that lawn every day. He's a genius when it comes to growing things in the desert."

"Looked great to me."

"You have a preference between the two that are left?" Lori nodded at the plate.

"I think I'm obligated to take the southwestern one, since I'm on vacation in Sedona."

She put one of the egg appetizers on a napkin. "So where are you from?"

"Colorado—little town called Fort Garland, about a nine-hour drive from here. I should have come out before. I haven't traveled a lot."

"I used to, but since I found my way here, I've stayed put. It just kind of felt like home right away."

Daniel got that. He hadn't explored much, but there was something about the place. . . . He could see himself becoming a regular at that dog bar, and he knew for sure he'd hit the food truck festival every time it happened, especially if Riley came with him to share the cheese.

"So if you're not much of a traveler, how do you spend your time? I hope you don't mind that I'm asking so many questions. People are like books to me. I love the stories." She pulled out one of the toothpicks holding the omelet sushi together.

"Uh . . ." He should be able to answer that. It wasn't a hard question. "I like to draw." And as of a few days ago, he'd actually been doing that.

"A creative type." Lori nodded approvingly. "Anyone who makes anything—a drawing, an invention, jewelry, anything—that's who I like to hang with. They usually have unique perspectives on things."

"Well, you qualify. Not everyone would have put mint with artichoke. Or made these."

"Why, thank you." She gave a little bow from her chair.

Daniel took another bite of his breakfast. Who knew tuna melt could taste like this? "There's something in it I can't quite identify."

"Aleppo pepper. Most people go with paprika for tuna salad, but I like the raisin-y flavor the Aleppo gives."

He could suggest the substitution to his mom, but it probably wouldn't help. Whatever was the cooking equivalent of a black thumb, that's what she had.

"You here by yourself, or do you just have a companion who likes to sleep in? And if I'm asking too many questions, you can tell me to stop."

"Flying solo." Lori seemed like the type who'd be sympathetic if he told her why he was really here. But just for a few, until he got the cactus candy and drove it to Ironwood, he thought he'd just be a regular guest.

"So no girlfriend? Or boyfriend?" she quickly added. "Person of any stripe who just makes you feel good?"

"Not right this minute." Riley made him feel good. But it was an enjoy-the-moment kind of thing. They both knew he'd be going home as soon as Sam got out. And after that—Daniel didn't really want to think about after that. He just hoped that the Ironwood stay was long enough to give Sam a real chance of turning things around. Assuming he wanted to.

"Me, either. I have a friend who says all it takes to find love is an open heart chakra. I have my doubts, because she also says cacao opens that right up. If that's true, why am I still waiting for my person of any stripe?"

"Hey, after eating here a few times, I'm half in love with you already."

"Sweet boy." Lori stood. "I gotta get back to the kitchen."

A hand ran lightly across his shoulder blades, sending hot tingles through his body. He knew the touch came from Riley even before she dropped into the empty chair and smiled at him. "Good morning."

He smiled back. Just looking at her made him smile. "Good morning."

Her smile widened. "Good morning." She took a sip of his coffee. Watching her mouth touch his cup made him want to drag her straight back to bed.

"I saw Lori sitting with you. She never does that. I've seen her venture out of the dining room exactly once before, and that was because Mr. Osborne wanted to compliment her on his dinner."

"My overwhelming charm."

She studied him for a long moment, long enough that he felt heat move up his neck and into his face. He better not be blushing.

"I have a kinetic sculpture workshop in about twenty minutes, but I've got the afternoon free. Want to do a little actual sightseeing on your trip to Sedona? I'm a pretty good tour guide."

"Absolutely. I've decided you're right about me missing out on an amazing place. Just don't talk in High Sky entertainment director mode all day. It makes me itchy."

She stuck her tongue out at him. "Go outside and draw. Starla says the light is inspired this morning. Something about the cloud layer."

He watched her go. He didn't need clouds to be inspired. He could just look at her. But he'd just been thinking about doing some drawing, and he'd been meaning to sketch the red rocks outside Riley's house. It was the perfect day for it. Starla was right about the light.

First things first. He needed to get that cactus candy. He couldn't forget the reason he was really here.

Riley felt—she thought for a moment, trying to come up with the right word. *Springy.* She felt springy. Her body felt light, and her legs had *bounce.* It's like—*boing*—she could go popping up to the ceiling as she headed into the employee dining room. This is what happened when you had sex after a six-month dry spell, she thought. Except she'd never experienced sensations quite like these, and this wasn't the first time she'd had a long stretch between guys.

"Hey, girlie!" Starla grinned as Riley joined her at the buffet table.

"Hey, you. What's gotten you so smiley?"

"Oh, nothing." Starla's eyes were glinting.

Had she and Bumper gotten back together? Since the breakup, she'd managed to put a smile on her face when she was in front of guests, but the rest of the time she'd been looking miserable. Whatever was going on with her, Riley would find out soon enough. Starla didn't have a private life. With her, everything was out there.

Riley selected a few of the omelet sushi, and Starla took a power-punch muffin. Riley wrinkled her nose. "Those taste good, but I just can't forget that they have sardines in them."

"But all blended up, no little chunks. And with Lori's magic blend of spices, it works. I feel healthier after one bite, with the kale and coconut oil and all the other good stuff. My body is still recovering from the tequila, even though I couldn't make myself drink much after that horrible night. I had to switch addictions early."

They sat down, the only two at the long table for the moment. "Is the addiction plan working?" Riley should have asked before. She'd been on a roller coaster. Getting another animal to deal with, losing her Vermont job—she had to get on that—the fight with Daniel, then telling him more about her life than she'd told anyone but Mary, then the sex. It had been just a little distracting.

"Every time I get a text, my heart—" Starla flapped her hands, and the brightness on her face faded. "I'm so excited it might be Bumper. Then I have to remind myself I don't want it to be Bumper. And when I remind myself, I don't completely believe myself. But I guess the plan is working, because when he texts me, which he still does a lot, I don't text him back. Sometimes I have to sit on my hands, for real, but I don't text him back."

"Good for you." This was the longest Bumper breakup Riley could remember. She took a bite of her omelet.

"You should see yourself." The grin had returned to Starla's face. So had the glint in her eye.

"What? Do I have tuna on my face?" She wiped her mouth, but it felt clean.

"No, but your chakras are definitely beating at a different frequency than they were a few days ago." Lori pushed open the door with her back, carrying pitchers in each hand. "Doesn't Riley look different to you?" Starla asked her.

Lori set down the orange juice and tea, then sat down across from them. She studied Riley for a moment. "There's some sparkle."

"Exactly!" Starla leaned toward Lori. "Do you want to know why?"

"Pretty sure I know. Pretty sure it has something to do with the cutie I saw her with at the bonfire last night."

Riley felt her face flush. "I wasn't with him, I was just chatting with him, the way I do with all the guests."

"You were chatting *and* sparkling." Starla shook her finger at Riley. "That's not what happens with all the guests."

"I have to admit, I noticed it, too." Lori poured herself a glass of the tea.

"It's like Garret when he's around you." Starla took a bite of muffin, then waved it at Lori. "Thanks for making these."

"Sure." Lori's forehead furrowed. "But Garret's not any different around me. He's just a sparkly kind of person in general, with his jokes and all those ideas he's always coming up with."

"It's different with you. I know these things. I knew Daniel liked this one, and I knew she liked him back before she did. I'm never wrong about love."

The sound of someone singing about a purple people eater interrupted the conversation. Lori almost knocked over her tea. "Stop talking! He's coming!"

Garret walked in a moment later and dumped a jumble of papers at the end of the table. When he saw Lori, he used his thumb and pinkie to smooth down his mustache, then made a show of arranging his notes. They were scribbled on napkins and in the margins of a flyer for a sale at Blooming Buddies, and—Riley craned her neck to get a better view. "You took a note on a leaf?"

"A dead leaf. I'd never use a live one." Garret pulled out a calculator and started punching in numbers.

"Is that for my science guy?" Starla asked. "Science people, I mean. Peggy told me you were going to try to figure out something for them. They were looking so down about their experiments last night that I decided to cheer them up with tacos. Lori's cooking makes people happy."

Garret jumped on that. "I'm never happier than when I'm eating Lori's food." Lori fiddled with her napkin, not even looking over at him. He tapped his papers. "I have a few ideas for tricking out their magnetometer so it'll amp up the vortex energies. It'll have to have a new name—that's how new and improved it's gonna be. This could be the one that gets me in—"

"*Invention Today,*" he, Riley, and Starla finished together.

Riley couldn't resist trying to give Garret a little boost. "Garret's going to be famous, Lori. Look at him. He's about to make a major scientific breakthrough."

Lori didn't look at him. Instead, she changed the subject. "I confirmed that your cutie is single, Riley."

"I couldn't believe you went out in the dining room to talk to him. You never go out to the dining room."

"I've never seen you sparkle at anyone. I needed to make sure he was worthy of you."

"Who's this now?" Garret set down his pencil.

"Daniel. Daniel something. I didn't get his last name."

Garret winked at Riley. "I believe I know the gentleman. He's the one who helped you out with your puppy, am I right?"

"Oh my god, it's not my pup! Why would it be my pup? Animals aren't allowed. And he's just a nice guy who has a soft spot for rescue animals," Riley cried. "Garret, you're going to get me in trouble with Ms. Aguilar."

"None of us are Ms. Aguilar, honey. Not a Tic Tac in sight." Lori laughed. "And you're right about him being a nice guy."

"Any man who's good with animals is a man you can trust," Garret agreed.

Lori nodded. "Listen to Garret. A man who knows how to read plants is a man who knows how to read people." She breezed back out the door, leaving a blushing Garret behind.

"Oooh, she gave you a compliment." Starla sounded so happy for him. Riley was happy for him, too. She wanted to yell at him for bringing up her against-the-rules behavior, but she couldn't bring herself to do it. Everybody should be as happy as she was today.

"There has to be one thing in Sedona that you haven't done," Daniel said. "How long have you lived here?" He and Riley were giving Petunia her eye drops before heading out for their afternoon sightseeing adventure, and he wanted it to be something new for both of them.

"Almost six months," she said.

"That's all? But you know everything about it."

"I always make sure to do absolutely everything in every place I go. That's how you know you've really lived."

Petunia stamped her back legs against his stomach, hard. It was unbelievable how strong rabbits were, and as she was feeling better, she fought harder. "Ouch! Where are we going to re-home this girl? It better be someplace that understands bunny behavior."

"I'm looking into elementary schools," Riley said. "Class pet seems like a good life, don't you think?"

"I'd take it."

Done with the drops, Riley picked up the bunny, kissed her on the top of the head, and deposited her back into the makeshift hutch Daniel had built out of some old milk crates Garret found. "There is one place I haven't been in Sedona, actually. It's the City of the Star People."

"Sounds mysterious."

"It is so mysterious that nobody even knows for sure where it is," Riley said. "But there's an area in Sedona that people think might be the place."

"Well, let's get our boy and check it out." Daniel shook J.D.'s harness, and the puppy came running, almost tripping over his feet in his haste to get to them. Once they were in the car, he settled down on Riley's lap as she read aloud from a website about the legend of Palatkwapi, the temple city of a group of people called the Kachinas.

"Hopi stories talk about it, but they don't say where exactly the place is," Riley said. "Just that the Kachinas—the 'Star People'—did a lot of ritual stuff there."

"So the place we're headed is what?"

"I guess it's a maybe site. Or a site that a lot of people hope is the correct place." She turned off her phone and looked out the window at the gorgeous scenery passing by. "Who cares? It'll be beautiful. We're going to skip the tour, unless you want to hear about aliens and how they're going to come back some-day, right here to Sedona."

He snort-laughed, then caught himself. "Wait, do you be-lieve in all this stuff? All the Sedona woo-woo things?"

"Well, if I did, you'd be pretty insulting calling it *woo-woo things*," she teased. "But no, I don't really. I mean, the vortexes are weird, there's no denying that. People claim to have serious transcendental experiences here. I got the tiniest bit dizzy once when I was hiking near the Bell Rock vortex, and maybe the vortex caused it. But maybe I was just dehydrated. Starla says I'm not open enough to experience something I can't explain, to touch the mystic wonder. Translation: I'm too much of a control freak."

"I hadn't noticed."

Riley swatted him on the arm, and he laughed. "Hey! I'm driving!"

"Well, drive on over to that parking lot up on the right."

"There's a parking lot near this place of mystery?"

"Of course, and we'll have to pay for it. Welcome to Sedona."

Once they'd parked and paid, they started down a red-dirt trail, heading toward those breathtaking red cliffs that were everywhere. That was the thing about Sedona. You didn't have to drive anywhere to find a stunning view. All you had to do was stop and look, no matter where you were.

"It always surprises me how much green there is around here." Daniel mentally flicked through his colored pencils, trying to decide which one he'd use to capture the scrubby vegetation. The set Riley had given him had the basics, but the other night when they'd been walking the dog around uptown Sedona, he'd bought a few more. It wouldn't even have occurred to him if Riley hadn't suggested it. He wasn't in the habit of thinking about what he wanted. But once she pointed out the pencils, he realized that, yes, they were something he'd really like to have.

"You're thinking about how you'd draw all this."

He looked over at her. "How could you tell?"

"J.D. had a fit because he saw a lizard he wanted to destroy, and you didn't even notice. You're like Garret when he's working out the details of one of his inventions. He doesn't register anything but what's in his head. Unless Lori's in the vicinity."

Lori. Interesting. Sounded like she might be the mystery lady who had Garret singing a love song the other day. "So Garret has inventing. I have drawing. What's the thing that makes you forget everything else?"

"I don't really zone out like that over anything. Control freak, remember." She reached over and grabbed his hand. "Actually, I just thought of something. When we're together, you know—" She gave his hand a squeeze. "It's all-consuming."

"For me, too."

They rounded a curve in the trail, and Daniel gave a burst of surprised laughter. "What?" Riley asked.

"That sign." He read it out loud. "Red Rock Secret Mountain Wilderness."

Riley gave that loud laugh that sounded like it exploded all the way up from her belly. He loved that sound. Even better, loved being the one to make her laugh like that. "Keep an eye out for the one that says 'This Way to the Undiscovered Alien Temple.'"

Now she was the one making him laugh. When's the last time he'd laughed this hard? A more sobering question hit him. When's the last time he'd been this happy? Had he ever been this happy?

CHAPTER 11

The sound of a text alert woke Riley, and she sat up with a start. Was she late for work? But a quick glance at her phone showed it was still only five in the morning. Next to her, Daniel and J.D. were both sacked out, snoring at two different—both cute—levels.

Riley checked the text. Mary, of course. Riley smiled. Mary was on East Coast time, and she never remembered to adjust her texting to wherever Riley was at that point in T.U.P. She was a little early for her three-times-a-year check-in, though, not that there was a strict schedule. *I hope everything's okay,* Riley thought.

Surprise! I'm retired. My last day was Friday, I have all my loose ends tied up & I'm taking a trip out to Sedona to relax before I start the next phase of my life, Mary wrote. **I didn't tell you I booked a room at your resort because I wasn't sure if you're still there.**

What? You're coming here? Riley typed back.

You made it sound so wonderful last time we spoke. I arrive tomorrow. Are you on the road to Vermont?

I should be, Riley thought, a finger of anxiety creeping up her spine. But she couldn't even give notice yet. She still didn't have a new job lined up in Vermont. She couldn't give notice if she didn't have a new job. And while she had a place lined up for Petunia as soon as she was finished with her drops, Riley hadn't found a home for J.D.

Chloe Campbell's statistics began playing through her mind like always: Twenty-five percent of girls like Riley didn't graduate from high school. Before they turn twenty-one, ten percent of former foster kids end up dead. Fifty percent develop a substance abuse dependence. Twenty-five percent end up homeless. Twenty-five percent end up in prison. Seventy percent of the female ones get pregnant, and less than five percent ever get a college degree. Before they turn twenty-one, ten percent end up dead. Fifty percent develop a substance abuse dependence. Twenty-five percent end up homeless. Twenty-five percent end up in—

Daniel rolled over in his sleep, resting his arm on her leg. It snapped her out of the panic, and she took a shaky breath. Those statistics were meaningless now. She'd beaten them, just like Daniel had said. Her chances of success were the same as anyone else's now. It was a strange thought to get used to.

No, I'm still here. I can't wait to see you! she wrote back to Mary. She couldn't even remember the last time they'd actually been in the same room, probably not since the final state-required meeting releasing Riley from the system.

Focus on the sensations, Riley told herself, trying to stop the intrusive thoughts of what it had felt like, leaving the system with no support, with Chloe's voice in her head. All she'd had was T.U.P. and her own determination. She'd managed to build the life she planned, even though it had taken all these years. She'd done it—and now it had all veered off course.

It was okay, though. She'd find a different job. She would. And the plan was going to take her about twenty-five years. A few weeks here or there shouldn't matter.

But it did. A few weeks here or there could start adding up. Weeks could turn into years. The whole thing could fall apart.

She tried to focus on the warmth of J.D.'s little body, curled up next to her. But it was finding J.D. that started this delay in her plan. So she focused on Daniel, the way his lips curved into a small smile when he slept, the way his hand gave a nice weight resting on her leg . . . the way she'd have to say goodbye to him when she left for Vermont. She'd never gotten as close to any guy as she was to him.

This wasn't working. Focusing on the sensations wasn't going to stop the panic that kept building up almost as soon as she managed to force it down. She needed action. Damage control. Right now. Riley gently extricated herself from Daniel and the puppy and climbed out of bed. She padded over to the kitchen table, pulled out her laptop, and opened the job-search board. She needed a new position in Vermont now, even if it meant waiting tables again. She'd been in management for the past five years, but if she had to take a step backwards to keep T.U.P. on track, then that's what she would do. Nothing could get in the way of T.U.P.

Starla wasn't feeling it. She was sitting right next to one of the crooked Joshua trees, which meant she was almost in the heart of the vortex, but she wasn't feeling that deep connection. Usually, it just happened. Usually, she stepped out of the van, and it was like she'd plugged herself into the same energy source that made those trees grow all twisty. But today she felt nothing except a staticky anxiety zigzagging through her body. All eight of her chakras were messed up. And right before this, she'd hit three garage sales. The shopping addiction wasn't helping. She kept compulsively rereading Bumper's texts, even when she had a basket—thanks to Adam, she'd gone prepared with a basket—crammed full of things to buy.

She glanced at the scientists. They were almost finished setting up their equipment around the juniper tree farthest from Starla. Nothing for her to do. But it's like Adam felt her looking at him, because the instant her eyes landed on him, he turned and gave her that shy smile of his. He returned his attention to helping Rissa with one of the EKG readers before she could smile back.

Bumper's smile was more like Miles's, big and bright and look-at-me. She missed that smile. She missed him. Maybe her chakras were all out of line because she'd separated herself from her soulmate. No other guy had made her feel as much as Bumper. Sometimes those feelings were hideous, sometimes euphoric, but always intense, all-consuming. That had to mean something, didn't it?

She clicked open his last text. It had arrived almost three hours ago, and for every minute of those three hours, her fingers had been itching to answer it. That had to mean something, didn't it? Wasn't she supposed to listen to her body? Weren't her itchy fingers telling her what she needed to do?

Her itchy fingers started writing a response without waiting for Starla's permission. She watched the words appear as if she had no control over them. **Bumper, I feel like I'm dying. It's like you're the sun and I'm a plant and I can't survive without you.**

What was she doing? Starla gave her fingers a vicious shake, sending her phone flying. She'd promised herself that she was done with him, and nothing felt worse than breaking a promise to yourself. She retrieved the phone, sat back down on her camp chair, then pulled off her shoes and socks and pressed her toes into the hard, hot ground, hoping that would send the vortex energy surging up into her. But she still felt nothing.

She leaned down and dug two little holes into the earth, then stuck her toes in and patted the dirt down on top of them. Nothing. This had never happened before. She'd never been at the vortex and felt nothing. Feeling nothing was like being dead. Maybe her fingers had known the truth. Maybe she really couldn't survive without Bumper.

And now her fingers were retrieving the phone and starting another message. If she sent it, she knew the horrible dead feeling would end. Maybe Bumper would even be waiting in the employee parking lot when she returned the van. He'd grab her and pull her into the back and—

No. Not this time. She hit the back key until the message disappeared. She just had to hang on a little while longer. She was off as soon as the scientists were done. Time for more shopping. If she couldn't find a garage sale, she could always hit a dollar store. But what was the point? Her addiction-switching plan wasn't working.

She looked over at the science crew. Adam was making adjustments to a shiny thingie Starla hadn't seen before, maybe the one he'd been talking about at the garage sale. He nodded and signaled to the rest of the crew. They each sat down on one of the X's they'd chalked onto the ground, the metallic studs on their latex caps glinting in the sun. Adam pressed a switch, and the thingie started to hum. Adam looked from Rissa to Miles to Dorothea, his expression intense. Miles gave him a thumbs-down. A few moments later, Rissa and Dorothea did, too. Adam turned a dial, and the humming turned into a high whine, so high it felt like it was drilling into Starla's ears. She used her index fingers to plug them.

The adjustment didn't seem to be working. Adam quickly got another thumbs-down from everyone. He cut off the device, and Starla took her fingers out of her ears. She watched as the four scientists got in a huddle. Adam crouched next to the device, and Rissa pulled some copper wire out of her pocket and handed it to him. As he soldered it into place, Dorothea walked in a tight circle, Miles trailing behind her. His body language was saying *let me help you*, his head tilted toward her, one hand reaching for, but not quite touching, her arm. Dorothea looked the way Starla felt, jangled and out of sorts and needing . . . something. Something she couldn't have.

"We're ready to go again." Rissa pulled her latex cap farther down on her head and got back into position on her X. As soon as Miles got in his spot, Adam flipped a switch. There was no sound this time, but the air around the machine seemed to *waver* the way it did coming off a hot stretch of highway.

Dorothea stared at the spot where the air seemed to almost breathe, eyes unblinking. Then her body sagged, and she gave Adam a thumbs-down. She ripped the latex cap off. "We're done for the day." She didn't help pack up the equipment, just strode to the van, got in front, and slammed the door. Her team gathered everything together in silence. None of the usual mock insults between Rissa and Miles. No description of the new improvements to his Oreo-splitting device from Adam.

Starla wanted to say something encouraging as they stowed the gear in the van, but she didn't understand enough of what they were doing—any of what they were doing, actually—to come up with anything. She fell back on her High Sky hospitality training. "Anyone want to go to a sound healing session? There's a fabulous woman in town who does them. She uses crystal bowls and Yavapai chants passed down through her family. We can go straight from here. Who's with me?" She was off, but Riley would approve the overtime if Starla explained the situation. She'd get brownie points from Ms. Aguilar and, bonus, keep herself from driving over to Bumper's, which she'd started thinking would be better than texting, although actually, it was worse.

Dorothea twisted around to look at Miles, Adam, and Rissa. "You three go. I can go over what little data we managed to collect tonight. No reason for all of us to stay cooped up."

"In the five-star resort." Rissa twisted her long mermaid hair into a bun on the top of her head. "If we're off, I think I'll spend some time poolside with some kind of healthy alcoholic beverages. There are such things, right?"

"Citrus Pomegranate Champagne Smash," Starla offered. "Champagne and pomegranates both have antioxidants."

Miles replaced the juice he'd just taken from the cooler. "I could go for something alcoholic, healthy optional."

Yep, they liked each other. Riley could call her a hormonal teenage girl all she wanted. Starla always got it right.

"A sound healing is something I've never experienced." Adam met her eyes in the rearview mirror.

"Great! We'll swing by the resort, then we're off." No one seemed to want to talk, and it felt like the silence had a weight and was pressing down on Starla's head, neck, and shoulders. She had to do something to stop it from crushing them all, so started up some of her usual tourist vortex-outing patter. "A psychic named Page Bryant is the first person to use the term *vortexes* for our energy centers in Sedona, although many of the same spots were used by Native Americans for ceremonies. Page was told about the sites by a spiritual being called Albion."

She timed the end of the anecdote perfectly, pulling up the long drive leading to the resort as she said, "In 1987, which the Mayan Calendar says is a time of transition, ten thousand people gathered here for a spiritual gathering. Spiritual seekers have been coming here ever since." She parked in front of reception and climbed out of the van, grinning as she heard "O sole mio" being belted at full volume. She loved hearing Garret sing. His voice was only okay, but his passion was off the charts.

As Starla slid open the side door of the van, Garret headed toward them. "The Palmer's agave needed some musical sunshine. I did, too. Can I assist?" He didn't wait for an answer, just took Adam's invention out of his hands. "Thing of beauty. A magnetometer but with some extra bells and whistles to pump it up, am I right?"

"In theory," Adam answered. "In practice at the vortex, no. I theorized a conducting cylindrical would enhance its sensitivity, but I was proved wrong."

Garret ran his finger lightly over one of the copper coils soldered to the device's side. "Were you able to do an accurate calibration? It's hard to find a place with no ferromagnetic materials in the area."

"We calibrated it at the university before we left."

"Hmm. I'm assuming the cylindrical was vertically aligned."

It's like the two of them had entered their own little science-guy bubble. Starla didn't think either of them was aware of anything other than the ideas flying back and forth between them. The rest of the team headed off with the remaining equipment, and they kept talking. And talking, and talking. Starla sat down on one of the wicker sofas and pulled out her phone. There was another message from Bumper. Damn it. She ordered herself not to read it. If she read it, she'd want to answer, and if she answered, that was it.

Adam and Garret were still geeking out, but she needed to get out of there. She grabbed Adam by the arm. "Sound healing, remember?"

"I'll think on it some more." Garret launched into "Walking on Sunshine" as he started away.

"Music is a strategy I've been considering applying to my work." Adam pushed his curly hair off his forehead as he spoke, and it immediately fell back in place. "In theory, it can take some of your brain's attention away from the problem you're attempting to solve, which would seem like a negative, but it may take your focus off the most obvious answers, leaving mental space for more creative solutions."

"Like with stars."

"How so?" His brow furrowed in a way that made Starla want to run her fingers across it.

"When you look straight at a dim star, it disappears," she explained. "But if you kind of sneak up on it and look at it from the corner of your eye—there it is."

"I didn't see the connection at first, but, yes. It's exactly like that." His usual shy smile turned into a grin. "You get me."

That's what she'd said to him when she'd explained her addiction-substitution plan. He listened to her, listened and remembered. Something Bumper wasn't that good at. "I guess we get each other." As they got back into the van, Starla felt her phone vibrate, and the staticky energy that had been fading a little as she talked to Adam surged. Maybe the healing session would center her, but if the vortex hadn't done it, Gouyen's bowls and chants probably wouldn't, either. "You up for a change of plans?"

Adam nodded. "Curiosity is the basis of science, so yes."

"There's a casino about twenty minutes from here. I've never been. Gambling's not really my thing, but since I'm working that changing-addiction plan, I wanted to check it out."

"I thought you were still laying down the shopping neural pathways."

"It's not helping enough. Maybe I need something completely new to me."

"Games improve neuroplasticity, so gambling encourages new neural pathways in several ways."

"So maybe gambling is the right choice."

Starla's brain started to ache as soon as they walked into the casino. Was it the new neural pathways already digging their way into her brain? Or just all the lights, all the electronic beeps from the slot machines, all the voices bombarding her at once, so the opposite of High Sky's soothing vibe. But opposite was good. Shopping probably hadn't been opposite enough. Hitting a garage sale probably felt too ordinary to be addictive. It hadn't hooked her. Some of these people—they looked hooked. Like that kind of scary blonde lady with her eyes flicking back and forth between the two slots she was working.

"What kind of gambling were you thinking, Starla?"

"I have no idea. What do you think is the most addictive?"

"I read an article that called slot machines the crack of gambling. The colors and shapes spinning in front of your eyes is enough to produce dopamine, and there are consistent small rewards, like a free spin."

Starla nibbled on her bottom lip. "Do you think I have to worry about getting addicted-addicted? My plan was to keep each addiction short-term. I don't want to end up with five addictions instead of one. I didn't feel like I was in trouble with shopping, which is maybe why it didn't work that well, but this. . . ." She looked over at the blonde lady again, wondering how long she'd been standing in front of those two machines.

"Being aware of your actual wins and losses can slow down addiction, from what I understand. The machines are designed to make you feel like you're winning more than you are by playing music and flashing lights that are similar to what happens when you win, even when you lose. I can track your wins and losses, so you don't get tricked."

"But then you can't play."

Adam shrugged. "I want to try out the Kelly criterion at the roulette table at some point in my life, mostly for curiosity."

"Your thing."

"My thing."

"But tonight, I'm happy to help you find the sweet spot between new neural pathways and addicted-addicted."

"Are you sure?" Starla wanted him with her, but the whole point of going out was to cheer him up after the bad day at the vortex.

"I always mean what I say."

Two more ways Adam wasn't like Bumper. Bumper lied, not all the time, but still. And if Bumper had wanted to play roulette sometime, he'd be playing roulette right now. Adam was like the anti-Bumper. She should be with someone like him. But even though he was so adorkable, she didn't feel that thing, that electric spark, that she did with Bumper. And anyway, right now she didn't want to be with anyone. Not until she was completely over the love addiction.

"Which machine?"

Starla glanced around. "What's the lowest we can go? I don't have a lot of money, so I need to make it last. I don't think I'd be able to play long enough on the five-dollar ones to make new pathways. Maybe just one little dirt trail."

"There's a nickel one. And you can get change over there."

One of the scary blonde lady's machines hit a jackpot, dozens of coins falling into the tray. She scooped them up with one hand, using her other hand to keep pressing the button on the machine that hadn't hit. Her expression didn't change. The first time she'd ever played, had it been fun? Because tonight, it looked like a job.

Starla got herself a cup full of twenty dollars' worth of nickels. "Do they still have ones where you pull a handle? The button seems. . . ."

"I agree that the handle would give more tactile stimulation and more novelty." Adam glanced around the room. So did Starla, and she couldn't help noticing how shabby it was—the roses on the carpet grubby, the walls in need of fresh paint. That's probably why they kept the lighting so dim.

"Notice how there aren't any clocks?" Adam asked. "They don't want there to be any sense of time passing, so you have no stimulus that signals it's time to leave." He took her by the elbow—warmth, but no fire—and steered her between two rows of pinging, ringing, flashing machines until they reached a nickel slot with a handle.

"Here goes!" Starla put in a nickel. The weight of the handle was satisfying when she pulled it, and so was the *thunk* when she let it go. Cherry, cherry! Starla gave a little bounce on her toes. Then a banana came up. Then a blueberry. Then a lime. The machine played a happy tune.

"See, you lost, but the music sounds happy, and only needing one more correct item makes you feel like you got very close to winning, both of which make you want to play again.

If you're aware of how the machine is manipulating you, the manipulation won't work as well. But the knowledge won't completely protect you."

"So the sweet spot." Starla put in another nickel. She racked up eight more happy-music losses before—jackpot. Not *the* jackpot, the big, big, big one, but enough to get some nickels spilling into the tray, glinting in the celebratory explosion of colored lights from the machine. It worked on her. "I can feel the squirt of dopamine right here—" She pressed the heel of her hand to her forehead.

"The prefrontal cortex is a key part of the reward. You get a dopamine hit when you lose, too."

"That makes no sense."

"A surprising amount of brain chemistry makes no sense. It's partly because when you pull the handle, pleasing lights and sounds are the result, win or lose. You're causing that out-come. You're in control, win or lose, and the brain sees that as positive and releases dopamine."

"Let's see if I can get a complete row of those beautiful cher-ries this time." Starla fed the machine a nickel, gave it a spin. Cherry, banana, cherry, blueberry, lime. She danced in place to the happy-loser music. Adam joined in, waving his hands over his head. He really was cute. *Bullfrog!* she reminded herself, forcing her eyes to the little birthmark.

She felt her phone vibrate, but didn't care. She. Did. Not. Care. The gamble-aholic was stronger than the love-aholic. "It's working! I probably just got a message from Bumper, my ex. Usually I'd be dying to read it, and I'd practically have to swallow my own hands to keep from answering it. But right now, I feel like I never have to read it." She smiled at Adam. "I'm good listening to the happy-loser music with you."

CHAPTER 12

"I wish I could get the night off to hang out with you, but I'm going to have to go in a few minutes." Riley couldn't stop looking at Mary, trying to accept that she was really here, walking with Riley on the trail behind the resort. "We're doing a jewelry-making workshop, and a mother and daughter staying here have personally requested me to lead it. Not teach it. That's not in my skill set. But be there to keep everyone happy, which is."

"When I asked about you at the check-in desk, they told me you're very in demand. Think of where you started, Riley. You've come so far."

Praise from Mary meant more than anything, even now that she was a grown-up, but suddenly, Riley felt a wave of longing for her mother, the mother she could hardly remember. This almost never happened, but for a moment, Riley was overcome with the wish that she could show her mother around, have her mom feeling proud of her.

She pushed the childish yearning away. Mary was right here. Her hair had gone mostly gray, and there were deeper lines around her eyes and new lines around her mouth, but her warm brown eyes were just the same. So was the way she was looking at Riley, making her feel the way it always had. Seen. Safe.

"They said you're the best entertainment director they've ever had."

"Oh, I doubt that. I'm probably the only one who's actually been willing to follow all of Ms. Aguilar's rules." Although she hadn't really been following the rules lately, and way too many people knew about it—Starla, Garret, Lori. She knew she could trust them, but the more people who knew, the more likely it was she'd get caught. She pushed that worry away. "I'm sorry you're only staying for a couple of days."

Mary paused to take a picture of the vista of red rocks. "All I can afford on a retired social worker's salary, I'm afraid. But this view is worth every penny. I knew it would be. You've raved about all the other places you've been, but I could tell this one was special."

"I could've gotten you a discount."

"Like I said, I wasn't sure you'd still be here. Six months is your usual, right?"

Mary was the only one in the entire world who knew about The Ultimate Plan. She'd been there through the years when Riley was forming it, and she'd always believed it could become reality.

"Yup, six months. But I ran into some delays here over the past few weeks."

"It happens."

But it didn't. Not to Riley. Before this, she'd always found a way to work the plan with no deviations.

"Anyway, who wouldn't want to stay in this place as long as possible?"

True. Riley should just find a way to relax and enjoy it, not something that came naturally to her. But the last bunch of days had been especially great. She'd loved sharing her favorite things with Daniel, even little things like eating Señor Tommy's loaded fries.

Mary shaded her eyes and pointed up the pathway. "If I keep going up this way, will I get to your house? I'd love to see where you actually live."

Riley hadn't been expecting the question. Daniel was in her house with J.D. and Petunia. "Um. Yes, but it's too far to walk."

"There's a way to get there on the road, right? Could I take one of the golf carts? They said at the desk they were at guests' disposal."

Riley chewed on her lip. She really had to get to that class. And why was she hesitating about letting Mary see her house, and the dog and Daniel? Mary was the closest thing she had to an old friend. Actually, kind of the closest thing she had to a real friend, period. Not that Starla, and Garret and Lori, weren't real. She loved them. They were the best work family yet. But they were only temporary. It was too hard staying in touch with people when she moved on every six months. The upside was there were always new people to meet.

She might even have lost touch with Mary if the older woman hadn't done the work. But she'd never stopped checking in. Of course, Riley should let her see what Riley's life was really like. "It's actually not that much farther. You're welcome to go on up. But I have to warn you, I'm hiding an illicit puppy. Also an illicit man."

Mary waggled her eyebrows. "I'm intrigued."

Riley laughed. "They're only illicit because of my boss's rules. Long story." She glanced at her watch. "I'm so sorry, I have to run. I'll text Daniel—that's the name of the illicit man—to be outside looking for you."

"Can't wait to meet him."

"If you're hungry, make him take you to dinner. And if you want to leave before dinner, make him drive you." Riley turned around and started back down the path. "You'll like him, I know," she called over her shoulder.

As she finished putting the awls and calipers away, Riley noticed Ms. Aguilar lurking in the hallway outside the supply room. Great. She'd been hoping to get finished quickly so she could spend more time with Mary, but clearly her boss had other ideas. The woman really didn't ever go home.

"We're having an impromptu meeting in my office," Ms. Aguilar told her, popping a couple Tic Tacs.

"Is everything okay?" Whatever was going on had to be big. Ms. Aguilar didn't do impromptu.

"I'd prefer to discuss it when we've joined your colleagues. Your session ended twenty minutes ago. Why don't you have everything back in order?"

Riley plastered a serene expression on her face. "Sorry, the guests wanted to chat afterwards."

That explanation should have pleased her, but Ms. Aguilar frowned. Apparently even guests weren't supposed to mess with the schedule. She turned on her heel and walked off without bothering to answer.

When they reached her office, Riley took the empty chair next to Garret and Lori. Lori shot Riley a *what's-going-on?* look as she twisted her hands together in her lap. Riley shrugged, wishing she could say that she doubted Lori had anything to worry about. Lori was as conscientious about the rules as Riley was—make that as she usually was.

Garret was picking some dirt off his khakis and flicking it onto the floor. Ms. Aguilar gave him the Ice Glare of Death as she took a seat behind her desk. Garret either didn't notice or didn't care.

Ms. Aguilar stuck one more Tic Tac in her mouth, then crushed it between her teeth. "Mr. Osborne is back, and he says he's got something serious to talk to me about." She let the words hang in the air like it was some kind of dreadful news.

"Well, what is it?" Garret finally asked.

"That's what I need to know. He'll be here shortly. I have to prepare myself," Ms. Aguilar snapped. "Does anyone know of any problems lately? Anything that's been going wrong, anything against the rules?"

Riley's heart slammed against her ribs. Was this about J.D.? Had the wrong person seen him?

Garret flicked more red dust from his pants onto the floor. "Maybe he's ready to break ground on that new pickleball court he was talking about. That would mean we'd have to move the bikes somewhere."

Ms. Aguilar looked like her face might explode. That's how red it was. "That's not something Mr. Osborne would consider serious. And in any case, he and I have exchanged several emails about how the construction should best be handled."

"I doubt it has anything to do with rule-breaking. I don't think Mr. Osborne takes all of them as seriously as you do," Riley found herself saying without taking the time to weigh Ms. Aguilar's reaction. Daniel spoke about the owner as if he were the most easygoing guy in the world, and that had been Riley's impression of him, too.

"I agree," Garret put in quickly. "I've known Ben since he bought the place. He's not a stickler."

"Are you suggesting because the owner is a tolerant man, we don't need to follow the rules?" Ms. Aguilar looked ready to fire Riley and Garret right that minute. "He doesn't have to be a stickler, because I'm here. I run a tight ship, so he has no reason to—"

A knock on the door interrupted her, and Ben Osborne stuck his head in. All eyes went to Ms. Aguilar.

"Hi, everyone. Maria, do you have a few minutes now?" he asked.

Ms. Aguilar nodded, reflexively adding another two Tic Tacs to her mouth. "You're dismissed." She flipped a hand. Garret and Lori jumped up and headed for the door. Riley followed quickly, afraid to even meet Ms. A's eye. What had she been thinking, talking like she was buddies with the owner?

As she passed him, he laid a hand on her arm. "Riley, nice work on the jewelry-making workshop. I ran into one of the guests afterwards, and she says her daughter hasn't smiled at her like that in at least a year. Teenagers, right?" He chuckled. "You have a way with people."

"Um, thanks." She felt a flush of pride creep up her neck. Maybe her job here was safe for the moment after all. "I appreciate that."

Lori grabbed her arm as soon as the door closed behind her, pulling her along to the little patio behind the spa that was usually empty this time of the evening. Garret was already there.

"What was that all about?" Lori asked. "Do you think Ms. Aguilar's in trouble?"

"Do you think *I'm* in trouble?" Riley couldn't help asking.

"I think you're both crazy," Garret announced. "I talked to him an hour ago about how well the new plantings are coming in. And he knows your quesadilla cake is on the menu tonight, Lori. How can he be anything but happy?"

"Am I allowed here?" Mary asked from the dirt walkway behind the patio. "I'm sorry, I saw Riley but I think maybe I stumbled into a staff meeting."

"No, come on over." Riley held out her arm, slinging it over Mary's shoulders when she got close enough. "Meet my coworkers—Lori, our chef, and Garret, our groundskeeper."

"Oh, I feel like I know you both already from the lovely meal I just enjoyed and the beautiful surroundings," Mary said.

"Mary is my old—" Riley stopped, suddenly realizing she'd never told anyone here about her past as a foster kid. Most people didn't have an old social worker to introduce.

"Friend," Mary finished smoothly. "We go way back to when Riley was a tween with pigtails."

"I bet she was a do-gooder then, too," Garret teased. "Rescuing puppies and stray men all alone at resorts."

"Oh, be quiet, you." Lori shooed him away. "Let's let these two catch up."

Mary gave them a wave, then turned to Riley. "All your friends here are so sweet. I met Starla up at your house with Daniel, then Daniel and I had dinner in the dining room. He went back up to walk your doggie."

"Not really my doggie. I'm surprised Starla was over there. She's been spending most of her free time with this group of scientists. They've been having kind of a hard time, and she's been trying to show them some fun."

"She said she needed a puppy fix. And boy, did she get one! That is one active little guy!"

"Did Daniel tell you the whole story?"

"Sure did. I can't believe someone would just leave that little thing in the desert. If they didn't want him, there are other options, easy ones!" Riley had heard that outrage in Mary's voice before. She was always ready to fight for the vulnerable.

"I'm glad I found him, but it really messed up my plans, having to take care of him. I should have already given notice, but I can't. I have to find him a place first. And then the bunny made it even worse! She still needs a few days of eye drops before I drop her off at her new home."

"Too bad you can't keep him. He's such a smartie. Daniel taught him to sit. Well, almost. I suspect J.D. knows what the word means, but sometimes he just has something he'd rather do."

"Most resorts don't allow pets," Riley said. "Although they should. So many hotels are allowing them now, and it doesn't impact reservations at all. In fact, people are happy to pay the extra fee to have their fur babies with them, which is a thing I'm starting to understand."

Mary winked. "Work your way up a little higher, and you can change the pet policy here. Although you might have trouble convincing that boss of yours. She sounds tough."

"And I'm not staying long enough."

"Ah, yes. The plan. But aren't you tempted to? Your friends are wonderful. And that guy! He's a keeper, helping out with all those rescues. Is it serious between you two?"

Serious? What kind of question was that? "Of course not. You know I don't get serious with anyone. It doesn't work with my life. He's been fun, though. And helpful. I wouldn't have been able to handle J.D. and Petunia without him."

"Fun, helpful, cute, nice to animals and old ladies. Guys like that don't come around all the time. He told me he works from home. Maybe you should just kidnap him and take him with you."

For a second, Riley allowed herself to imagine what it would be like, exploring a new place with Daniel. But letting the two animals into her life, even for a few weeks, had given T.U.P. a serious hit. Adding another person? It would never work. She could make J.D. and Petunia do what she wanted them to. Mostly. But people didn't work that way. They wanted to be consulted on—well, basically everything. It absolutely would never work.

"Yeah, he's great, but I kind of wish I hadn't depended on him so much with the animals. He almost got J.D. caught one time. He took a risk I'd never even think of taking, and I realized I'd taken a risk, too, by letting him help. Wrong call."

"It's impossible to get through life without taking any risks, Riley."

"Okay, but more people means more risk. Garret, Lori, and Starla all know about J.D. They all helped me out by keeping my secret, and I appreciate it. But having three more people involved makes it three times riskier. And it was already too risky with just Daniel. I should have remembered what you taught me. Take care of yourself, and you won't have to worry."

Mary's mouth fell open. "I never told you that."

"Yes, you did. About a million times. Remember after I took the Casey Life Skills Assessment? We came up with that whole list of things I needed to learn so I could take care of myself, so I wouldn't need anybody but me."

Mary looked at her for a long moment. "Sweetie, I wanted you to know things like how to make a budget, and how to get health insurance, and how to decide what to wear on an interview. Basic life-skill stuff. I never meant you should never need any help from anyone. We all need help sometimes. It's part of being human."

"It wasn't just about—" What had Mary called them? Riley felt like she'd been twirling in circles like a little kid and was about to fall on her butt. She forced herself to focus. "It wasn't just about basic life skills. It was about being able to follow the plan. You said if I stood on my own two feet, I could do it. You said." Now she sounded like a little kid. *You said!* But Mary *had* said. And Riley had believed her.

"Riley, listen to me." Mary took her hands. "I only meant that you were strong enough to stand on your own two feet, that you would be able to take care of yourself. More than that, that you were strong enough to go after your dreams. But I never meant you had to do everything on your own, without help. Never."

Riley pulled her hands away. "I'm doing fine on my own. Yes, I've had a setback, a momentary setback. But I already have a couple job prospects in Vermont. I'll find a home for J.D. He's little and cute. That's all it really takes. The rabbit is a done deal as soon as her eye is good."

"I don't doubt it. You've made your plan work for years; I have every confidence you'll be able to keep it going. But it's a lonely life. That's the last thing I wanted for you." Mary was keeping her voice soft and soothing, the same voice Riley had used on J.D. when he was out in the desert. Did Riley seem like she needed reassurance?

"Like I said, momentary setback, but I have it all under control."

"Look at it another way." Mary reached for Riley's hands again, but she crossed her arms. "You help people all the time, human or not. Starla was telling me how you helped her through her breakup, and Daniel said you've really been there for him while his brother's in rehab. Everyone here raves about how thoughtful you are with guests, anticipating their needs. Don't you deserve some of what you're always giving? You've got to allow other people to do that for you sometimes, too."

"The difference is, I don't need it." And it was too risky, way too risky. "I need to go back to work for a little. I left the jewelry-making stuff out, and my boss will not be happy with me if she sees it." Riley realized the excuse didn't quite make sense. "I was just taking a quick break out here with Lori and Garret. Do you want me to walk you back to your room?"

Mary looked at her, and it was like when Riley was a kid and it felt like Mary could see right into her. She was sure Mary knew Riley had been lying so she didn't have to listen to any more of what Mary had to say. But Mary didn't call her on it. "No, you go on. I don't want you to get in trouble." She gave Riley a quick hug before she walked away.

Riley took a deep, shaky breath. She was in control, and she better start acting like it. There were a couple obstacles keeping her from moving on. She was working on the job, but she had to deal with J.D. He needed a home. Now.

She did a quick check for Ms. A, then got out her phone and pulled up SmoochiePoochie. All she needed was a decent place. Her problem was that after the Jen and Jason debacle, she'd been looking for the perfect home. She more than anyone should know perfect homes didn't exist.

Someone wanted her puppy. She skimmed his details, then gave a nod. This would work. The guy sounded fine. He worked full-time, but had roommates and a girlfriend, so J.D. wouldn't be alone too, too much. No yard, but walks would be enough, and there were lots of parks around. Decent. Definitely.

The roommate thing, though. . . . What if they didn't want a dog? What if they just tolerated J.D.? She imagined him trying to start up a game of Squidward tug and being ignored. He wouldn't understand.

He'll be okay, Riley told herself. *It's not like you can keep him.* This was the best thing for the puppy, even though it felt so wrong.

She messaged the guy, Charlie. He messaged her back before she could slide her phone in her pocket. He couldn't take J.D. until day after tomorrow, but then it would be done.

Now she just had to tell Daniel.

Daniel made his way down the long hallway to the group therapy room, but this time, it was only him and Sam with Sydney the therapist.

"How's it going?" he greeted his brother.

Sam didn't answer, looking like a sullen teenager. Great. He'd been hoping maybe Sam would be more himself this time around. They hadn't spoken, but Daniel had told himself it was because that group therapy had been weighing on his brother, same as him.

If Daniel was being honest with himself, it had been kind of a relief. He'd been dropping off candy for Sam every day, doing the "I'm here for you" thing, but that's it. He'd started feeling like he really was on vacation, drawing every morning, hanging out with Riley whenever she wasn't working, watching J.D. do his crazy puppy show, sometimes with the bunny joining in.

Well, vacation over. And for what? Sam didn't want him here. He wasn't even acknowledging that Daniel was in the room.

Sydney jumped right in. "Sam has been starting to come up with some ideas for what to do when he's released."

"Idea. I've come up with an idea. Which is to go back home and live my life." Sam's tone was a mix of defiant and petulant. Daniel tried not to let his reaction—his *oh, hell no* reaction—show. Sam didn't do well with *no*s, especially from Little Brother. There was no point in starting off the session with a confrontation.

"Perhaps not the best choice." Sydney's voice was calm. "I don't know that living alone is going to help you maintain your sobriety."

Daniel was glad she'd been the one to say it. He'd made the right call. Let the professional handle it.

"We already talked about halfway houses, and I already told you no. Living with a bunch of other addicts is asinine. You know someone will start using, and then, boom, chain reaction." Now Sam was on to his know-it-all voice. That was the one that drove their mom the craziest.

It didn't seem to get to Sydney. Her voice was low and calm when she answered. "There are rules in place to prevent that."

Daniel had done the research, and he'd unearthed a few horror stories. People OD'ing right there in a halfway house. So-called support staff selling drugs and alcohol to the residents. But the stats showed halfway houses were the best chance for someone to get clean. He opened his mouth to back Sydney up, bring up the curfews, the visitor restrictions, and drug testing, but Sam didn't give him a chance to speak.

"That's crap. Come on. We all know it. There's no rule that a junkie can't get around."

"Is that how you think of yourself? As a junkie?" Sydney pushed her hair behind her ears.

Junkie. The word was like a punch in the gut. It sounded so hardcore. Daniel had never called Sam that, never even thought of him that way. Was Sam a junkie? Obviously. The reason he'd lost his last job, the job he'd been pretending he still had? He'd been stealing stuff off the delivery trucks. He'd stolen from

Daniel, too, and his parents. Classic junkie behavior, stealing for drug money.

Sam crossed his arms and leaned back in his chair. "Just using the word you'd use. It's not like I'm Matthew Perry."

Of course, Sam didn't think of himself as a junkie. He probably thought of himself as someone who'd just had a couple incidents of bad judgment. That's what their parents always called it. Bad judgment. Even when that bad judgment got a judge to send him to rehab.

Thinking of his parents made Daniel's gut tighten. He knew what they'd want him to do. What they expected him to do. He took a swig of water, delaying. But really, he had no choice. "Sam can stay with me for a while. It would be tight quarters, but we can make it work."

"Sharing a bedroom with Little Brother?" Sam didn't even glance at him. "Not an option."

"Well, let's talk it through." Sydney brushed her hair behind her ears again, a nervous gesture Daniel wondered if she was aware of. "Why do you say it's not an option?"

"First off, Daniel doesn't want me to live with him."

"I'm the one who just suggested it."

"Yeah, but who suggested it to you? Mommy and Daddy, am I right? Rhetorical question. And you couldn't say no." He looked at Sydney. "Daniel never says no to them."

"What's wrong with that? I love them."

Sam completely ignored him and continued with his rant. "Daniel never says no to anyone. If you asked him to loan you a hundred dollars, you probably wouldn't even need to tell him why. He'd just hand it over."

Daniel thought about how many times he'd done exactly that with Sam. Just given him a loan that they both knew wasn't a loan. And now Sam was throwing it in Daniel's face?

But he was right. Daniel shouldn't have done it. He had this thing about being nice. Everyone always said he was the nicest guy. But it wasn't because he wanted to be a nice guy, a good guy, a decent human being. It was because he was a wimp. Saying no made him feel nauseous, so he didn't do it much. He never did it with Sam. Which made Daniel an enabler. It was exactly what they'd been talking about in group therapy. He was sure a part of him had already known that. He'd just ignored it.

It was different with his parents. They'd gone through enough. If Daniel could make things a little easier for them, why not? He'd told himself that's all he'd been doing with Sam. Sam had already had so much hurt, so why not make things easier, giving him whatever he could, including money? But making things easier for an addict was enabling.

This wasn't about him. He was here to get Sam's life back on track so their parents could actually just be retired people, golf and play bridge or whatever, without worrying all the time that they were going to end up losing another child. He looked over at Sydney, but she didn't step in.

"We're not talking about me, Sam. I'm not the one in rehab. I'm not the one who has no place to live. You say you want to go back home? How? I talked to your landlord, and you were about to get kicked out for not paying rent. I also talked to your boss."

That got his attention. Sam jerked his head toward Daniel. "Yeah, I know you lost your job." He leaned toward his brother, holding his gaze. "You don't want to go to a halfway house, and you can't live alone. So you'll stay with me." *And I won't give you any money,* he silently added.

No more enabling.

By the time he left Ironwood, Daniel felt completely drained. But his day wasn't over yet—he'd promised Riley that he would drive them out to J.D.'s new home. It was the last thing he wanted to do. Right about now, he wished he could keep the puppy and trade his brother in instead.

CHAPTER 13

Riley was in as bad a mood as he was, it seemed. She didn't speak the whole ride out except to read directions from her phone.

"This is it," she told him.

He pulled to a stop. "Are you ready?"

"Nope."

Riley opened the door before he even had time to turn off the ignition. She looped the strap of the carrier over one shoulder, grabbed the pet store bags with one hand and the leash with the other, and started for the modest house—a manufactured one, going by the skirting. He had to trot a few steps to catch up to her. It looked like her whole body was clenched, from the cords in her neck to the tightness of her fingers on the handles of the bag, to the stiffness of her stride. Letting go of the puppy was getting to her, too.

A kid in a University of Sedona T-shirt came out to meet them. "Here's the guy!" He crouched down to greet J.D., and the puppy danced around him, leaping up to give his face a lick. Daniel felt a jab of jealousy. J.D. seemed almost as happy to see this stranger as he was to see Daniel when he got home. He pushed the silly feeling away. He wanted J.D. to like his new person.

"Charlie, I assume?" Riley's voice sounded strained. The guy nodded. "Here's his toys and bowls and some food and a carrier." Riley thrust J.D.'s supplies at him.

"Hey, thanks. This is great." Charlie dropped one of the bags as he stood.

Daniel handed it to him. "I didn't even know there was a University of Sedona."

Riley shot Daniel a *what-are-you-doing* glance. She clearly didn't want any unnecessary conversation, but Daniel wasn't ready to walk away yet.

"It's all online courses, but the more I heard my professors talk about the place, the more I wanted to be here. I just moved out last month." He fingered his almost nonexistent mustache. If he'd told them he was a tenth grader, Daniel would have believed him. "When I saw this guy's story about being abandoned in the desert, I had to take him." Daniel had been right when he'd gotten Riley to revise J.D.'s profile after the disastrous adoption. "Standing against systemic violence against non-human creatures is a key part of metaphysics. That's what I'm getting my degree in."

Riley frowned. "Will you get a job with that?"

"I'll be an ordained minister when I graduate."

"Cool." Daniel wondered if Charlie knew he could get ordained in less than two minutes online.

"You know you can get ordained in about two minutes online, no degree necessary," Riley informed him.

Well, he knew now. Riley was letting her pain at giving up the puppy come out in out-of-character snarkiness.

J.D. suddenly whipped around. Then around again. Then around again. Charlie stared at him. "Why's he doing that?"

Daniel turned to Riley. "I think our puppy just realized he has a tail. Or at least he realized there's something wiggly behind him."

"Our puppy?" Charlie repeated. "On the app you said you found him."

"I did. He's not ours. We were only taking care of him until we could get him settled in a real home." Riley smiled down at the spinning dog.

"He just feels a little like ours." J.D. gave a yelp, so Daniel leaned down and removed the puppy's tail from his mouth. He'd managed to catch it and didn't have the capacity to realize it was his own sharp teeth causing him pain.

"You'll need to get him to a vet so he can get started with his shots," Riley said briskly. "You have enough food for a few days. You should keep him on that brand. Or if you have to switch, start by mixing the new food with what we gave you, otherwise, his stomach could get upset. And you should let him sleep on your bed. It'll create a stronger bond."

"Can't. My girlfriend is a germaphobe. She's not even that happy having me in the bed if I don't take a shower first. But I'm planning to buy him a crate and a dog bed."

"He still needs to go out every two hours. His bladder is small, remember that. And he doesn't understand English. You can't just say *no* and expect him to understand." Riley's words came fast and clipped, and she wasn't even looking at Charlie. "Even if he does start to understand, he's not going to automatically know what behavior the *no* applies to. You've got the bigger brain. You have to try to understand him, not vice versa."

Charlie held up both hands. "Got it. And don't worry. I don't think I'm above any other species. I'm thinking I can learn a lot from my new buddy, probably more than he can learn from me."

His perspective was a little out there, but Daniel found it reassuring. This would-be minister seemed like he was committed to treating every living thing like his equal. He probably wouldn't even kill a spider. Actually, Daniel didn't like to kill them, either. He usually nudged them onto a piece of paper and deposited them outside.

Riley nodded. Nodded again. "Okay, well, that's it, then."

She reached down and gave J.D. two quick pats on the head, then turned and headed for the car, moving fast.

Daniel knelt down next to J.D. and picked him up for a cuddle. "You're a good, good boy. The best boy." The puppy looked up at him, and Daniel would swear he was smiling, even though he knew dogs didn't smile. He handed J.D. to Charlie. "His Squidward toy is his favorite. He really likes to play tug with it."

"You can come visit him if you want."

"I'm only here on vacation." Behind him, Riley laid on the horn. "I gotta—" He gestured toward the car.

"Don't have to tell me about not keeping the girlfriend waiting."

"Yeah." Daniel didn't have the heart to correct him. "Take care." He turned and left the puppy howling after him.

Riley made her way into the dining room after breakfast, hoping she didn't look as bleary-eyed as she felt. When she'd scheduled back-to-back chocolate-making workshops, she hadn't expected to be giving away a puppy she loved the night before and then staying up late trying to pretend she wasn't desperately sad about it. She hadn't even let Daniel stay over after dropping off J.D., not that he'd put up much of a fight. He seemed as depressed about the whole thing as she was. She'd used the alone time to fill out two more applications for entertainment-director jobs in Vermont. Well, assistant director. All the positions at her level were clearly taken already.

A time check told her the first workshop would be starting in fifty minutes, which was plenty of time for prep. Any rational person would agree. Ms. Aguilar would not. She would be expecting everything to be in place in about ten minutes. Thanks, Petunia. Riley had left later than she'd planned, because the rabbit had kicked her way out of her bunny burrito three times. It wasn't easy doing eye drops without Daniel there to help.

Starla, bless her, already had six tables set up with the utensils and ingredients for the class, the scent of red chile pepper, marshmallows, and cinnamon spicing the air.

"Everything looks great, Star. Thanks for starting without me. Has Ms. Aguilar been in here?"

"Just left."

"Did she ask where I was?"

"Yeah, I said you were taking care of your bunny." Riley's heart gave a kick, even though she knew Starla was kidding before she said, "Sorry. Not funny. I said you and Lori were going over final details."

Riley nodded. "Perfect. I actually should go check in with Lori. Let's put out chocolates on a few of the empty tables, so people can do tastings before we start."

In the kitchen, Lori was humming Garret's purple people-eater song as she stirred something on the stove. "Morning, sunshine," she called. "Have you seen Ms. Aguilar?"

"No. Why?" Riley's breath caught. "Wait, did she tell you what her serious talk with Osborne was about?" She couldn't believe she'd forgotten to ask Starla about that first thing. She really was sleep-deprived.

"Whatever it was, it did something strange to her." Lori raised her eyebrows and whispered. "It made her cheerful."

"What?" Riley had never seen Ms. Aguilar even crack a smile.

"I know, it's unsettling."

As if their words had summoned her, Ms. Aguilar appeared, heels clicking as she walked into the kitchen. "There you are! Riley, Mr. Osborne is looking for you."

"I have a chocolate-making workshop now. I was just checking with Lori that everything's ready on her end."

"Oh, I'll take over until you're done," Ms. Aguilar offered, popping a Tic Tac. "No worries."

No worries? Riley glanced at Lori, who gave her an *I-told-*

you-so look. "Okay, thanks." She headed toward Mr. Osborne's office, a Zen retreat that she'd only ever been in once before. The owner was sprawled on the couch with a laptop when she stepped inside, his desk completely bare.

"Ah! Riley, good." He jumped up, depositing his computer on the desk. She had a feeling he never sat there at all. "Thanks for coming in; I have a question for you."

"Sure," she said. "Whatever you need."

"You know I have another resort in Phoenix." Riley nodded. "Well, we're expanding there. It's not as extensive as High Sky, but I'd like it to be. And things are going so well here that I've decided to bring Maria over to manage that facility. She really seems on top of things."

"Ms. Aguilar? She's definitely on top of everything."

"Which means I need someone to take over her job here, and she's recommending you for the role."

Riley stared at him. "Me?"

"That's right. She says the activities have run without a single glitch since you've been here, and the guest reviews are phenomenal. I know it hasn't been long, but you've done such an impressive job that we know you're ready."

"I don't understand," Riley said. "You want me to take over Ms. Aguilar's job? But she runs the whole resort."

"Yes, it's a big step up." He smiled. "I took the liberty of calling your last two employers, the inn in Ocracoke, and the resort in Cape Elizabeth. Both said they were sorry to see you go, and that you'd make a terrific general manager."

"Oh." She realized how stupid she sounded, but she couldn't think of anything else to say.

"You move around a lot, huh? It's a good way to get experience, but I'm hoping you'll agree to stay here and take the next step in your career."

"I—I need. . . ." She needed to get to Vermont is what she needed. But she still didn't have a new job lined up there. She couldn't turn down a job offer here if she didn't have one there. "I need to think it over. Would that be all right? I'm really surprised."

"Of course. I'll be here for at least a week; just let me know." He held out his hand, and she shook it.

"Thank you so much."

"You've earned it," he said. "Good work."

"Bunny burrito nice and tight?" Daniel asked. Riley nodded. "If I wasn't holding a rabbit, I would do a drumroll for her very last medication session!"

"It's so much easier giving her the drops with two people."

"Most things are easier together." He shook his head. "Though I'm probably not the right one to say that."

Riley finished with Petunia and lifted her back into her makeshift hutch. "How come?"

"You know, single guy in his thirties, works remotely, lives alone. I'm not the poster child for team work."

She made a face. "Me, either."

"Don't you lead entertainment teams? Isn't that your whole thing?"

Riley brushed her thumb across her bottom lip the way she always did when she was thinking. It was both adorable and incredibly hot. "Yes. But somehow I've always managed to be on teams without ever feeling like part of the team. I know it doesn't make sense when I say it, but that's how it feels. I've never been anyplace long enough to dig in deep."

"I didn't know it was so seasonal."

She shrugged, leaning over to offer a carrot to the bunny. "That's another reason having a pet doesn't work for me." Riley made little kissing noises at Petunia.

"It feels weird not to have J.D. doing his zoomies around the room. Do you think he's okay?"

"I'm sure Minister Charlie is taking good care of him." Daniel heard the quiver in her voice, but couldn't come up with any-thing comforting to say. "Maybe you can get a dog when you go home. Then you won't be the single guy living alone, you'll be the cute guy taking his dog for a walk."

"Nah, I can't. Sam's allergic to dogs."

Riley turned to look at him, frowning. "So?"

"Oh, at rehab they're making a plan for when he gets out, and he's not supposed to live on his own. He doesn't want to go to a halfway house, so he's going to move into my apart-ment for the time being."

She sank down onto the kitchen chair opposite him. "You're letting Sam live with you? Right after rehab?"

"I don't have much choice. His therapist said he's likely to relapse if he's on his own, and I know that's right. I think even Sam realizes that. He's done it before."

"So you're going to babysit him?" she asked. "You're sup-posed to be responsible for him not relapsing?"

"No, it's not like that."

"How is it not like that? Why is he living with you if it's not like that?"

Daniel opened his mouth, then closed it. He hadn't thought of himself as being a babysitter, but he knew he was definitely in for a lot of watching Sam's behavior, keeping an eye on his stuff, searching for signs of him using again. All the same old things he'd done before, but this time in his own place. This time, when Sam called in the middle of the night to come bail him out and take him home, it would mean taking him *home*. To Daniel's apartment. There'd be nowhere to escape Sam's ad-diction anymore.

"He has nowhere else to go," he finally said.

"He could go to a halfway house," Riley replied. "I know there are a few right here in—"

He didn't let her finish. "I don't need your entertainment director crap. I told you Sam doesn't want to do that."

Riley studied him for a moment. "But what do *you* want?"

"It's not about me."

"Of course it is. You said yourself that you're miserable because of Sam's addiction. Are you planning to just be unhappy the rest of your life?"

"My brother needs a place to stay! I told you, he'll relapse if he's not with me. What don't you get about that?" His stomach started to churn. He didn't need this. Being with Riley was supposed to be fun, his time to forget about all the crap in his life.

"Maybe you're right. But maybe not. If Sam can't conquer this on his own, though, living with you won't help. You can't solve this kind of problem for somebody else, Daniel. I've known enough people with addiction to learn that."

"Well, you don't know him. He won't make it by himself."

"It's really scary to think of him alone, I get that. Believe me, I do. I was entirely alone the minute I turned eighteen. No support system at all, but I managed. I was strong enough, and Sam will be, too. Only he can decide to save himself, Daniel. You can't do it for him."

She didn't get what it would do to his parents if they knew Sam didn't have anybody looking out for him. And Daniel was it. It had been hard enough convincing Sam to live with him. Daniel would never have gotten him to go to a halfway house.

He shoved himself away from the table and stood up. "You know what? This is none of your business. There's no way you could possibly understand what I'm going through. You don't even have a family."

Riley's face drained of color, and instantly he knew he'd crossed the line. But what did it matter? She and her house and the puppy had been a way to escape, a little vacation. Now the puppy was gone, vacation was over, and he had to go back to his real life.

CHAPTER 14

The alarm chimed, and Adam gave a start. Nine o'clock already? He'd gotten so absorbed in Garret's notes and sketches that he hadn't been aware of so much time passing. Reluctantly, he set the papers on the desk. The first step of his sleep system was a consistent bedtime. He now had an hour to prepare, starting with brushing his teeth, washing his face, and changing into his pajamas. It was the least relaxing part of the system, which is why he did it first.

Next, he turned off every light except the small one on the bedside table. He put his phone in the table's drawer. Studies showed exposure to blue light decreased melatonin production, which could lead to a decreased amount of REM sleep. He'd tried blue-blocking glasses, but ended up spending more time than planned on his phone, dismantling his routine. Routine gave his brain less to process, preparing it for sleep.

That done, he sat on the edge of the bed for his fifteen minutes of worry time. He'd found if he allotted time to worry, he had an easier time falling asleep. His first concern was Dorothea. They hadn't been able to collect any significant data at the vortex again. He understood it could be frustrating, but her level of emotion didn't correlate with what he'd observed. He'd developed a twenty-five-level emotion scale, and Dorothea was —

A series of fast, loud knocks interrupted his thoughts. Rissa and Miles had been informed of his sleep system. Dorothea never came to his room. As Adam stood and walked to the door, the knocking started up again, even though it had only been moments. He pulled open the door while recalculating his new bedtime and saw Starla standing there, face flushed, breathing fast and shallow. "Bumper's here. I saw his car in the parking lot. He's here!" She rushed past him and shut the door.

He needed information, quickly. "Who is Bumper?" He wasn't the best at reading people, but she looked scared. "Why is he here?"

"Bumper's my boyfriend. My ex-boyfriend. I never told you his name. I thought it would be easier not to think about him if I didn't say it."

"Should I call security?"

"No!" Starla exclaimed. "Staff isn't allowed to have visitors. I'd get in big trouble. Like getting-fired trouble."

"If you feel threatened, that should —"

She shook her head, her mix of blue and black hair swinging around her face. "Bumper would never hurt me."

"I don't understand." If he were better at reading cues, maybe he'd be able to better interpret what had gotten Starla into such a state of agitation.

Starla let out a huff of air. "You know how I've been doing my addiction-substitution plan to cure my love addiction?"

"Yes." She knew that he knew. He'd gone to the garage sale with her, and the casino. They'd spent one evening betting on the Suns game. He'd created some on-the-spot systems for calculating the time of the first point, the number of rebounds for an assortment of players, as well as the number of assists. Adam usually didn't spend time watching sports. He didn't need the brain clutter, but watching with Starla, with her clutching his hand the whole time, had been worth the brain space. And when she'd wanted to explore an exercise addiction, he'd calculated her maximum heart rate and periodically checked her pulse.

"Well, Bumper is who I was addicted to. This time. I've had . . . issues before. But I'm not even close to being ready to see him. What if I tell him I'm sorry for everything, even though I don't have anything to be sorry for? Or what if I start screaming at him for how bad he hurt me? That would be even worse. Because every time we fight, we end up having makeup sex. And it's—" She pressed her hands against the top of her head, then yanked them off, making an explosion sound. "So I can't see him. I can't. I'm so close to running outside and shouting his name until he finds me. Which is why I came here. I need help. I brought these." She pulled a pack of Westhaven Naturals cigarettes out of her pocket. "I don't have time to bet on a game online. I need something fast." She ripped open the pack and pulled out a cigarette, her fingers shaking.

Adam plucked the cigarette out of her hand. "Too dangerous."

Starla grabbed the cigarette back. "But the beauty of the plan is that I won't do anything long enough to hurt myself. I'm only going to smoke for a week, tops."

Adam took the cigarette again. "Even one cigarette can change your metabolism. It will take two days for the nicotine from just one to leave your system, and in those two days, your sense of taste and smell will be reduced." When he was fifteen, he'd done extensive research on the dangers of smoking and created a PowerPoint presentation for his father. It had worked. His dad had given up cigarettes using the short-term nicotine-replacement method Adam's research had indicated was the most successful.

Starla gave the cigarette pack a shake. "I chose organic ones. They have fewer chemicals. It's like a clean smoke."

"You're getting your information from a biased source." He suspected the source was Westhaven Naturals commercials. "A clean smoke doesn't exist. Natural cigarettes have the same nicotine, carbon monoxide, heavy metals, tar, and toxins as nonorganic." His father had briefly tried to convince Adam that switching to organic was a feasible option.

Starla spun in a circle. "Well, what am I going to do? I have to do something. Now. Or I'm going to do something very, very stupid."

"The first thing you should do is sit down." Adam guided her to the overstuffed armchair in the small living room. "Stay right there. I'm going to help you." He hurried to the bathroom, soaked a washcloth with cold water, then wrung it out and returned to Starla. "Lean your head forward." He gently pressed on the back of her head, then brushed her hair away from her neck. Her hair was very silky, he noted, and decided that should be added to his list of attributes. He pressed the cloth against her neck.

"Yikes. Cold."

"Cold will stimulate your vagus nerve, which will lower your blood pressure and heart rate. You need to leave it on for fifteen minutes. Just get through the next fifteen minutes, and you'll feel calmer and be more likely to act on logic rather than emotion."

"Okay, okay, fifteen minutes. I can do that. I can do that."

Adam sat on the sofa across from the armchair and leaned forward, watching Starla intently. After five minutes, he took her hand and turned it palm up, so he could press his fingers against her wrist. Eighty-two bpm. Her resting pulse was sixty-eight. She was agitated, but not at a level to cause concern. He noticed that she had the cigarette pack clenched in her other hand. He considered pulling it free, but thought that might increase her stress level.

"He's probably gone, right? Bumper is an instant-gratification kind of guy. If he didn't see me right away, he probably just left. It's probably safe for me to go out."

"Don't make any decisions for—" He checked his smartwatch. "Eight more minutes. Close your eyes. Try not to talk."

As he watched, her chest began to rise and fall more slowly. The cold stimulating her vagus nerve was working. He checked his watch and wasn't surprised to see that exactly fifteen minutes had passed. He had an excellent internal clock. He stood and removed the washcloth from Starla's neck. "How are you feeling?"

She took a long breath. "Better. I think I can toss these now." She gave the pack of Westhaven Naturals a shake. Adam took them from her, threw them away, and returned the washcloth to the bathroom.

"I really need to watch *Blue's Clues*," Starla said when he returned. "I always watch it when I'm sick, and it makes me feel better. It works when the sick is just here, too." She pressed both hands over her heart.

Adam retrieved his phone from the bedside table and found an episode of the show on YouTube. He thought her impulse was a useful one. He'd read a study once about how re-experiencing familiar media from the past allowed a safe space for psychological decompression and gave the viewer a sense of control.

"Do you have a comfy blanket? It works better with a comfy blanket." She moved over to the sofa and tucked her legs under herself.

Adam was familiar with data about how weighted blankets eased anxiety. None indicated blankets of standard weight had the same effect. But if she thought a blanket would help, he would get her a blanket. He grabbed the comforter from his bed and brought it to her. She pulled it up to her chin, then patted the spot next to her. "Come watch with me."

He sat next to her and was surprised when she spread part of the comforter over him. She started the *Blue's Clues* episode he'd found, holding the phone so they could both watch. "Thank you, Adam. You got me through. If it wasn't for you, I might be having sex with Bumper right now." She rested her head on his shoulder with a contented sigh.

Adam let out a sigh that matched hers and reminded himself to add to his observation notes on Starla. A quick mental calculation told him she was two attributes away from being over seventy percent. He estimated that with between one and seven more hours together, he'd be able to ask her out.

"Daniel! How about I take my favorite guest to lunch?" Ben clapped Daniel on the shoulder. "I haven't seen you since I got back."

"I was going to eat out on my patio." Daniel held up a paper sack. "Chef Lori made me a to-go bag." The truth was that he'd been hiding from Riley since their argument yesterday. Throwing it in her face that she had no family was the worst thing he could have said. It was unforgivable after she'd basically told him that she'd never opened up to anyone about being in foster care.

There was no point in trying to fix it. Even if he wanted to, it was impossible. Riley was going to be mad as long as Daniel was going to let Sam live with him. And Sam was mad even though Daniel *was* going to let him live with him. Daniel was mad, too. Mad at himself. He couldn't make everybody happy, no matter what he did.

"I'll come along. I've been working all day. I can use the fresh air."

"She gave me enough to share. Much as I love her food, I can't eat all this myself." They headed toward the casita. "It really is a beautiful resort. Thanks again for letting me stay. I'm sure my parents have been emailing you every day how grateful they are."

"Only every other day." Ben chuckled as he started unpacking the food. Daniel went inside for drinks.

"I continue to be amazed by the way Lori comes up with new enchilada recipes," Ben said when Daniel returned and sat down with him. He took a bite and closed his eyes with pleasure as he chewed. When he opened them, he smiled at Daniel. "I can keep doing more small talk, or we can talk about Sam, whichever you want. Sometimes you just need distraction."

Daniel sighed. "I tried distraction for a while this trip. I think that's over now." An image of Riley came to him, smiling as she leaned in for a kiss. He shook it off. "Things got too real with Sam again."

"So . . . what's going on?"

He'd been conditioned not to talk about his family situation, meaning Sam's addiction. But Ben already knew everything. Still, he hesitated.

"It can be a relief to get everything out," Ben added.

"I appreciate that. But in my family, getting everything out isn't usually an option. Can you believe I didn't even know I had another brother until I was eight? There were no pictures up of Kevin. I'd never heard his name, not even from Sam, and Sam usually sucks at secrets. He told me what I was getting for Christmas pretty much every year."

He hadn't expected to go there. No one had ever said not to talk about Kevin, but they hadn't had to. The absence of pictures, the silence, had made it clear it was forbidden. Now he was talking about it twice in a couple weeks. Riley wasn't someone who already knew the truth like Ben, but he'd still been able to tell her. It had taken months for him to have the conversation with Mila, and even then, he'd left a lot out.

"I'm not surprised." Ben ran his fork through his rice but

didn't take a bite. "Your dad and I were close back then, back when it happened, but he didn't really talk to me about it. He told me it happened, in as few words as possible. And that was it."

"When I was, I don't know, twenty-one or something, after college, I finally asked Sam about it, about what he remembered. He just said he put it all into a closet and shut the door."

Ben raised his eyebrows. "It would take a lot to keep that door closed. He was right there. He saw it all."

"That time I asked, he told me there was no point going there, that it had nothing to do with his life now." Daniel took a swallow of water. "I've done a ton of reading about addiction. That's what I do when I'm stressed. I research. Like that will help me deal with things."

He took another drink of water. His throat kept drying up. "Big connection between childhood trauma and drugs and drinking. Pretty much everybody agrees. Maybe he thinks what happened has nothing to do with his life now, but—" Daniel gave a helpless shrug. "I mean, I wasn't even born when Kevin died, and it made me who I am, at least partly."

"How so?"

"Because it was always there, in the back of my mind, from the time I found out back when I was a kid. I never wanted to do anything that could possibly hurt my parents, because they'd already been hurt so much. I felt really protective of them."

"Sounds like a lot of pressure." Ben's tone was sympathetic, but talking was making Daniel feel squirmy, just like at group therapy.

"Nah, it was just secondhand smoke, you know? Nothing happened to me directly. I didn't see my brother pulled out of the pool, watch someone pounding on his body trying to bring him back to life. I didn't bury my kid. Nothing happened to me."

"That's not true. You said it yourself, Kevin's death is part of what made you who you are."

"But Sam . . . how much of what he's going through right now is because of what happened back then?"

Ben let out a long breath, leaning back in his chair, eyes on the wispy clouds stretching across the sky. Daniel wondered if maybe he shouldn't be talking about addiction to a recovering addict. "Sam's going to have a lot of work to do," Ben finally said.

"He's not interested in doing the work. He's just going through the motions. It was rehab or jail, so he chose rehab. He'll be going home pretty soon. Did I tell you he's going to be living with me? At least that's what my parents want. We're going to be home, and he's going to be doing the same shit he always does, and I won't be able to stop him, and—" Daniel dug the fingertips of both hands into his forehead. "Sorry. I wasn't planning on saying all that. You asked about Sam, and it just came spewing out. And most of it wasn't even about him. It was about me. And it needs to be about him. I need to figure out what to do about him."

Ben studied him for a long moment, a long, uncomfortable moment. What was he thinking? "It's okay for it to be about you some of the time, Daniel. How did your brother react when you talked about how his substance abuse has affected you? That's come up in group, right?"

"Right. He thinks that I'm being a dramatic little weenie."

"It can be hard accepting that you've hurt someone. I know that from experience."

"He's hurt my parents so much, over and over, for years."

"Yeah. But they're not the only ones."

"But they've already been through . . . everything, and he doesn't even think about that. He doesn't think about them at all. They don't deserve more."

"It's not about deserving, is it?"

"I guess not. If people deserved what they got, Kevin wouldn't have drowned in the first place. He and Sam would be, I don't know, opening a restaurant together. Competing on *The Amazing Race*. Only seeing each other at Christmas. Doesn't matter what."

"And you? What are you doing in this scenario?"

"Me? I'm not in existence."

Ben held up a hand. "Hold on. In your mind, the only reason you're here is to replace Kevin?"

"No. I don't even know why I said that. I mean, Kevin was six when he died. Would my parents have waited six years if they wanted to have another kid? Maybe, I guess. I don't know." He took a breath, tried to pull his thoughts together. Ben's question had rattled him. "I guess I just feel like I'm the only one who didn't have this huge family tragedy, so it's kind of my job to handle things, like the Sam situation."

"No," Ben said firmly. "That's not true. It's not your responsibility, Daniel. Something terrible happened to your family, but that does not mean you should be expected to put your life on hold to take care of your brother."

Daniel's heart was beating so fast that it felt like he'd been running. Ben had it wrong. "My parents expect me—"

"No," Ben said again. "I love your father. I was best man at his wedding. I know with certainty he does not expect you to take care of Sam forever. I'm sure of that. And you can't, anyway."

"What do you mean?"

"You told me what would happen if he comes to live with you. He'll go back to his old shit, and nothing will change. You're right about that."

Daniel immediately wanted to argue, to defend Sam, even though he was the one who'd said it.

"Nobody can change Sam's behavior except Sam. That's how addiction works. Take it from me, I've been where he is. He has to save himself, and you can't control whether he does that or not. I'm sorry, Daniel, it's a hard thing to hear. But only Sam can stop this cycle."

Something loosened in Daniel. It felt like his lungs had more room for air. "That's what Riley said. She said he'd be strong enough to do it on his own once he decided to."

"Riley?" He gave Daniel an appraising look. "Well. She's a smart woman. That's why I offered her the job managing this place."

"Thanks for coming with me, Star," Riley said. "I know you hate how my car smells."

Starla had the window down as far as she dared while holding Petunia in the box on her lap. "No problem! I'm not sure how you could drive and bunny-wrangle by yourself."

"True." Riley had assumed Daniel would be around when it was time for her to deliver the rabbit to her new home, but after their fight, she didn't want any more help from him. She didn't even want to see his face, and he must feel the same way, because he'd been keeping his face away from her since yesterday.

"Where's Daniel today?" Starla asked, as if she could read Riley's mind.

"I have no idea." The words came out more aggressive than she'd intended.

Starla gave a whistle. "I knew you two were going to fall in love."

"We aren't in love. Even for you, that makes no sense." Riley realized that could be insulting. "Sorry. I'm a little tense today. It's sort of sad to see Petunia go."

"No worries." Starla grinned at Riley. "It's okay to say that since we're not at work. And you're not the only one I confuse. I baffle Adam all the time. He's a brain guy, and I'm a heart girl, but we're figuring out how to communicate."

Riley was glad to have a subject change. "Seems like you two have been hanging out a lot."

"Which is perfect. I get to have fun with a guy with no worries—I said it again!—about relapsing into my love addiction. Adam and I get along too well for that."

"Uh, confused again."

"I explained it to you, remember? I told you about my parents and their fighting and making up and how much they love each other. Adam and I don't have that passion. You and Daniel do. I can tell you're furious with him. If I took you to the energy bazaar for an aura photo, there would be red everywhere. Red is the color of rage, but also the color of passion, so it proves my theory. Big anger equals big love."

"Daniel will be going home as soon as his brother's done at Ironwood." It seemed like the fastest way to end the conversation.

"You have to keep in touch. Your chakras balance each other so perfectly. That's rare. I'm pretty sure he's your soulmate."

Riley wasn't touching that one. Fortunately, they'd arrived. "We're here!"

"Look at this little school!" Starla cooed as they pulled into the circular drive. It was after-hours, so there wouldn't be any kids, but that didn't seem to dampen her enthusiasm. "Petunia, you're going to be so happy as a kindergarten bunny."

"She is." Riley parked and took a minute to reach over and pet the rabbit's soft fur. She was looking good now, her eyes normal and her nose back to a constant inquisitive twitchiness, which seemed like how a rabbit should be. Riley wished she had gotten contact info for that little boy at the food trucks. He would be so happy if he could see her now. "Good girl, Petunia. Let's get you to your new life."

A dark-haired woman with a wide smile was waiting on the walkway. "Riley? I'm Deanna. And this must be Petunia!"

"In the fur," Starla announced. "I'm Riley's friend Starla, occasional rabbit-sitter."

"It's great to meet you both," Deanna said. "I can't tell you how excited the kids are to meet their new class pet. They each drew pictures to decorate the wall behind her hutch."

"Oh my gosh, how adorable," Starla cried.

"I'm thrilled she'll be so loved. Her last owner really loved her, too." Riley felt a pang of sadness as Deanna took the crate.

"Bye, bunny!" Starla wiggled her fingers at Petunia.

"Oh, one more thing!" Deanna called as they headed back to the car. "The kids made you a thank-you card. Maybe you can grab it from my pocket? My hands are kind of full."

Riley pulled the large construction-paper card from the roomy pocket of Deanna's jacket and opened it to see a drawing of a somewhat misshapen rabbit with crayon names scrawled all around it. It was the cutest gift she'd ever gotten. "Please tell them how much I appreciate it. And take good care of Petunia!"

As soon as she got back in the car, her cell buzzed with a notification. A text from the job board. "Just one sec," she told Starla, quickly opening it up.

We're pleased to offer you the position of Associate Entertainment Director at Mansfield Lodge in Stowe was all she needed to see. She'd done it! She had a job in Vermont! And it was perfect timing. If she was Starla, she'd say the universe recognized that she was free to leave. Riley took a deep breath for what felt like the first time in a week. Everything was back on track. J.D. had a home, Petunia had a home, and she had her next job lined up. She could give her notice at High Sky tomorrow, get the car fixed, and in two weeks, she'd be on the road.

The Ultimate Plan is secure again, she thought as she pulled out of the drive, but all she felt was numb. Once she was on the road, she'd feel better. Once she saw WELCOME TO VERMONT, she'd feel good. And when she saw that spot from page twenty-eight, then she'd get excited.

There'd just been so much pressure, trying to situate two animals, find a new job, and get her car going. Of course, right now it was hard to feel anything but numb.

Trevor gave Daniel directions to a small meeting room, then pointed to his 2% tattoo, his shorthand version of a pep talk. Daniel nodded and headed down the hall, walking a little slower than he needed to. He was tempted to stop and study a couple of those close-up photos hanging on the wall, but knew it was mostly because he wanted to delay what he was about to do.

At least Sam had agreed to see him when Daniel asked to be on the visitors' list. He wasn't so pissed off about last time that he refused. Although that would definitely change once Daniel said what he'd come there to say.

You got this, he told himself, then opened the door. The room had clearly been designed to be soothing: sage-green walls; lots of plants; art with inspirational slogans. He took a seat in the armchair across from Sam. "No Sydney?"

"Sydney is for therapy, not visits."

Daniel would have liked to have a voice of reason—other than his own—but he could deal. "Which you would know if you visited," Sam added.

Give him a break. He's detoxing, Daniel thought. But that wasn't right. Why did he automatically try to rationalize Sam's unfair behavior? He didn't know exactly what Sam had been taking, but he should be past any withdrawal symptoms by now. Not cravings. But the physical stuff. So this was mostly just Sam being a dick.

"You were the one who could call me. I couldn't call you. I didn't hear from you, so I assumed you didn't want to see me."

"You didn't even make the attempt." Sam pulled a leaf off the aloe vera plant on the table next to him and split it open with his thumb.

This was about to turn into an endless grown-up version of "I know you are, but what am I," and Daniel wanted to make the visit as short as possible. He launched into the speech he'd been rehearsing in the car. "I've had some time to think, and I've decided the best thing for both of us is for you to go to a halfway house."

Sam just stared at him, shocked. The silence stretched out for what seemed like ten minutes, but was probably only one, before the familiar anger filled Sam's eyes. "Best for both of us. Is that what you said? Best for both of us." He started grinding the leaf between his fingers, turning it into pulp. "Because it sounds like you'd be living in an apartment, able to come and go as you please, getting laid—if you can manage it—eating whatever you want, going to—"

"Okay, you're right," Daniel interrupted. "It's only better for me. But I'm not the addict, so I get dibs on my apartment."

"Oooh. Little Brother standing up for himself. Impressive. Let me ask you this—what do Mom and Dad think?"

Daniel flinched. He should have known Sam would go there, but when he'd been playing out this conversation in his head, it hadn't even occurred to him. And Sam could see the surprise on his face. "You didn't tell them."

Daniel tried to get himself back on track. What had Riley said? And Ben? "Ultimately, it's not going to help you to keep depending on me. You're the one—"

Sam cut him off. "You are in trou-ble." He stretched the word into a schoolboy taunt, then leaned back in his chair and laughed.

"This has nothing to do with Mom and Dad. It's about me and you. I'm not taking care of you anymore, Sam. You're on your own. You can flush your life down the toilet—although I hope you won't—or pull it together. Up to you."

"Call them. Right now. I want to watch you tell them what a selfish little prick you are. It will take Mom about fifteen seconds to start crying, and you won't be able to take it." His sneering laughter made Daniel want to punch him. How could he laugh about something like that?

"Suddenly you care about how Mom feels? That's new. You haven't given a shit about that in I guess forever. Because she's spent years crying over you. And Mom and Dad have spent who knows how much money on you. You think neither of them retired until they were almost in their seventies because they loved their jobs so much?"

Sam was on his feet, hands balled into fists. Daniel thought he was about to throw a punch, but Sam didn't even yell. He sat back down, looked Daniel in the eye, and said, "Get out of here. Don't come back. I have no use for you."

"Oh, hey, that's my big brother, ladies and gentlemen. Always in my corner. Always looking out for me," Daniel said. "As long as I'm giving him what he needs. Screw this. I'm happy to go—right back to my own apartment."

He heard the nastiness in his own voice, almost as bad as Sam's. But he didn't care.

"Don't pretend that it's so great. It's a rathole. You hate it there. You hate your whole pathetic life. You're miserable, remember?"

That hurt more than any punch Sam could've thrown, mostly because it was true. "Yeah, miserable because I've wasted my entire life taking care of you. But you know what, I do hate my apartment. I don't need to stay there if I'm not trying to be your babysitter anymore. I'm going to move out. I'm going to move here."

The words surprised him, but as soon as he said them, he knew that's what he wanted. He loved this place. He'd been so much happier in Sedona than he'd ever been before. "And, you know what else, I'm getting a dog. And maybe a girl, if she doesn't hate me, thanks to you. And I don't have to worry that you're allergic, because you won't be coming over."

"I wouldn't even if you—"

"Whatever, I'm not sticking around for more abuse." Daniel felt good being the one to cut off the conversation for a change. "I'll stay in town until you're released, and I'll drive you to whatever halfway house Sydney thinks is best. You can thank me later, if you ever get your head out of your butt and realize that I've been here for you my whole freaking life." Then he turned and left. He loved Sam, but it felt so damn good to realize that he was allowed to walk out and leave Sam here and go get himself an actual life.

CHAPTER 15

Maybe she should go check on the S'mores and Stargazing setup. Peggy was heading it up, because Riley had the night off. She'd wanted to have Starla in charge. She was ready for the responsibility, but Starla was taking the science crew to the vortex. They'd wanted to try getting readings at sunset.

Riley was sure Peggy could handle it. She'd worked the event with Riley a bunch of times. But it couldn't hurt just to stop by. See if she needed anything. Riley reminded herself that in a few weeks, she'd be gone. She'd accomplished everything on her list. Petunia—check. J.D.—check. Car repair—check. She'd accepted the job offer in Vermont. Tomorrow she'd give notice. It was time to let her team start handling things without her, so when she left, they'd be ready.

S'mores and Stargazing made her think of s'mores, and she was suddenly craving one. Lori had probably come up with a new flavor combo, and Riley didn't want to miss it. She needed to get as much of Lori's cooking as she could. She'd had a lot of good meals at her other jobs, but nothing could compare to Lori's creations. She'd miss them. She'd miss Lori.

She stood and started for the door, then returned to the sofa. Checking on Peggy, getting a s'more—they were just excuses to get out of the house. She'd always been someone who liked alone time, needed it to recharge, but now she hated being in the house by herself. She'd gotten too used to J.D.'s company. Petunia had given her something warm and soft to cuddle, but now she was gone, too. And Daniel—

Daniel was a bastard. She'd trusted him with the truth about her childhood, and he knew how hard it had been for her to open up. He knew, and he'd used it against her like it meant nothing. She was glad he'd been keeping out of her sight.

She wished she didn't have to stay here even two more weeks. She'd made so many good memories in Sedona, but what Daniel had done had made her happy memories of these last few weeks with J.D. turn dark. She'd feel better when she was moving on.

Riley noticed a white hair on the pillow next to her and plucked it off. She kept finding puppy hair everywhere, in the house, on her clothes. It was making her crazy. Everything was making her crazy. She couldn't sit here one more second. She wouldn't go to the resort. She wouldn't be Ms. Aguilar and hover, making her people feel like she didn't trust them, but she could at least go out for a walk. She'd walk until she was too tired to do anything but sleep.

She grabbed her hiking boots, but before she could pull them on, someone knocked. Couldn't be Starla, but Riley couldn't think of anyone else who'd just show up. She opened the door. Daniel. Of course it was Daniel. She'd hoped she was going to make it out of here without seeing him again, but he wasn't the type to let it stand when people were mad at him. "What do you want?" She didn't move out of the doorway. There was no way she was letting him in.

"To apologize. I regretted what I said as soon as the words were out of my mouth. I'm so sorry, Riley. You trusted me, and I screwed it up."

"Yup."

"I would've come sooner, but I was honestly too angry with myself. It was unforgivable, and I'm just . . . I'm so sorry."

At least he understood that much. "Fine. Apology accepted." But that didn't mean things were going back to how they had been, all sex and fun. What was the point? Even if she could forgive him, which was a lot different than just saying "apology accepted," she was almost out of there. "Is that all?"

"Yes. No! I wanted to tell you that you were right, what you said about Sam. I think I knew it right away, and that's why I freaked out and attacked you. I didn't know how to face it."

What she said about Sam? Riley's mind was spinning. What had she even said? His comment about her having no family had replaced everything else in her memory. "When I said he shouldn't live with you after rehab, you mean?" That made no sense. "I was trying to look out for you. You were about to do something that was going to make you so unhappy. Why was it a bad thing for me to try and stop you? Why would that make you so furious?"

"You're right. It makes no sense. I'm trying to think how to explain it." Daniel ran his hands over his face. "Basically, my life has always been about taking care of my mom and dad."

"Oh." Riley didn't know what to say. Had she missed the fact that his parents were ill or something? "Was there a health issue?"

Daniel gave a harsh laugh. "No, that would make actual sense. It's nothing like that. It's just—you know how I told you I had that brother who died before I was born?"

Riley nodded, not sure where he was going with this. They'd been talking about how horrible he'd been when she'd tried to talk to him about Sam.

"I always felt like they'd had enough pain, and from when I was a kid, I felt protective of them."

"Okay."

"I didn't want to do anything that would cause them any more hurt. I mean, not like I walked around thinking, *will this hurt them or not?* It was an instinct, part of who I am. Was. I don't want to keep being like that. Taking care of Sam was part of it. I took on as much of it as I could so they wouldn't have to."

Riley felt her anger toward him melting away. She could practically see the little boy in his eyes, just trying to carry that huge emotional load. She remembered the feeling of attempting to handle big, confusing adult emotions that a child shouldn't have to understand. It's how she'd felt when her parents died.

"That's a lot for a little kid."

"Yeah, but I'm not a little kid anymore," Daniel said. "It just never occurred to me to . . . reevaluate. It would have been like reevaluating whether or not I needed to breathe. I mean, I took care of Sam because I thought I was supposed to. It didn't feel like I was making a choice."

"So when I said you had to stop taking care of Sam, it was the same as telling you to stop breathing?"

"That's kind of what it felt like."

Which did sort of explain why he'd lashed out the way he did. "All I meant to do was give you some tough love, get you to take care of yourself for once instead of only thinking about Sam."

He nodded. "I cut Sam too much slack, because I knew he'd been hurt, too, when he was little. He was there when Kevin drowned. I thought I was helping him. You were right, though, I was making it worse. So I did it. I told Sam he couldn't live with me."

"You did?" After listening to him, she realized that was huge.

"Yep. And he was not happy." Daniel's warm brown eyes clouded. "Understatement, obviously. He was pretty awful about it."

"You did the right thing. I know it probably feels like crap, but in the long run, this will be better for Sam. And for you,

Daniel. That's all I ever meant, that you deserve to think about what you want, too."

"Telling him actually felt good. I wasn't expecting that. It felt really good. I feel a hundred pounds lighter. Thanks for helping me get there. That's the other thing I needed to say. I'm sorry, and thank you."

"I'm proud of you." She hugged him, intending for it to be brief, friendly. But as soon as she touched him, she didn't want to let him go.

He hugged her back, holding her gently. "I've missed you."

"Me, too," she admitted. Her arms tightened around him, her fingers clutching the back of his shirt. But she needed more. She needed to be even closer. She slid her hands up to the back of his neck and pulled him down for a kiss.

Riley could feel the same urgency in him. Together they stumbled back through the doorway. The bed was too far away. The couch was too far away. Daniel obviously felt the same way. He kicked the door closed and maneuvered her down to the carpet without breaking their kiss. And the world faded away, until it was only Daniel and her. No one else. Nothing else.

When the rest of the world came back into focus, Daniel was grinning down at her. "Thank you for that, too."

Riley laughed. "You're welcome." She ran her fingers down his cheek, over his stubbly jaw. "I don't want to move, but the floor is getting a little hard."

"I don't want to move, either, but I might need some food before we find a softer place to continue this."

"Taco truck?" Riley suggested as they collected their clothes from the tangled heap and started to dress.

"I was thinking more like fridge. Faster." Daniel zipped his jeans, then buttoned her shirt for her, taking his time. "There was something else I was going to tell you before we got"—he raised his eyebrows—"distracted."

"Hmmm?" She was still feeling a little distracted.

"I've decided to change my miserable life. I'm moving to Sedona."

"Oh. Wow." Was he thinking that she . . . ? That they . . . ? She hadn't told him she was leaving, but she also hadn't given him any reason to think they were anything more than a—

"You should see yourself." Daniel opened his eyes wide with exaggerated shock. "Don't freak. I'm not moving here because of you. It's everything about the place. All the people searching for some kind of enlightenment, whatever that means to them. All the colors that make me want to draw again. I really need a change, and this feels right."

"You're going for happiness."

"Yes. I want to be here no matter what, but I hope we can see where this might take us." He brushed her hair away from her face. "I know you'll have a lot going on. Ben told me about your promotion. That's so great. Congratulations!"

Riley sucked in a breath. She'd completely forgotten about his relationship with Ben Osborne. "Oh. Right." Guess they'd be having the I'm-leaving-in-two-weeks conversation right now. "I was thrilled to get the offer. Completely unexpected. I can't take the job, though."

"What? Why?"

"It'd be great. If I had two lives, I'd definitely say yes. But I can't stay in one place. It's just not me. I love seeing new places, meeting new people. I have a job in Stowe, then after that, I'm going to Polson, as close to Flathead Lake as I can get, then New Orleans, French Quarter, definitely. Sedona's gorgeous, but I want to see the whole country." She was talking too fast. She made herself stop and looked at Daniel to see his reaction.

It wasn't that exaggerated I'm-so-shocked face he'd teased her with, but it was close. "What's the job?"

"What job?"

"In Vermont."

Wasn't he listening? That wasn't the important part. It was

about the *where*, not the *what*. "Associate entertainment director at a ski resort."

"Aren't you the entertainment director here? So this new job is a step down?"

"Yes. I had another job lined up, but then there was J.D. and Petunia. . . . But it's okay, because the resort is amazing. The gondola between Mount Mansfield and Spruce Peak goes right over the grounds."

"Like in the book. Like in *Beautiful America*."

Riley felt the air whoosh out of her lungs. "How do you know about that?"

"It was on the coffee table. I flipped through it a few times when I was staying with J.D. There were photos taken from that gondola. You—I'm assuming you—wrote *I'm going to ride that gondola* in the margin."

Riley fought the urge to vomit. Or run. Or something she couldn't even define. To have him, to have anyone, talk about her book felt like an invasion, even though she *had* left the book out. She wasn't used to people being in her place when she wasn't there. "Yeah. Like in the book."

"Sedona was in the book, too. When I saw the picture, I thought it could have been taken on the drive up to the summit or from your porch. Is that what you're doing? Visiting all the places there are pictures of?"

Riley nodded. "It's my plan, my . . . life plan."

"To travel everywhere?" He didn't sound judgmental, or like he wanted to laugh at her, but Riley still felt like a raw nerve, exposed. "I came up with the idea when I was sixteen. I called it The Ultimate Plan." She realized she'd never said those words to anyone but Mary. It felt like she was letting someone read her diary. "It took me a bunch of years. I had to sling a lot of burgers before I got the experience to move up and start making enough money to travel. But I made it. I've lived in six of the places, counting Sedona. Stowe will make seven."

"But it's a step back. And Ben's offering you a job managing a four-star resort in one of the hottest tourist destinations in the country. You're going to walk away from it? It's an incredible opportunity."

Riley felt the familiar anxiety rising in the pit of her stomach. She'd outgrown all the foster-kid statistics, but that didn't erase her fear about losing track of T.U.P. "I know. I agree. But it's not me. I don't stay in one place. There's too much I want to see."

"So do both. Take the job and go on vacation to all those places. You'll definitely be making enough money to afford it."

"That's not the plan." She could tell he wanted more of an explanation, but Chloe Campbell's words were pounding through her brain now—substance abuse, pregnant, no future, dead—making it impossible to think. She needed to be alone. She needed him to stop asking questions.

"And you can't change the plan? You're the one who—"

Daniel was interrupted by a string of high yips.

"That's J.D.!" His barks broke through the chaos in Riley's head. She rushed to the door and flung it open. The puppy hurled himself at her, his paws scrabbling against her leg.

"He's bleeding," Daniel cried. "Look at your pants."

Riley looked and saw a streak of red. She dropped to her knees and picked J.D. up. Daniel gently took one of his paws in his hand, and J.D. gave a whimper. "Oh, man. It's all torn up, and he's really panting."

"Did you run all this way? Did you?" Riley gave the puppy's head a stroke, then handed him to Daniel. "I'll get the first aid kit."

She rushed to the kitchen and pulled the kit out from under the sink, then hurried back to where Daniel sat on the couch, cradling J.D. on his lap. She popped open the latches and found the packages of alcohol wipes, then hesitated. Something in all those articles she'd read that first night she had J.D. was making her brain prickle. She grabbed her phone and did a quick search.

"It says not to use alcohol wipes. It says in a pinch to use warm tap water. I'd say we're in a pinch."

"What do you think happened?" Daniel called, as she returned to the kitchen for the water.

"He obviously got out and ran here. I should have known it wasn't the right place for him. I should have known as soon as that minister kid said his girlfriend was a germaphobe. I'll deal with them later." Riley sat next to Daniel and carefully cleaned the wound, then took another fast look at the article she'd found. "Antibiotic ointment next. Then gauze."

"You're doing so good, J.D. Such a good, brave boy."

Riley met his eyes as he dabbed on the ointment. "Just like last time." Except completely different. Last time he'd been an inconvenient stranger, ruining her plan by appearing in a casita that was supposed to be empty. Now . . . now she didn't know what to call him. A good memory, she decided.

"Last time, you were so impressive. In about twelve seconds, you'd figured out the kind of cactus spines and how to deal with them. And this time—I wouldn't even have thought to check about the alcohol wipes."

Riley wrapped J.D.'s paw in the gauze, then wrapped an Ace bandage on top of that and clipped it in place. "You are not going back to them." She put her hand on J.D.'s head.

Daniel put his hand on top of hers. "Absolutely not. He's staying with me. I'm keeping him."

For the first time since she'd found the puppy, Riley felt exactly right about his future. This was the perfect home for him. "He'll love that." Riley slid her hand away.

Daniel looked at her hand, and seemed to get it. "Listen, I'm not trying to meddle in your life. But you'd be a great manager. You think fast. You stay calm. I've seen you in bad situations with J.D. and Petunia. And Starla, now that I think about it. You're amazing. You handle whatever life throws at you, and you make it look easy."

"I'm faking it," she mumbled.

"Fake it till you make it—that's a thing, right?"

Riley smiled. "It is."

"Well, you did that. Ben wouldn't let just anybody run his resort. You should think about taking the job, Riley. You deserve it."

Rissa, Miles, and Dorothea did not look happy as they trooped toward the van. Starla was used to her scientists being bummed or angry after an unsuccessful session at the vortex, but they hadn't even attempted one of their experiments yet and were already acting as if they'd failed. She wondered where Adam was. It wasn't like him to be even a minute or two late. He took punctuality very seriously. He took almost everything very seriously, part of his nerdy appeal.

It was obvious all three of them had a blocked solar plexus chakra, struggling with self-trust, which made sense. They made trip after trip to the vortex without getting the results they were looking for, or any results at all. From what Adam had told her, even their high-tech equipment wasn't getting readings from the Juniper site. Of course they were doubting themselves.

She slid open the van door to let them in, wishing she had brought a few of her essential essential oils. A little lemon, peppermint, and ginger wouldn't completely unblock their chakras, but it would give the team at least some relief.

As was almost always the case, she heard Garret before she saw him. But there was a second voice joining in with his enthusiastic, slightly off-key rendition of "Don't Stop Believin'"— Adam. It was Adam, head tossed back, singing away, swinging the magnetometer as he and Garret walked around the corner of the main building and headed toward the van. Both of them looked like their energy was flowing freely, no blocked chakras. It made Starla feel a little bubbly inside just watching him. No, not just Adam, Garret, too. She always loved watching Garret let loose.

She wondered if working with her on her sugar addiction yesterday afternoon had given Adam some extra pep. They'd eaten a ton of Oreos, which had given him a chance to work on his device while she worked on overcoming Bumper. Although the last few days, she hadn't really been thinking about him much. Yesterday, she'd actually thrown away Waddles, the stuffed penguin he'd given her last Valentine's, and she hadn't even cried. Well, only a little, not even close to ugly crying. Usually she would have donated the penguin. She didn't believe in throwing things away when they could be rehomed. But the idea of Waddles being out there in the world—no.

"Good luck out there," Garret said, after Adam stowed the magnetometer in the back.

"You're not coming with us?" Adam shut the door. "You need to be there when we field-test it."

"I was hoping you'd ask!" He and Adam climbed into the van, and Starla got behind the wheel. "Gang, I think we did it! We added the mu-metal, and this thing is more sensitive than a *Mimosa pudica*." Garret grinned.

"What again now?" Miles grabbed a prickly pear lemonade. Starla always made sure to stock extra in the cooler. The whole team had become, well, addicted.

"*Mimosa pudica*. Also known as the tickle-me plant. Its leaves fold up when you touch it or give it a tiny shake. With the new adaptations, the magnetometer is going to pick up everything at the vortex and give it a boost. I'm sure of it."

Adam adjusted his glasses. They were always sliding halfway down his nose. "Based on the tests we performed here, I'd say there is more than a ninety percent chance we'll be successful."

Starla took another glance at the crew in the rearview mirror. She could see a faint yellow glow around all of them. That infusion of hope from Garret and Adam had gotten rid of a chunk of the chakra blockage. She looked over at Dorothea in the shotgun seat. She stared out the window in silence, so different from the cheerful woman she'd been on their first trip to the vortex.

As Starla drove, she visualized Adam operating the tricked-out magnetometer, with the rest of the team in their rubber caps giving him a big thumbs-up. She visualized Dorothea giving a huge smile. Today was the day. She could feel the knowledge making her bones tingle. She was so happy for Adam. And everyone. Especially Garret. As long as she'd known him, he'd wanted to get a mention in *Invention Today*. This could do it for him. She loved his little make-the-perfect-marshmallow spinner, but this, assisting in a big-money university research project, was magazine-level impressive.

When they got to the site, Miles and Rissa grabbed the metal suitcases, while Adam retrieved the magnetometer. Starla hurried over to him, the vortex sending vibrations through her body with every step, even through the sensible closed-toed shoes Ms. Aguilar insisted on. Her ability to sense the immense power of the place had gradually returned since the horrible day after the breakup, when nothing she'd done had allowed her to feel it. It was because her unhealthy connection to Bumper was fading. Her switching-addiction plan was working with a big assist from Adam.

"I'm super proud of you." She gave him a quick hug, careful not to bang the magnetometer.

Adam pulled the little golf pencil from behind his ear, took his notebook out of his pocket, and began to make a note in his neat all-caps handwriting.

"What are you writing down? Nothing's happened yet. Or wait. Has it?" Adam definitely noticed things Starla didn't. And vice versa. It was doubtful he had the ability to perceive the colors emanating from open chakras, although he'd be open to trying. Open-mindedness was another one of his anti-Bumper qualities. He had so many.

"Observations of you."

"Me?"

"I have a list of forty-seven—make that forty-eight—attributes of the perfect woman—" He stopped and corrected himself. "*My* perfect woman. You just indicated you have one of the attributes—acknowledgement of accomplishments—so I made a notation. That puts you at sixty-eight-point-seven percent. If I observe one more attribute from my list, I'll be able to ask you out."

"Be able to ask me out?" Starla repeated. He'd thrown a lot of words at her—*attributes, percentage, observation, notations*—and she was having trouble understanding how any of them had anything to do with her. And why had he been talking about asking her out? She was trying to get over a love addiction. He was her addiction-switching buddy. Buddy! He knew that. Maybe with all the words, she hadn't really understood correctly. "Can you explain more?"

"It started when I went to the eighth-grade homecoming dance with Holly Zimmerman. The results were . . . not satisfactory. I had the realization that it was unlikely I'd have a satisfactory experience unless the girl, now woman, had specific attributes, and I made a list of them."

"Oh, boy," she heard Garret mutter. She hadn't realized he'd been close enough to hear, but he was walking away fast, and the other three were too busy adjusting their caps to be paying attention.

"And you've evaluated me and decided I have enough of these *attributes* for me to be acceptable to you?" She couldn't believe he'd been studying her like that, like a bug under a microscope.

"Almost enough. I don't ask a woman out who has less than

seventy percent of the forty-eight attributes. You currently have thirty-three. One more, and you'll—"

"Meet your requirements?"

"Yes." Adam shoved his glasses up his nose, a gesture she usually found adorable. Not today.

"Well, thanks, thanks a lot, Adam."

He frowned. "I don't always do well with detecting sarcasm. When you said—"

"Let me make it easier. If I do manage to make it over seventy percent, don't bother to ask me out, because I will absolutely say no. Ab-so-lute-ly. Is that clear enough?"

"Yes."

"Good. You better get over to your spot. Everyone's waiting for you."

Adam seemed to be thinking in slow motion, the way she'd been when he threw all those words at her. For a moment, he just stood there, then he flexed his fingers on the magnetometer's handle and walked away. Garret joined him and clapped Adam on the shoulder, which was not nice. Garret was supposed to be her friend.

It didn't matter. What did it matter if she didn't meet Adam's expectations? What about *her* expectations? Except she tried not to have expectations. She tried to stay in the moment. And that's what she needed to do right now. She grabbed her camp chair and umbrella out of the van and got herself set up. She pulled off her shoes and socks and planted her feet on the earth, which was beginning to cool as the sun set, then took a sip of juice, and closed her eyes. She was finally able to feel the full force of the vortex, and she wasn't going to waste it. Except. . . .

Her eyes popped open, and she straightened up. Adam—not just Adam. This wasn't about Adam. The team of scientists she'd been spending a lot of time with might be about to make a breakthrough, and if they did, she wanted to see it.

Adam flicked a switch on the magnetometer, and a high whine started up, rhythmically changing pitch in a way it hadn't before. Garret grinned, and then it was almost as if her vision had materialized. Dorothea, Miles, and Rissa all gave a thumbs-up. Then Miles pumped his fist in the air, Rissa gave an excited bounce. But Dorothea didn't give the huge smile Starla had envisioned. Dorothea squeezed her eyes shut and tilted her head down. Starla could see the tension in Dorothea's body as she focused all her concentration on what was happening.

Then Dorothea ripped off her rubber cap, hurled it to the ground, and strode over to the tree that was farthest from the others. She rested one hand on its twisted trunk and leaned forward, as if she wouldn't be able to stand without the tree's support.

Miles and Rissa slowly removed their own caps. Adam turned off the magnetometer, and the sudden silence made Starla's ears twinge. She stood and joined them. "What happened?" she asked Rissa.

Rissa twisted a section of her long hair, then released it. "I don't know. Everything worked this time. The magnetometer was registering changes in our brain waves, right?" She glanced at Adam, and he nodded.

"That's what we hypothesized would happen, and it did. The magnetometer readings clearly showed that the vortex was changing your brain waves." Adam ran his hand down the magnetometer's handle. "It just wasn't sensitive enough to register the changes until we layered the new shell with the mu-metal, the way Garret suggested."

"So why is she so upset?" Miles shot a quick glance at Dorothea. "This is what she's been working toward."

"I don't know, but I'm not going over there to find out, that's for sure." Rissa opened one of the metal suitcases and began replacing equipment.

"I'm not going over there, either." Miles knelt down next to Rissa.

"I've barely even met her, so. . . ." Garret jammed his hands in the pockets of his khakis.

Adam looked at Dorothea and gave a helpless shrug. "I don't know what to say. I don't understand what's happening."

"Fine. Someone has to do it, and it clearly has to be me." Starla walked toward the tree where Dorothea stood, slowing down when she got close to the woman, the way she would with a cornered animal. "Are you okay?" It wasn't the right thing to say. It was obvious Dorothea wasn't okay. She was trembling, enough to make the wide sleeves of her gauzy shirt flutter. Her eyes stared, unseeing, out into the desert.

Words weren't going to do it. Starla gently rested her hand on Dorothea's back, and began rubbing in slow circles, feeling the tremors of Dorothea's body moving into her own. She waited until the tremors began to subside, then asked, "What happened?"

Dorothea pushed herself away from the tree and took a step away from Starla, then turned to face her. "What happened is I'm an idiot. I read an article, one article, and I know better than to consult just one source. It said that the Juniper Vortex is the strongest in Sedona, strong enough to change brain waves, and that that change can allow. . . ." Dorothea stopped and shook her head, her two pigtails flopping.

"Allow. . . ." Starla prompted.

"Allow people to see into another dimension, to see spirits, to communicate with the dead." Her voice was thick, like it was having to push its way through a ball of unshed tears. "See? Stupid. I just wanted to . . . I really wanted . . . I needed. . . . I wasn't with my granddad when he died. I didn't get to say goodbye. I just wanted to say goodbye. It's not like he wasn't old. He was ninety-two. Every time I saw him these last years,

I was kind of saying goodbye. But I wanted to be there. I tried. But I just didn't get there. There wasn't time."

"The first day you all came up here, I thought all your equipment and all your knowledge wasn't going to let you understand the vortex. It's not a head thing. It's a soul thing. You feel it. You don't analyze it."

"But that's what I do."

"You know what—take your shoes off." Dorothea stared at Starla. At least her eyes were focused now, not staring off at nothing. After a moment, she sat down and pulled off her hiking boots. "Socks, too." Dorothea obeyed. "Now stretch out on your back and let your whole body connect to the earth, then close your eyes." When she did, Starla leaned over her. "We're all energy, when we're alive, and when we're dead, and this is a place where energy is always flowing. It's flowing from you and to you. Let yourself feel it. I'm going to leave you, but I'll be close by. Don't think, just feel."

As Starla walked away, her feet pressing into the warm earth, she could feel the spirits, so many, surging around her. Were they the vortex's electricity? Did it come from them, and not from the earth, the way she'd always believed?

"What did she say?" Adam asked when Starla got back to the van.

"Not much, really. I think maybe finally having a breakthrough was a little overwhelming. She's just going to stay out there for a little, take everything in."

It was full dark when Dorothea returned to the van. Starla opened the passenger door for her.

"I felt him. He's not really gone, so it doesn't matter that I didn't say goodbye." Dorothea gave Starla's hand a hard squeeze as she climbed in. No one talked during the short ride back to High Sky, but the silence didn't feel uncomfortable or awkward. It felt like everyone was kind of . . . taking a moment, going deep inside themselves.

"Great work, everybody," Dorothea said when Starla pulled up to reception. "We'll go out tomorrow morning, get some more readings. Garret, you get a mention in the article we're writing."

Garret smiled so wide, Starla thought it must hurt his face. He whistled "Don't Stop Believin'" as he walked away. Adam fiddled with the magnetometer until he and Starla were the only two left.

"I don't know exactly why you're mad at me," he said, "but even I can tell you are, and I'm sorry. Isn't it a good thing that you have a lot of the attributes on my list? Isn't it a compliment?"

He just didn't get it. She looked into his face and saw confusion and regret. He just didn't get it! He honestly didn't. Because his list made logical sense to him.

"Adam, there are lots of things I like about you. I like the way you smile, and the little chip in your tooth, and your corny pumpkin pi T-shirt, and the way you listen to me, and the way you get me, and your super smarts, and the way your sweat smells, and I think it's adorable how you have a system for everything, like eating Oreos, and going to bed, and wearing the same clothes to keep your brain clear."

"Not the same. I have multiples."

"Right. I guess I forgot for a little that systems are your thing. And even if I don't have a list of attributes and a notebook and a tiny little pencil, I notice things about you. And when I notice enough of them I like, then I'd want to go out with you. The only difference is you do systems and I don't."

"But the addiction-substitution system is a system."

She laughed. "You're right. And most people would think my system was wackier than yours." And maybe the wackiest part was that she'd created the system to prevent herself from falling in love, when falling in love was awesome, in the true sense of the word.

"My hypothesis is that the only reason you don't have all the attributes on the list is that I haven't known you long enough. Every time I'm with you, I observe another one. Like tonight, just now, I observed that you're forgiving. Which puts you over seventy percent. And once you're past seventy percent, you're only eight attributes away from being someone I could fall in love with."

"I don't have a list, so I could fall in love with you at any moment. But if I do, what if I never get to the percentage where you'd love me back?"

"If the system doesn't indicate that you are someone I can love, then the system is flawed and needs revision." He gave her that adorable shy smile. "So have you noticed enough positive qualities in me that you'd go out with me?"

"Definitely."

Then it hit her. Before they went on a date, there was something he needed to know. "But I just realized no matter what, I won't fall in love with you."

"I don't understand. You said you could fall in love with me at any minute."

"But I was forgetting that we never fight. Today was a misunderstanding, and we talked it through."

"I don't understand."

"Bumper and I never talked things through. We had massive screaming fights and broke up, then we got back together and had insanely hot sex. I can't be in love without all that passion."

"I think your hypothesis that there can't be passion without fighting is flawed and needs revision." He took her face in his hands and kissed her, really kissed her, a kiss that had to be turning her aura a million shades of red, none of them angry.

"Definitely, definitely flawed." She was almost too breathless to speak.

CHAPTER 16

"Mom? I have to tell you something, and I need you to just let me get through it before you say anything." Daniel stared at himself in the mirror. His voice sounded shaky, and he looked pale and terrified. He'd been practicing for this phone call for at least half an hour, and his delivery was getting worse each time. *It shouldn't be scary to call your parents*, he told himself.

He just had to do it. He had to tell them about Sam's new living arrangements. The longer he waited, the more he allowed doubt to creep into his mind. He grabbed his cell and hit his mom's number.

She answered right away. "Daniel, I'm so glad you called. I just had the strangest message from Sam."

Every word he'd practiced went right out of Daniel's mind. "Sam called you?"

"Yes, and I was in the shower, can you believe that?" His mom sounded so upset, and Daniel felt his pulse speed up, the familiar stress spreading through his body. "He hasn't called once since the arrest, and I just had to go and miss it."

"Did he try Dad?" He could hardly believe that Sam was calling to tell on him. That was the only explanation. And the thought made Daniel so angry that he didn't even wait for her answer. "Because he will. He wants to complain about me. That's why he's finally bothering to be in touch with you guys. Like a little kid running to tattle."

He heard his mom's gasp, but he kept going.

"I'm sick of it, Mom. I'm sick of him and his attitude. He's a complete dick to me. Sorry. But he is, and it's not only the drugs talking, or withdrawal or whatever. He treats me like a doormat, and I allow it, and I'm done."

"Daniel, I don't know what—"

"Since I was a kid, Sam's been a mess, and he expects me to cover for him," Daniel rushed on. "In middle school, he'd come home drunk and tell me to lie to you and say he was sick. I've never even told you and Dad how many times I got calls to go pick him up from bartenders who threw him out or cops who were taking pity on him and didn't want to arrest him."

"Oh, sweetheart, I had no idea." She was crying. Of course she was. What kind of jerk made his mother cry?

"I'm sorry. I didn't want to upset you." He slumped down onto the overstuffed couch in the casita. "I had a whole speech I practiced to break it to you so you wouldn't cry."

"What? What do you mean?" She sounded baffled.

"I changed my mind, Mom. I don't want Sam to stay with me when he gets out. I told him he has to go to a halfway house."

"I see."

The bleakness in her voice almost broke him.

"I'm sorry, I'm so sorry. I've tried really hard to keep him safe so you didn't have to feel this way again, Mom. I did everything I could, but I can't—" A sob broke free from Daniel's throat, surprising him. He swallowed it down and kept going. "I can't live like this anymore. I want to have my own life. I want to be happy, or at least try. I'm so sorry that I'm letting you down."

He didn't know what else to say, so he stopped talking. His mom didn't answer, but he could hear her crying softly.

"The therapist at High Sky thinks it's actually better for his recovery," Daniel finally added. "And so does Ben. I think I've been enabling him."

"I agree."

"You do?" He was shocked.

"Sam wouldn't have called me if he wasn't desperate. I'm not naïve enough to think otherwise. I hate that. But they say that addicts have to hit bottom, right?" She sounded utterly defeated, and Daniel wished he could hug her.

"I don't know, Mom. I have a . . . friend here, and she says people have to solve some problems on their own in order to learn how strong they are, that Sam will be able to do that. Ben thinks so, too."

"It's not Sam I'm worried about right now, sweetheart, it's you. I had no idea that you were holding all this in. I never thought you were taking care of Sam because of me or your dad. We always figured it was because you two were so close."

"I wanted to be close to Sam. He was my big brother. I don't know how he felt. But mostly I thought it was my job. My role in the family, or however they put it. To keep the peace."

His mom was full-on sobbing now. "I'm a terrible parent; I didn't mean to make you feel that way. We never thought it was your job. Oh my god, Daniel, you poor thing."

"Mom, stop! I'm not blaming you. Nobody did any of this on purpose. Please don't cry. That's like my kryptonite."

She laughed through a sob. "Sorry."

"Stop saying that!"

"Only if you do."

"Deal." Daniel drew a deep breath. "Sedona is this mind-opening place. It's all about enlightenment. I get why Ben wanted to stay here after he got clean. I've started drawing again, and I adopted a puppy. I'm beginning to feel happier, and it made me realize that I haven't been allowing myself to do anything that I wanted to do, not for years. Maybe not ever."

"That's not fair. Sam's troubles shouldn't keep you from having a life, Daniel."

"I know that. But the same goes for you and Dad," he told her. "I don't want to hear that he's moving in with you. Because the whole cycle will start over again. He'll go back to his old habits, and you two will be miserable."

"I think you're right. He should follow the therapist's advice."

"Then we're all on the same page." Daniel felt a strange lightness seep through his limbs. Relief. "Thanks for understanding, Mom."

"I love you, Daniel."

Riley opened her phone, then hesitated. She'd never called Mary. They'd just done the thing where they texted a few times a year, at least until Mary came to visit. Seeing her after so long had felt so good. She was the one through line of Riley's life, the one person who'd known her almost forever. Mary understood her the way no one else could.

She hit *call*. Mary answered almost immediately. "Riley! I'm glad you called. Seeing you face-to-face was so wonderful. Going back to just texting felt all wrong."

"I know! I think we got spoiled, hanging out in person."

"I definitely got spoiled at that resort of yours," Mary joked. "How are things?"

"Weirdly amazing. I got offered a job managing High Sky. Me, running the whole place." She hadn't been calling to talk about the job offer, but telling Mary about it was a must. Only Mary could really comprehend exactly how far Riley had come. She'd barely graduated from high school, and now some-one thought she was capable of handling a resort that brought in tens of millions of dollars a year. She was still having trouble believing it. Thinking about it made her feel a little dizzy.

"That's amazing! Or not amazing at all. Everyone I talked to there told me how wonderful you were. You deserve this. Congratulations! I'll have to come out and visit again now that I have an in with the manager."

Riley felt her pride balloon instantly deflate. "I'm not taking it, though. Obviously."

Mary had thrown out the idea of Riley staying at High Sky with her friends and Daniel when she was here, but Riley had made it clear T.U.P. was still her dream. You didn't give up your dream for anything. Mary might even have been the one who told her that.

"Oh, Riley, no. This is a once-in-a-lifetime chance. You move around so much that even though you're fabulous at your job, you don't have the résumé to get this kind of offer. Someone has seen past that, has seen how special you are. You've got to grab this with both hands."

If Mary had started spouting Chloe Campbell's statistics about foster kids, Riley wouldn't have been more shocked. "What?" was all she could manage to say.

"I know you focus on that plan, sweetie, but somebody who only stays in a job for six months at a time gets a little suspect after a while. You have to admit. It's okay for a twenty-five-year-old, but eventually employers are going to start wonder-ing why you won't settle down. You're not twenty-five any-more."

"I don't want to settle down. That's not my Ultimate Plan." Riley felt like she was taking crazy pills. Or Mary was. "You know that—I'm going to live all the places in my book. I don't care about the jobs. It isn't even about that."

"Obviously not, or you wouldn't turn down an incredible promotion in order to be. . . ." She waited.

"Associate entertainment director." Riley mumbled the title, knowing a comment about it being a step backwards was coming. "But that's not the point. The point is, it's in Stowe."

"Okay, I'm going to pull rank here. Or age, I guess. It's time for me to remind you why you came up with The Ultimate Plan to begin with, because you were just a kid then, but I was a full-grown woman. I think I remember it more clearly than you do."

Excuse me? Riley thought angrily. "It's *my* plan."

"Yes, and you were a child when you came up with the idea, a child who had no security in her life, no future prospect of college or a high-paying career, and no older family members to depend on. What you had was a dream of a better life, one where you could be in control of your own destiny. And it was a dream you could actually accomplish! You didn't want to walk on Mars. You just wanted to see all these places. You could work in any of them. So we figured that out together."

"Exactly. And I did accomplish it. I worked my ass off to make enough to buy a car, and to get higher-paying jobs. Each time I do that, it makes the next leg of the plan a little easier because. . . ."

Mary finished the thought for her. "Because you have more money, and more money equals more security. That's what I'm saying."

Riley suddenly realized that she was sitting scrunched up on her l0͡ hugging her knees to her chest like a scared little girl. She ͡ d herself out. "It's not all about money, and an ͠ work my way back up. This is just a little glitch becau͠ ming got messed up by taking care of J.D. and Petunia."

"Why'd you do that?"

"They needed help." An image of J.D. lost in the desert popped into her head: his sad, frightened brown eyes.

"And you liked helping them, I think," Mary said. "You like your job at High Sky. You like the people and Daniel, though I know he's leaving—"

"Actually, he's not."

"Ah." Mary cleared her throat. "So you have a lot of good things there. Your schedule got off track because you were busy living your life. That's okay, Riley. You're allowed to have other things in life besides your plan."

"Not if they get in the way of the plan."

"Do you hear yourself? Truly? Sweetie, this isn't a plan anymore. It's a prison."

"How can you say that? I thought you were the one person who understood how important it was to me."

"I do. And I'm telling you that the plan did its job. You grew up strong and capable and made your own way in the world. And because of your ultimate plan, you earned what you were lacking—security and a good-paying job and people to depend on. You made all that happen! But you're going to give it up . . . why?"

Riley's eyes filled with tears. She didn't know anymore. "Because it's The Ultimate Plan."

"Well, I'm glad you called me, then. I think it's time for us to make you a new plan."

"Lori, this is ridiculous!" The chef had just appeared with cake number four. *Four!*

"Only a couple more." Lori winked at Riley as she added the cake to the table already loaded with cakes, cakes, cakes, cakes, and pretty much High Sky's entire appetizer menu.

"What's that one?" Garret called from the other side of the rooftop patio.

"Orange and ancho chile, with just a hint of cayenne."

"That's already way too much." Riley turned to Daniel. "This is too much." And not just the food, everything. Ben Osborne had insisted they use the resort's most exclusive event location. At least it was after hours, so they weren't missing out on a booking. Riley didn't want to start out as the High Sky general manager by losing him money. And after hours meant all her coworkers could come.

Riley felt a little lightheaded. She'd had some big dreams, and she'd made a lot of them come true for herself. But she had never dreamed of something like this. You couldn't dream of things you couldn't even conceive of. What would Chloe Campbell make of her now? "This is too much," she repeated.

"I think it means they're happy you took the promotion." Daniel slid his arm around Riley's waist and leaned close to whisper in her ear. "Not as happy as I am."

J.D. gave a short, *hey-what-about-me* bark, and Riley swept him into her arms. He let out a little sigh, as if being held by Riley while still being close enough to lick Daniel's hand was his dream come true. She knew how he felt. Being held by Daniel while still being close enough to get a lick from J.D. was a dream come true. Another dream she couldn't have conceived of back when she was under the covers with *Beautiful America,* just trying to make it through the night.

Daniel smiled at her. "Can you believe you almost walked away from this? And the puppy. And there was something else. What was that other thing?"

"Lori's cooking?" she asked as Lori appeared with another cake, but then she kissed him, getting as close as she could with J.D. in between them. "Ah, now I remember the other reason." She gave him another kiss. She'd really believed that short-term boyfriends were all she needed or wanted. Daniel had managed to convince her she was wrong, starting with being a Boy Scout.

"I knew you two should be together," Starla called as she headed toward them, leading Adam by the hand.

"Did you have some bad fights?" Adam adjusted his glasses.

"Uh, a couple," Daniel admitted.

"Another data point." Adam pulled a golf pencil from behind his ear.

Starla slapped him on the arm. "Stop. I already admitted I was wrong about people needing to fight to have a passionate relationship. You don't have to make a Venn diagram."

Riley shook her head at her friend. "I never thought I'd hear the words *Venn diagram* come out of your mouth."

"I've learned about Venn diagrams, and Adam learned about the five virtues." Starla plucked the pencil away from Adam and stuck it back behind his ear. "I want to dance with you."

But suddenly, the music stopped. "Attention, attention everyone!" Ms. Aguilar smoothed her already smooth slickback bun. "I wanted to stop by to congratulate Riley one more time. As you all know, her exemplary—" Her body stiffened. Riley hadn't known Ms. Aguilar's spine could get any stiffer. "Is that a dog?"

Before Riley could answer, J.D. was scrabbling out of her arms and running straight toward her manager. No, Riley was the manager now. Toward her *former* manager. It was still hard getting used to thinking of Ms. Aguilar—*Maria*—as a colleague.

Daniel tightened his grip on her waist. "Nothing's going to save us this time."

J.D. launched himself at Ms. Aguilar. She recoiled, dropping her purse. As she bent down to retrieve it, J.D. stuck his teeth into the pocket of her blazer. He shook his head violently back and forth.

"J.D., no!" Riley cried as the puppy ripped the pocket free. She raced across the patio, Daniel right behind her. J.D. had lost interest in Ms. Aguilar. He was greedily eating. Riley leaned closer. "Is that bacon?"

"Of course not!"

"It looks like bacon," Daniel said.

"I would say with ninety-eight percent certainty that it's bacon," Adam agreed.

Garret came over for a look. "Of course it's bacon!" He gave J.D. a pat on the head. "What else would the doggie be after?" J.D. licked his lips, having finished every scrap.

"You're a bacon eater?" The way Starla asked, she might as well have said, *You're a Satan worshiper?*

Daniel grabbed Riley's arm. "That's why J.D. went running after her that day. Bacon!"

So much was suddenly making sense to Riley. "The Tic Tacs! The Tic Tacs are to cover up the bacon breath!"

Ms. Aguilar opened her mouth, shut it, opened it again, but no words came out. She swallowed hard. "I tried to stop. But I love it. I know I shouldn't eat it. We're a vegetarian establishment, and it was my duty to set a good example for my staff. I've failed."

"It's all right, Maria." Ben put down the plate crammed with appetizers he'd been holding. He'd clearly wanted to try everything Lori had to offer. "There was never any rule about employees eating meat, as long as they weren't on the grounds."

"My goal is not to simply follow the rules. It's to be exceptional."

Ben laughed. "And you are. That's why I'm bringing you to Phoenix. I know you'll make it just as exceptional as High Sky."

Ms. Aguilar gave a nod. "Thank you." She looked down at J.D. "There is a rule against animals at the resort."

"Actually, that's something Ben and I discussed at our last transition meeting," Riley told her. "Resorts that allow pets bring in more revenue, so we've decided to make High Sky pet-friendly. More than that, pet-encouraged. We're going to add a dog massage to our spa treatments, and I'd love to do a program with a pet psychic. You want to get started on that, Star?"

Starla clapped her hands. "Love, love, love it!"

One of the other things Riley had discussed with Ben was moving Starla up to entertainment director. He'd said that as manager, that was her call, and she'd made it. Starla had a gift for engaging with guests, and now that she'd left behind her relationship drama, Riley was sure she'd be able to handle everything else.

Lori waved her hand. "I have a question about another rule."

Ben grinned and gestured to Riley. "You're on."

"What about the rule that says coworkers aren't allowed to have relationships?"

"I know how *you* feel about staff and guests having relationships," Daniel said, keeping his voice low enough that only she could hear.

Riley thought for a moment. "New rule," she announced. "Relationships between coworkers are fine." She heard Ms. Aguilar give a stifled gasp. "As long as they don't interfere with work."

"Hallelujah!" Lori strode over to Garret, took his face in her hands, and kissed him. He looked stunned when she let him go. Riley shot Starla a smile, and Starla mouthed, *Told you so.*

"But I haven't heard back from *Invention Today* about if they want to do a profile on me," Garret protested.

"Uh, why are we talking about this now? I just kissed you."

"And I didn't think that would ever happen until I was something other than the plant guy."

"Garret, you're not just the plant guy," Riley protested. "You're a huge part of what makes High Sky a place so many people want to visit."

"Agreed." Ben took a bite of *calabacitas.* "You should have a profile in *Landscaping Today.*"

"The 'plant guy' is what my ex-wife called me. She wanted someone who was more impressive to her friends."

Lori reached over and took Garret's hand. "I love that you're the plant guy. That's one of my favorite things about you."

"Look at you. You make one decision, and you change lives." Daniel smoothed Riley's hair away from her face. "And your decision to stay changed my life. Not that I think we're—"

She put her fingers over his lips to stop him from speaking. "I think we both made some good decisions lately. We both go for happiness."

EPILOGUE

All right, my puppies, you know how to choose the right humans and how to make them choose you back. But that's just the beginning. Once they're yours, you need to know how to train them. Salvador, get Andy's tail out of your mouth. Andy, don't let him get away with that. He deserved a nip to teach him to behave himself. Next time, give it to him.

Most humans, even Good Humans, think they should be in charge. They think they know better than dogs when they can't even smell a delicious piece of bacon from a block away. One block! Don't try to change their minds. It won't work. Instead, you have to train them. No, Savannah, not by giving them a nip. Shut your jaws, please.

Here's an example. My human Riley—you all know her—once expected me to sleep in a box by her bed. It was nice enough. There was a very fluffy towel for me to lie on. But it was a box! By the bed! Dogs sleep with their humans. It's good for you, and it's good for them. But humans don't always know what they need. If you choose a human who doesn't allow you on the bed, there's only one thing to do. Don't let them sleep. At all. They don't sleep with you, they don't sleep. It usually only takes a few nights for most humans to learn this lesson. But some are stubborn or maybe not that smart. Have patience and don't give up. I promise they can learn, and they will.

Mackinac, that's especially important for you. You're going home with my human Daniel's brother. He wants you so much that he's going to get shots so you can live together. There were a few times when Sam came to visit that Daniel had to put him outside. He didn't call Sam a Bad Human. He would never do that. But he needed to give Sam a little more training. And it worked. Daniel hasn't had to put Sam out in a long time.

Even with everything Sam's learned, he might still need a little work. He has difficulty with sharing food. So many humans have this issue. It's one of those behaviors that's instinctive. They really can't help being territorial when they're feeding.

Training them out of this behavior is another time where you'll need your puppy dog eyes. Everyone look at Georgia. She really knows how to work them. When your human is eating something you want, just give them the eyes. Your goal is to look pathetic. Like you're starving. Try not to blink until you get what you want. After a few times, they'll get the idea. They'll understand that whenever they eat, you eat.

And you're asleep again. Well, we can review tomorrow. Puppies are a lot like humans. It takes time and patience to train them. And love. I forgot to tell the pups that, and it's the most important part. It takes time, patience, and love.